喚醒你的英文語感！

Get a Feel for English !

喚醒你的英文語感！

Get a Feel for English !

商英教父的
單字勝經
Biz Vocabulary

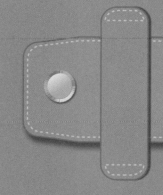

提升英語競爭力
商務人士爭讀的單字寶典！
★★★★★

500大企業 *Top1*講師

繼暢銷第一名書系《愈忙愈要學英文》，
再次推出風行商務人士的速效學習方案！

附MP3

作者◎ **Quentin Brand**

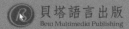 貝塔語言出版
Beta Multimedia Publishing

 IRT 語言測驗中心
Language Testing Center

推薦序

Quentin effectively demonstrates the use of English vocabulary precisely helping me to avoid those common mistakes which Taiwanese usually make due to cultural differences and preconceptions.

Quentin's experience of coaching senior managers' English for years provides excellent knowledge in terms of coverage, depth and mind set.

Quentin 以有效的方式精確示範英文字彙的用法，幫助我避免台灣人由於文化差異和錯誤認知而常犯的錯誤。

Quentin 多年教導高階經理人英文的經驗，在廣度、深度和觀念方面都提供了絕佳知識。

湯森路透台灣
總經理

Michael W.J

（推薦者依姓氏筆畫排序）

Quentin is a wizard who makes learning business English a summer breeze. He is an alchemist who turns any novice in English study into a proficient business English speaker or writer in a very short time. You will learn to use simple, appropriate, and convincing terms and idioms to present and communicate business ideas with impact. Business English has never been so easy to pick up before. Practicality and ease of learning are always the pillars of Quentin's pedagogy.

Quentin 是個把商英學習變得有如夏日微風的天才。他是個可以在短時間內把英語初學者變成商英說、寫高手的專家。你會學到如何使用簡單、適切和有說服力的用語，來提出和溝通你的商業想法。商務英語從來沒有這麼容易學會。實用和易學一直是 Quentin 教學理念的基石。

全球直效行銷股份有限公司
總經理

在國際型態的外商公司工作多年，英文書信、溝通及簡報已成為工作的主要部分，尤其是書寫溝通表達上，總希望能夠妙筆生花。

Quentin是我所接觸過最瞭解華人英語學習問題的老師。他用很簡單的學習方式來讓你能夠迅速地引用道地字彙和字串，自然而然地習慣使用它們，進而成為英文高手。有如打通英語學習的任督二脈，書寫、溝通變得好簡單。就像Quentin常說的一句話：「學習英文想太多，一定學不好！」現在有了這本「單字勝經」學好英文就更容易了！

嬌生股份有限公司 行銷處
專業行銷資深經理

林秀玲 Olivia Lo

Quentin's method of teaching English is perfect for business people. He helps you combine the words you already know so that you can increase your power of expression. He shows you how to learn new language easily and effectively. His teaching has had great results with my staff, and everyone enjoys learning with him.

Quentin 的英語教學法是為商務人士量身打造。他幫助你使用學過的字彙來提升表達能力，也教你如何輕易又有效地學習新用語。他的教學對我的工作伙伴有顯著效果，每個人都很樂於和他一起學習。

戴爾電腦 人力資源處
資深經理

張譯心 Vivienne Chang

我是在一個偶然的機緣下，知道有一位商英大師 Quentin。於是主動去尋找，而且非常幸運地能夠直接跟老師學習英文。Quentin 老師的字串英語學習法，突破了傳統的英語學習方式，並對「語言學習 v.s 文化差異」提供了新的思考方向。

　　我非常敬佩 Quentin 老師！他是一個很願意付出的人，在他身上你可以深深感受到英國紳士的風範與自在。因為，他不斷地在台灣用他的專業與熱情，想要幫助本地更多的上班族們，更有系統、有效率地學習英文。

　　我誠摯地推薦這本書，它絕對會是您英語學習上的墊腳石！

禾伸堂企業股份有限公司
消費元件事業群處長

黃俊諒

目錄
CONTENTS

前言　字串學習法

對很多商務英文的使用者而言，最大的挑戰就是字彙。雖然很多人擔心文法，實際上字彙才是語言中傳達想法最重要的部分。我總是告訴我的學生：Ideas equals vocabulary, vocabulary equals ideas.，不管你在事業上剛起步，或是在事業上已經很有成就，總是有很多新字要學！

學新字彙有三個主要的困難。

第一，找出你該先學什麼字彙。字彙如此之多，你需要有所選擇，先學最重要的字。**第二，學習字彙的用法**。大部分的字典與字彙書把焦點放在新字的意思，大部分人學習新字彙的時候也是如此。但是你仍然必須學會如何使用新字彙。每一個字彙都有它的意思與用法，你兩者都必須學會。本書將會教你如何做。**第三，學習哪些字可以搭配在一起使用**。字的組合搭配得好，英文就會漂亮。舉例來說，你可能已經知道 analysis 這個字，你也可能已經知道 preliminary 這個字。但是你可能不知道這兩個字經常搭配一起使用，preliminary analysis 是用來形容一項初步、不是很深入的分析。或許你認得這些個別的單字，但可能從來沒有把這兩個字搭配在一起使用過。

在繼續說明之前，我們先來做個 task。

Task 1 請思考以下問題，並記下你的答案。

1. 你購買本書的原因為何？
2. 你希望從本書中學到什麼？
3. 你在用英文交談和寫作時遇到哪些問題？

下面列出可能的範例答案，請勾選出最貼近自己想法的項目。

1. 你購買本書的原因為何？
- [ ] 我想找到一個學習英文的方法，來滿足我專業上的需求。
- [ ] 我看過《愈忙愈要學英文》系列的書，我想繼續按照相同的方法來增強我的英文。
- [ ] 我看過《愈忙愈要學 100 個商業動詞》，而我知道這本書可以和它搭配使用。

☐ 我知道我的英文字彙不夠，我想要擴建我的字庫。

☐ 我想要一本可以放在電腦旁邊隨時查閱的書，有一點像商務英文的聖經。

2. 你希望從本書中學到什麼？

☐ 我想學會商務英語中最常見的關鍵字彙，並且知道如何使用這些字。

☐ 我想學會如何把我已經知道的字彙依正確的方式組合起來使用。

☐ 我總是重複使用一樣的字彙，我想增加我英文表達的多樣性。

☐ 我想學會如何使用英文，對英文為什麼要這樣用沒什麼興趣，我沒時間，更何況我沒有語文學的背景，所以有時候看到一大堆文法解釋就像在讀天書。我覺得這是我以前都學不好英文的原因。

☐ 我想學會如何自己加強英文能力。我在英文環境中工作，但知道自己沒有充分利用這個優勢加強專業的英文能力。我希望這本書可以教我怎麼做。

3. 你在用英文交談和寫作時遇到哪些問題？

☐ 有時候我怎麼都找不到適當的詞或慣用語來表達，可能我懂的詞彙太少了。

☐ 我不知道自己犯了哪些錯誤，所以不知道我說的或寫的英文正不正確。

☐ 我很害羞，不敢和外國人說英文，因為我不知道自己有沒有說錯話。我不想說錯話，冒犯到別人。

☐ 我知道我的發音不精準，但是我不大知道該怎麼改善。

☐ 聽力是我的罩門。外國人講話好快，有時候二個字聽起來像一個字，有些字我學過卻聽不出來。有的口音我也聽不懂。

　　你可能同意以上這幾點的部分或全部，你也可能有其他我沒有想到的答案。不過先容我自我介紹。

　　我是 Quentin Brand，我教了將近二十年的英文，對象包括來自世界各地的商界專業人士，就像各位這樣，而且有好幾年的時間都待在台灣。我的客戶包括企業各個階層的人士，從大型跨國企業的國外分公司經理，

到擁有海外市場的小型本地公司所雇用的基層實習生不等。我教過初學者，也教過英文程度非常高的人，他們都曾經表達過上述的心聲。他們所想的和各位一樣，那就是要找到一種簡單又實用的方法來學英文。

各位，你們已經找到了！這些年來，我開發了一套教導和學習英文的方法，專門幫像各位這樣忙碌的生意人解決疑慮。這套辦法的核心概念稱作 Leximodel 字串學習法，是以一嶄新角度看待語文的英文教學法。目前 Leximodel 已經獲得全世界一些最大與最成功的公司採用，以協助其主管充分發揮他們的英語潛能，而本書就是以 Leximodel 為基礎。

本章的目的在介紹 Leximodel，並告訴各位要怎麼運用。我也會解釋要怎麼使用本書，以及要如何讓它發揮最大的效用。看完本章後，各位應該就能：

☐ 清楚了解 Leximodel，以及它對各位有什麼好處。
☐ 了解 chunks、set-phrases 和 word partnerships 的差別。
☐ 在任何文章中能自行找出 chunks、set-phrases 和 word partnerships。
☐ 清楚了解學習 set-phrases 的困難之處，以及要如何克服。
☐ 清楚了解本書中的不同要素，以及要如何運用。

但在往下看之前，我要先談談 task 在本書中的重要性。各位在前面可以看到，我會請各位停下來先做個 task，也就是針對一些練習寫下答案。我希望各位都能按照我的指示，先做完 task 再往下閱讀。

每一章都有許多 task，它們都經過嚴謹的設計，可以協助各位在不知不覺中吸收新的語言。做 task 的思維過程比答對與否重要得多，所以各位務必要按照既定的順序去練習，而且在完成練習前先不要看答案。

當然，為了節省時間，你大可不停下來做 task 而一鼓作氣地把整本書看完。不過，這樣本書無法發揮最大效果。因為你要是沒有做好必要的思維工作，就無法逐步熟悉、吸收書中所教的用語。請相信我的話，按部就班做 task 準沒錯。

➔ Leximodel 字串學習法

在本節中，我要向各位介紹 Leximodel。Leximodel 是看待語言的新方法，它是以一個很簡單的概念為基礎：

Language consists of words which appear with other words.
語言是由字串構成。

這種說法簡單易懂。Leximodel 的基礎概念就是從字串的層面來看語言，而非以文法和單字。為了讓各位明白我的意思，我們來做一個 task 吧，做完練習前先不要往下看。

Task 2 想一想，平常下列單字後面都會搭配什麼字？請寫在空格中。

listen   _____

depend   _____

English   _____

financial   _____

你很可能**在第一個字旁邊填上 to**，**在第二個字旁邊填上 on**。我猜得沒錯吧？因為只要用一套叫做 corpus linguistics 的軟體程式和運算技術，就可以在統計上發現 listen 後面接 to 的機率非常高（大約是 98.9%），而 depend 後面接 on 的機率也差不多。這表示 listen 和 depend 後面接的字幾乎是千篇一律，不會改變（listen 接 to；depend 接 on）。由於機率非常高，我們可以把這兩個片語（listen to、depend on）視為固定（fixed）字串。由於它們是固定的，所以假如你不是寫 to 和 on，就可以說是寫錯了。

不過，**接下來兩個字（English、financial）後面會接什麼字就難預測得多**，所以我猜不出來你在這兩個字的後面寫了什麼。但我可以在某個範圍內猜測，你在 English 後面寫的可能是 class、book、teacher、email、grammar 等，而在 financial 後面寫的是 department、news、planning、product、problems 或 stability 等。但我猜對的把握就比前面兩個字低了許多。為什麼會這樣？因為能正確預測 English 和 financial 後面接什麼單字

的統計機率低了許多，很多字都有可能，而且每個字的機率相當。因此，我們可以說 English 和 financial 的字串是不固定的，而是流動的（fluid）。所以，與其把語言想成文法和字彙，各位不妨把它想成是一個龐大的字串語料庫；裡面有些字串是固定的，有些字串則是流動的。

總而言之，根據可預測度，我們可以看出字串的固定性和流動性，如圖示：

字串的可預測度是 Leximodel 的基礎，因此 Leximodel 的定義可以追加一句話：

Language consists of words which appear with other words. These combinations of words can be placed along a spectrum of predictability, with fixed combinations at one end, and fluid combinations at the other.

語言由字串構成。每個字串可根據可預測度的程度區分，可預測度愈高的一端是固定字串，可測預度愈低的一端是流動字串。

你可能在心裡兀自納悶：我曉得 Leximodel 是什麼了，可是這對學英文有什麼幫助？我怎麼知道哪些字串是固定的、哪些是流動的，就算知道了，學英文會比較簡單嗎？別急，輕鬆點，從現在起英文會愈學愈上手。

我們可以把所有的字串（稱之為 MWIs = multi-word items）分為三類：chunks、set-phrases 和 word partnerships。這些字沒有對等的中譯，所以請各位把這幾個英文字記起來。我們仔細來看這三類字串，各位很快就會發現它們真的很容易了解與使用。

我們先來看第一類字串：chunks。Chunks 字串有固定也有流動元素。listen to 就是個好例子：listen 的後面總是跟著 to（這是固定的），但有時候 listen 可以是 are listening、listened 或 have not been listening carefully enough（這是流動的）。另一個好例子是 give sth. to sb.。其中的

give 總是先接某物（sth.），然後再接 to，最後再接某人（sb.）。就這點來說，它是固定的。不過在這個 chunk 中，sth. 和 sb. 這兩個部分可以選擇的字很多，像是 give a raise to your staff「給員工加薪」和 give a presentation to your boss「向老闆做簡報」。看看下面的圖你就懂了。

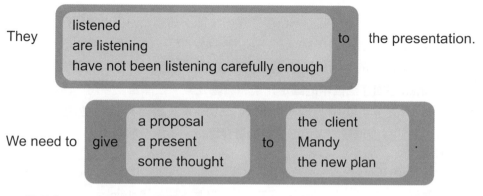

■ 部分為 fixed　　■ 部分為 fluid

相信你能夠舉一反三，想出更多例子。當然，我們還可以把它寫成 give sb. sth.，但這是另外一個 chunk。它同樣兼具固定和流動元素，希望各位能看出這點。

Chunks 通常很短，由 meaning words（意義字，如 listen、depend）加上 function words（功能字，如 to、on）所組成。相信你已經知道的 chunks 很多，只是自己還不自知呢！我們來做另一個 task，看看各位是不是懂了。務必先作完 task 再看答案！

Task 3　請閱讀下列短文，找出所有的 chunks 並畫底線。

Everyone is familiar with the experience of knowing what a word means, but not knowing how to use it accurately in a sentence. This is because words are nearly always used as part of an MWI. There are three kinds of MWIs. The first is called a chunk. A chunk is a combination of words which is more or less fixed. Every time a word in the chunk is used, it must be used with its partner(s). Chunks combine fixed and fluid elements of language. When you learn a new word, you should learn the chunk.

There are thousands of chunks in English. One way you can help yourself to improve your English is by noticing and keeping a database of the chunks you find as you read. You should also try to memorize as many chunks as possible.

中譯

每個人都有這樣的經驗：知道一個字的意思，卻不知道如何正確地用在句子中。這是因為每個字都必須當作 MWI 的一部分。MWI 有三類，第一類叫做 chunk。Chunk 幾乎是固定的字串，每當用到 chunk 的其中一字，該字的詞夥也得一併用上。Chunks 包含了語言中的固定元素和流動元素。在學習新字時，應該連帶學會它的 chunk。英文中有成千上萬的 chunks。閱讀時留意並記下所有的 chunks，將之彙整成語庫，最好還要盡量背起來，不失為加強英文的好法子。

現在把你的答案與下列語庫做比較。假如你沒有找到那麼多 chunks，那就再看一次短文，看看是否能在文中找到語庫裡所有的 chunks。
- 注意，語庫中的 chunks，be 動詞以原形 be 表示，而非 is、was、are 或 were。
- 記下 chunks 時，前後都加上 …（刪節號）。
- 注意，有些 chunks 後面接的是 V（go、write 等原形動詞）或 Ving（going、writing 等），有的則接 n.p.（noun phrase，名詞片語）或 n. clause（名詞子句）。「本書使用說明」會對此詳細說明。

… be familiar with n.p. …	… be used with n.p. …
… experience of Ving …	… combine sth. and sth. …
… how to V …	… elements of n.p. …
… be used as n.p. …	… thousands of n.p. …
… part of n.p. …	… in English …
… there are …	… help yourself to V …
… kinds of n.p. …	… keep a database of n.p. …
… the first …	… try to V …
… be called n.p. …	… as many as …
… a combination of n.p. …	… as many as possible …
… more or less …	
… every time + n. clause …	

好，接下來我們來看第二類字串：set-phrases。Set-phrases 比 chunks 固定，通常字串比較長，其中可能有好幾個chunks。Set-phrases 通常有個開頭或結尾，或是兩者都有，這表示完整的句子有時候也可以是 set-phrase。Chunks 通常是沒頭沒尾的片斷文字組合。Set-phrases 本質上比較是功能性用語，也就是說可用來達到某個功能，例如在餐館點菜，寫電子郵件請對方幫忙，或者在講話時釐清誤解。因為描述性較高之故，報告和提案中很少會見到set-phrases，不過本書部分章節還是會教到一些。現在請做 task。

Task 4 請看以下常見的商務英文set-phrases，把認識的打勾。

( ) Apologies for the delay in getting back to you, but …
( ) Thanks for your reply.
( ) Going on to n.p. …
( ) I look forward to hearing from you.
( ) I'd like to draw your attention to the fact that + n. clause
( ) I'd now like you to look at n.p. …
( ) If you have any questions about this, please do not hesitate to contact me.
( ) If you look at this (chart/graph/table), you can see that + n. clause
( ) If you look here you can see that + n. clause
( ) Just to confirm that + n. clause
( ) Just to let you know that + n. clause
( ) My recommendation here is to V …
( ) My suggestion here is for n.p. …

- 由於 set-phrases 是三類字串中最固定的，所以各位在學習時，要很仔細地留意每個 set-phrases 的細節。稍後對此會有更詳細的說明。
- 注意，有些 set-phrases 是以 n.p. 結尾，有些則是以 n. clause 結尾。稍後會有更詳細的說明。

學會 set-phrases 的好處在於，使用的時候不必考慮到文法。你只要把它們當作固定的語言單位背起來，原原本本地照用即可。接下來我們來看第三類字串：word partnerships（搭配詞組）。

這三類字串中，word partnerships（搭配詞組）的流動性最高，其中包含了二個以上的意義字（不同於 chunks 包含了意義字與功能字），並且通常是「動詞 + 形容詞 + 名詞」或是「名詞 + 名詞」的組合。Word partnerships 會隨著行業或談論的話題而改變，但所有產業用的 chunks 和 set-phrases 都一樣。舉個例子，假如你是在製藥業服務，那你用到的 word partnerships 就會跟在資訊業服務的人不同。現在來做下面的 task，你就會更了解我的意思。

Task 5 看看下列各組 word partnerships，然後將會使用這些 word partnerships 的產業寫下來。請見範例。

1

government regulations	hospital budget
drug trial	key opinion leader
patient response	patent law

產業名稱：　　*製藥業*

2

risk assessment	share price index
non-performing loan	low inflation
credit rating	bond portfolio

產業名稱：＿＿＿＿＿＿＿＿＿

3

bill of lading	shipping date
shipment details	letter of credit
customs delay	customer service

產業名稱：＿＿＿＿＿＿＿＿＿

4

latest technology	repetitive strain injury
user interface	input data
system problem	installation wizard

產業名稱：＿＿＿＿＿＿＿＿＿＿＿＿

請核對以下的答案。
2. 銀行與金融業
3. 外銷／進出口業
4. 資訊科技業

　　假如你在上述產業服務，你一定認得其中一些 word partnerships。搭配詞組正是本書主要的學習焦點，但是在起初的幾個單元裡我也會教一些實用的字串。

　　現在我們對 Leximodel 的定義應要進一步修正了：

Language consists of words which appear with other words. These combinations can be categorized as chunks, set-phrases and word partnerships and placed along a spectrum of predictability, with fixed combinations at one end, and fluid combinations at the other.

　　語言由字串構成，這些字串可以分成三大類──**chunks**、**set-phrases** 和 **word partnerships**，並且可依其可預測的程度區分，可預測度愈高的一端是固定字串，可預測度愈低的一端是流動字串。

　　新的 Leximodel 圖示如下：

可預測度

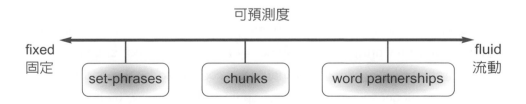

fixed 固定 ← → fluid 流動

set-phrases　　chunks　　word partnerships

學英文致力學好 chunks，文法就會進步，因為大部分的文法錯誤其實都是源自於 chunks 寫錯。學英文時專攻 set-phrases，英語功能就會進步，因為 set-phrases 都是功能性字串。學英文時在 word partnerships 下功夫，字彙量就會增加。因此，最後的 Leximodel 圖示如下：

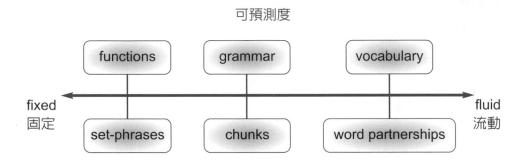

Leximodel 的優點以及其對於學習英文的妙用，就在於說、寫英文時，均無須再為文法規則傷透腦筋。學習英文時，首要之務是建立 chunks、set-phrases 和 word partnerships 的語料庫，多學多益。而不是學習文法規則，並苦苦思索如何在文法中套用單字。這三類字串用來輕而易舉，而且更符合人腦記憶和使用語言的習慣。本節結束前，我們來做最後一個 task，確定各位對於 Leximodel 已經完全了解。如此一來，各位就會看出這個方法有多簡單好用。在完成 task 前，先不要看語庫。

Task 6 請看這份報告和翻譯，然後用三種不同顏色的筆分別將所有的 chunks、set-phrases 和 word partnerships 畫底線。最後請完成下表。請見範例。

Dear Mary,

Thanks for your email. Just to update you on the situation, the clinical trial of the new drug is going smoothly and we have not encountered any problems. We expect the trial to be completed by the end of this quarter. If all goes well, we can get approval for the drug by the end of the year. Our team has already started working on the marketing strategy for the drug. We intend to have a public awareness campaign using TV, print ads, and bus posters. We are also assembling a team of doctors to help introduce the product to hospitals throughout the north.

I hope this helps with your plans. Once we get the go-ahead from headquarters, I'll be in touch to finalize the plans for the advertising campaign.

Best regards,
Albert

中譯

瑪莉，您好：

謝謝您的來信。向您報告一下目前情況，新藥的臨床試驗進行順利，我們尚未遇到任何問題。我們預期試驗將在本季末以前完成。如一切順利，藥在年底以前便可獲得核准。我們的工作小組已經開始為此藥研擬行銷策略。我們計畫透過電視、平面廣告和公車海報等來做公共宣傳活動。我們也正在延攬一組醫生，幫助我們在北部各地的醫院引薦產品。

希望以上報告對您的計畫有所幫助。一收到總部的許可，我便會和您聯絡，確定公共宣傳活動的計畫。

祝　安好
亞伯特

set-phrases	chunks	word partnerships
Thanks for your email.	*... the end of sth. ...*	*marketing strategy*

請利用下面的語庫核對答案。

- 注意，set-phrases 通常是以大寫字母開頭。
- 刪節號（...），表示句子的流動部分。
- 注意，chunks 的開頭和結尾都有刪節號，表示 chunks 大部分為句子的中間部分。
- 注意，word partnerships 均由意義字組成。

set-phrases	chunks	word partnerships
Thanks for your email.	… update sb. on sth. …	clinical trial
Just to update you on …	… any problems …	new drug
If all goes well, …	… be completed by …	go smoothly
I hope this helps …	… expect sth. to V …	encounter problems
I'll be in touch …	… the end of sth. …	get approval
	… this quarter …	marketing strategy
	… approval for sth. …	public awareness campaign
	… work on sth. …	print ads
	… intend to …	bus posters
	… a team of …	get the go-ahead from
	… introduce sth. to sb. …	advertising campaign
	… plans for sth. …	
	… help with sth. …	

　　假如你的答案沒有這麼完整，不必擔心。只要多練習，就能找出文中所有的固定元素。不過你可以確定一件事：等到你能找出這麼多的字串，那就表示你的英文已經達到登峰造極的境界了！很快你便能擁有這樣的能力。現在有時間的話，各位不妨找一篇英文文章，像是以英語為母語的人所寫的電子郵件，或者雜誌或網路上的文章，然後用它來做同樣的練習。熟能生巧哦！

⊙ 本書使用說明

　　到目前為止，我猜各位大概會覺得 Leximodel 似乎是個不錯的概念，但八成還是有些疑問。對於各位可能會有的問題，我來看看能否幫各位解答。

26

我該如何實際運用 **Leximodel** 學英文？為什麼 **Leximodel** 和我以前碰到的英文教學法截然不同？

簡而言之，我的答案是：只要知道字詞的組合和這些組合的固定程度，就能簡化英語學習的過程，同時大幅減少犯錯的機率。

以前的教學法教你學好文法，然後套用句子。用這方法學習不僅有如牛步，而且稍不小心便錯誤百出，想必你早就有切身的體驗。現在只要用 Leximodel 建立 chunks、set-phrases 和 word partnerships 語庫，接著只需背起來就能學好英文了。

本書如何使用 **Leximodel** 教學？

本書介紹在不同的商務領域和工作中會使用到的關鍵名詞。也會教你可以與關鍵名詞一起使用的搭配詞組（word partnerships），並且幫你能夠有信心地使用這些詞組在聽、說、讀、寫四項能力中。

為什麼要留意字串中所有的字，很重要嗎？

不知道何故，大多數人對眼前的英文視而不見，分明擺在面前仍然視若無睹。他們緊盯著字詞的意思，卻忽略了傳達字詞意思的方法。每天瀏覽的固定字串多不勝數，只不過你沒有發覺這些字串是固定、反覆出現罷了。任何語言都有這種現象。這樣吧，我們來做個實驗，你就知道我說的是真是假。請做下面的 task。

Task 7 看看下面表格中的 set-phrases 和 chunks，並把正確的選出來。

- Regarding the report you sent me, …
- Regarding to the report you sent me, …
- Regards to the report you sent me, …
- With regards the report you sent, …

- … contact sb. …
- … get in contact sb. …
- … contact with sb. …
- … get contact with sb. …

> 我敢說你一定覺得這題很難。你可能每天都看到這個 set-phrase 和 chunk，但卻從來沒有仔細留意過其中的語言細節。（每一組的第一個才是對的，其他都是錯的！）

如果多留意每天接觸到的固定字串，久而久之一定會記起來，轉化成自己英文基礎的一部分，這可是諸多文獻可考的事實。刻意注意閱讀時遇到的字串，亦可增加學習效率。Leximodel 正能幫你達到這一點。

本書內有許多 task，其目的即在於幫你克服這些問題。學字串的要領在於：務必留意字串中所有的字。

從 Task 7 中，你可能已發現自己其實不如想像中那麼細心注意 set-phrases 和 chunks 中所有的字。接下來我要更確切地告訴你學 set-phrases 和 chunks 時的注意事項，這對學習非常重要。

學習和使用 set-phrases 時，需要注意的細節有四大類：

1. **短字**（如 a、the、to、in、at、on 和 but）。這些字很難記，但是瞭解了這點，即可以說是跨出一大步了。Set-phrases 極為固定，用錯一個短字，整個 set-phrase 都會改變，等於是寫錯了。

2. **字尾**（有些字的字尾是 -ed，有些是 -ing，有些是 -ment，有些是 -s，或者沒有 -s）。字尾改變了，字的意思也會隨之改變。Set-phrases 極為固定，寫錯其中一字的字尾，整個 set-phrase 都會改變，等於是寫錯了。所以發音時也得注意這個細節。

3. **Set-phrase 的結尾**（有的 set-phrases 以 n. clause 結尾，有的以 n.p. 結尾，有的以 V 結尾，有的以 Ving 結尾），我們稱之為 code。許多人犯錯，問題即出在句子中 set-phrase 與其他部分的銜接之處。學習 set-phrases 時，必須將 code 當作 set-phrase 的一部分一併背起來。Set-phrases 極為固定，code 寫錯，整個 set-phrase 都會改變，等於是寫錯了。

4. **完整的 set-phrase**。Set-phrase 是固定的單位，所以你必須完整地使用，不能只用前面一半或其中的幾個字而已。

Set-phrases 是 Leximodel 中最固定的字串，因此以上大部分的須知都圍繞著 set-phrases，但這些須知在使用 chunks 時往往也都能派上用場。學習和使用 chunks 和 set-phrases 時，重點就在於留心檢查小地方。最常出錯的正是那些小地方，英文就有一種說法：The devil is in the details!

　　教學到此，請再做一個 task，確定你能夠掌握 code 的用法。現在請做 Task 8。

Task 8　請看以下 code 的定義，然後按表格將詞組分門別類。請看範例。

n. clause = noun clause（名詞子句），以前你的老師應該是稱之為 SVO，這樣說也沒錯。n. clause 一定包含主詞和動詞。例如：I need your help.、She is on leave.、We are closing the department.、What is your estimate? 等。

n.p.　　 = noun phrase（名詞片語），這其實就是 word partnerships，不含動詞或主詞。例如：financial news、cost reduction、media review data、joint stock company 等。

V　　　 = verb（動詞）。

Ving　 = verb ending in -ing（以 -ing 結尾的動詞）。Ving 是看起來像名詞的動詞。

arrange	go ahead with	prepare to
Can you help?	having	require
doing	he is not	return
general meeting	helping	sending
get on with	It's not right	talking
annual report	knowing	telephone call
	Mary is on leave	we are going to
		we don't know

n. clause	n.p.	V	Ving
	annual report		

n. clause	n.p.	V	Ving
he is not	telephone call	arrange	helping
we are going to	annual report	return	knowing
Mary is on leave	general meeting	require	doing
we don't know		prepare to	having
It's not right		go ahead with	sending
Can you help?		get on with	talking

總而言之，在學習 set-phrases 時，要留意的細節有：

1. 短字

2. 字尾

3. Set-phrases 的結尾

4. 完整的 set-phrases

不會太困難，對吧？

有沒有哪些問題需要注意？

有。在這裡我想提醒你三個問題。

首先，由於本書的主要焦點在商務常用搭配詞，大部分由名詞搭配動詞和形容詞組成，你必須先將名詞弄懂。從**文法**上來看，有三種名詞：可數名詞，例如：investment；不可數名詞，例如：assessment；以及可為

可數和不可數、但意思隨之不同的名詞，例如：business。

　　從**意義**上來看，也有三種名詞：形容人物的名詞，例如：client；形容活動或過程的名詞，例如：marketing；與形容事物或觀念的名詞，例如：market。當你閱讀本書的時候，請記得這幾點。

　　第二個問題是中式英文的思考方式。大部分字典都會給你單字的翻譯。有些字典也會提供你一些與字彙一起使用的字。這些字的組合並不容易翻譯。舉例來說，「參加開會」，如果你以中文式思考翻譯這些字，「參加」就變會成 join 或是 attend，「開會」則是 meeting。但是在英文裡，attend a meeting 和 join a meeting 是不自然的說法，因為這些字並不常搭配在一起使用。當你翻譯句子時，記得這點。要確保你翻譯的是文意與意義，而非字面意思。要做到這一點的關鍵在於：不要將學習焦點放在單一的字上，而是放在整個搭配詞組的意義上。因此，「參加開會」（視為一個語言單位）應翻成：go to a meeting。

　　第三個問題是字詞的搭配。字詞的搭配指的是字與字配對組合在一起的方式。在這裡要說明的是哪一個動詞或形容詞可以與關鍵名詞一起搭配使用。有時候，改變字的組合，也改變了一個或所有字的意思。舉例來說，如果你說 join a party，party 代表的是一個你可以加入成為會員的政黨；如果你說 go to a party，party 指的是某種慶祝會，像是生日會或是喜宴。**本書的焦點在於學習商務英文情境中常用的搭配詞。搭配詞能幫助你說出自然的英文，使你的英文更精確、更容易被瞭解。**字詞如何搭配並沒有法則可循，只要把那些搭配在一起使用的詞組學習起來即可。

➔ 本書的架構

　　本書分成四部分。第一部分教你談論工作程序的字彙，不管你從事哪一種工作都可以用到。你在開會、參加電話會議與簡報，不管什麼主題這些字彙都可派上用場。

　　第二部分的重點在管理。不論你從事哪一行，這個部分提供最常用的搭配詞組來從事與談論專案管理和策略管理。

第三部分的重點在於四個核心商務功能：行銷、財務、銷售與生產中使用到的字彙。如果你在這四個部門工作，或是工作上需與他們進行業務往返，不管是哪一行，你都會發現這些單元非常實用。

第四部分會教你兩個支援性商務部門：人力資源與資訊科技會使用到的字彙。

另外，每章皆分為「上手篇」與「工具篇」。如果時間充裕，建議你從「上手篇」逐步閱讀、做練習，有助於你吸收內化每章所教的用語。如果臨時需要惡補、快速學到所需用語，則可閱讀「工具篇」中所整理出的重點語彙。

你可以把本書從頭到尾讀完，或只專注於最符合你需要的單元。學習的方法操之在你，但是記得，每天讀一點要比一週讀2小時的效果來得好！

我如何充分利用本書？

在此有些自習的建議，協助你獲致最大的學習效果。

1. 建議用鉛筆做書中的task。寫錯時方便訂正。
2. 建議你在有空時，練習抄寫task中所教的用語。還記得當初是怎麼學中文的嗎？抄寫能夠加深印象！
3. 做聽力練習的時候，請先將MP3至少聽三遍，然後再查閱答案或對照錄音稿。
4. 做口說練習的時候，請錄下自己的口說，聽過錄音之後再練習一次。你可以比較二次練習的錄音，看看自己進步了多少。請把音檔儲存在電腦中，並花一點時間整理。
5. 利用機會練習自己新學到的用語，請記住以下重點：
   • 選擇困難、奇怪或新的用語。
   • 如果可以的話，避免使用你已經知道或覺得運用自如的用語。
   • 刻意多運用這些新的用語。
6. 如果你下定決心要進步，建議你和同事組成K書會，一同閱讀本書和做練習。

祝學習有成！

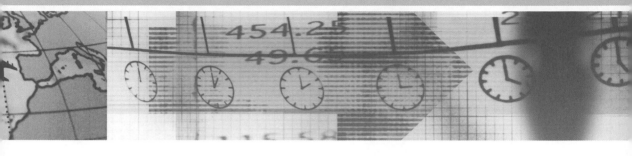

Part 1 | 商務作業
Working in Business

在一開始的兩個單元裡，我們要來看看你在商務工作中能夠使用的一些基本語言。首先，我們會學一些用來談論你的工作的關鍵名詞。然後我們要看看在不同的商業環境裡：不管你從事哪一行，或者你的工作是什麼，都能夠使用的一些關鍵名詞。

Unit 1

工作程序 Job Procedures

For many people a job is more than an income — it's an important part of who we are.

Paul Clitheroe

agenda 議程	appointment 約定	job 工作
manager 經理	meeting 會議	minutes 會議記錄
negotiation 談判	presentation 簡報	procedure 程序
proposal 提案	report 報告	system 制度
trip（因事）外出		

這些都是我們在這個單元裡要學的關鍵名詞。你將學習如何使用它們來說出與寫出你的工作程序。看完本單元，你將達到以下的學習目標：

☐ 有自信地談論你的工作
☐ 瞭解與關鍵字彙一起使用的主要搭配詞
☐ 瞭解一些關鍵字彙的複合名詞
☐ 能夠運用關鍵字彙與它們的搭配詞，做一些聽力、口說與寫作的練習

上手篇

一開始我們先來學一些動詞與名詞的搭配用語。

Task 1 請看這些工作任務，在你工作中通常或經常會做的項目旁打 ✔ 。

(   ) do a good job

(   ) draw up an agenda

(   ) have an appointment

(   ) report to your manager

(   ) go to a meeting

(   ) read through the minutes

(   ) hold negotiations

(   ) give a presentation

(   ) read a proposal

(   ) carry out a procedure

(   ) read a report

(   ) implement a system

(   ) make a trip

有的字彙不認識，別著急！本章最後的「工具篇」收錄了這些用語並附上中譯，做完練習後可參考中譯核對你的答案。

🎧 02

Task 2 現在請聽賴利談談他的工作，並找出賴利需負責哪些工作任務。

如果你覺得困難，多聽幾次。注意，賴利可能會提到某些不是他負責的工作程序。請閱讀書末的「錄音稿」來核對你的答案。

Task 3　請再看這些不同的工作任務，在你工作中通常或經常會做的項目旁打 ✓ 。

(　) put something on an agenda

(　) confirm an appointment

(　) inform your manager about something

(　) arrange a meeting

(　) take meeting minutes

(　) conduct negotiations

(　) attend a presentation

(　) write a proposal

(　) follow a procedure

(　) receive a report

(　) establish a system

(　) arrange a trip

本章最後的「工具篇」收錄了這些用語並附上中譯，做完練習後可參考中譯核對你的答案。

🎧 03

Task 4　現在請聽崔西談談她的工作，並找出崔西需負責哪些工作任務。

多聽幾次直到確定你完全瞭解為止。請閱讀書末的「錄音稿」來核對你的答案。

Task 5　現在請看這些不同的工作任務，在你工作中通常或經常會做的項目旁打 ✓ 。

(　) approve an agenda

(　) miss an appointment

(　) act as manager

(　) chair a meeting

(   ) sign meeting minutes

(   ) open negotiations

(   ) see a presentation

(   ) put together a proposal

(   ) introduce a procedure

(   ) submit a report

(   ) develop a system

(   ) cut short a trip

 做完練習後可參考「工具篇」的中譯核對你的答案。

🎧 04

Task 6 現在請聽瑪麗談談她的工作，並找出瑪麗需負責哪些工作任務。

多聽幾次直到確定你完全瞭解為止。請閱讀書末的「錄音稿」來核對你的答案。

⊙ 配對練習

Task 1、3、5 所介紹的用語，都是在談論工作程序時非常實用的語彙。為了幫助你們更熟悉這些用語，現在我們用這些動詞與名詞的組合來做一些配對的練習，練習題的答案請參照書末的解答。

Task 7 將左欄動詞與最常搭配的名詞配對。請看範例。

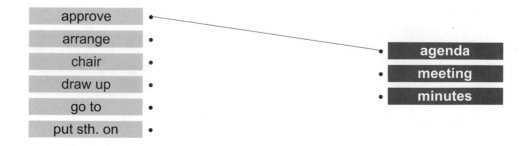

read through	•	•	agenda
sign	•	•	meeting
take	•	•	minutes

注意：書中的字彙配對練習，以組成最常見的搭配詞為主。並不代表其他可能的字彙組合就一定是錯誤的，只是使用頻率較低。以 Task 7 為例，approve 與 agenda 配在一起，是因為使用頻率高。但是，你當然也可以說 approve meetings 與 approve minutes。練習目的不在於探討一個正確的答案，而是幫助你熟悉使用頻率最高的搭配組合，好讓你學會在口說與寫作中使用它們。

Task 8 將每個動詞與最常搭配的名詞配對。

conduct	•		
confirm	•		
have	•	•	appointment
hold	•	•	negotiation
miss	•		
open	•		

Task 9 將每個動詞與最常搭配的名詞配對。這當中至少有一個動詞可以使用兩次，找找看是哪一個？

attend	•		
give	•		
put together	•		
read	•	•	presentation
receive	•	•	report
see	•	•	proposal
submit	•		
write	•		

40

Task 10　將每個動詞與最常搭配的名詞配對。

act as　　　•

arrange　　•

cut short　 •

inform　　 •

go on　　　•

report to　 •

　　　　　　　　　　　　　　　• **manager**

　　　　　　　　　　　　　　　• **trip**

Task 11　將每個動詞與最常搭配的名詞配對。

carry out　 •

develop　　•

establish　 •

follow　　　•

implement　•

introduce　 •

　　　　　　　　　　　　　　　• **system**

　　　　　　　　　　　　　　　• **procedure**

參考本書後面的解答。當你使用 verb-noun 搭配詞組，記得調整動詞時態。接下來藉由一連串的 task，我們要來探討如何使用 verb-noun 搭配詞組談論不同的時間。

🎧 02-04

Task 12　現在再聽一遍 CD 02 、 03 與 04 。說話者使用什麼時態？為什麼？

說話者用現在簡單式談論一些他們每天都要做的程序與固定行程。如果你很難聽出來，建議你一邊讀錄音稿一邊聽。當你閱讀時，在動詞下方畫線，並注意它們是什麼時態。

Task 13　現在練習用你剛剛學到的用語，說出你自己的工作程序或一些你每天在工作中做的事。記得要使用現在簡單式。

我們來聽聽賴利談他今天做的事。

🎧 05

Task 14 聽取 CD05。你可以聽出哪些在 task 1、task 3、task 5 出現過的搭配詞組？在聽的過程中將它們寫下來。

接著，把注意力放在賴利今天完成的事，以及尚未完成的事。

Task 15 請再聽一次並完成下列的表格。請看範例。 🎧 05

completed results	uncompleted activities
I've had three appointments today already	

 請參考本書後面的解答核對你的答案。注意，賴利用現在完成式（have + p.p.）談論他今天已完成的事，用現在進行式（be Ving）談論仍在進行的事。我們接著來練習這個技巧。

Task 16 談談你今天一天之內發生的事。用正確的時態說出你完成的事與你正在進行的事。練習使用 task 7 至 task 11 當中出現的搭配詞組。

 替自己錄音，然後聽錄音檢查自己使用的動詞時態是否正確。

🎧 06

Task 17 現在我們來聽崔西談論她昨天一整天發生的事。仔細聽，並找出她使用了 task 1、task 3 與 task 5 裡頭哪些搭配詞組，以及她用什麼時態說話。

你可以閱讀本書後面的錄音稿以找出搭配詞組。崔西用了過去式談論她昨天一天發生的事。記得，當你在談論過去時間裡發生過的事件或行動時，應該要使用過去簡單式的動詞。

Task 18 現在請你談談昨天工作時做過的事。練習利用 task 7 至 task11 當中的 **verb-noun** 搭配詞組，並確定動詞為過去簡單式。

替自己錄音，然後聽錄音檢查自己使用的動詞時態是否正確。

🎧 07

Task 19 現在我們來聽瑪麗談論她明天一整天要做的事。仔細聽，並找出她使用了 task 1、task 3 與 task 5 裡頭的哪些搭配詞組，以及她用什麼時態說話。

你可以閱讀本書後面的錄音稿以找出這些搭配詞組。當瑪麗在說明她的時間計畫時，她用了下列的 chunks：
- be Ving
- have to V
- be going to V
- have got to V

🎧 07

Task 20 請再聽一次，聽聽看這些 **word partnerships** 如何與 chunks 搭配使用。

你可以參照錄音稿。記得，當你在談論關於未來的計畫或時間表時，要使用這些 chunks，而不要用 will，因為這個字不能用來談論計畫與時間表。

Task 21 現在請練習談談你明天或下星期的時間表。利用 task 7 至 task 11 出現的搭配詞組，以及 task 19 的 chunks。

替自己錄音，然後聽錄音檢查自己使用的動詞時態是否正確。

到目前為止，我們學習的都是出現在名詞前面的動詞。現在，我們來看看出現在這兩個名詞：job 與 negotiation 後面的動詞。

Task 22 請研讀下列語庫。

job	involve n.p. involve Ving require that n. clause

Task 23 閱讀這則工作說明。將文章中出現先前語庫中的 **verb chunks** 畫線，並學習它們的使用方法。

Junior Sales Manager

The job involves a wide range of responsibilities. The job involves demonstrating the product to prospective clients, working on the road and going to different locations around the country. The job requires that you are independent, responsible and can work without close supervision.

中譯

初階業務經理

此份工作包含廣泛的工作職掌。工作包含向潛在客戶展示說明產品、外出工作、在國內各地奔波。工作需要你獨立、負責，並能在沒有就近管理下作業。

Task 24 請研讀下列語庫。

negotiation	take place go well go badly continue involve n.p. involve Ving break down

The negotiations took place at the Westin Hotel. The negotiations involved teams from both companies, and involved reaching agreement on the terms of the merger. At the beginning the negotiations went well. Both parties were eager to exchange points of view and make compromises. However, after the second day, the negotiations went badly, due to the issue of staff redundancies. Nevertheless, the negotiations continued. On the fourth day, it was obvious that due to differences of opinion regarding staff redundancies, the merger was going to be impossible under current conditions. Negotiations broke down over this issue.

中譯

談判在 Westin 飯店舉行。談判包含來自雙方的人員，包含在合併條件上達成協議。談判一開始進行得很順利，雙方急切地交換意見、妥協。然而，第二天過後，受到冗員議題的影響，談判進行得不順利。不過談判還是持續進行。第四天時，顯然受到冗員議題意見相左的影響，合併在目前的條件下無法達成，談判由於此議題而宣告破裂！

Task 26 請研讀下列語庫。

report	recommend that n. clause
	recommend n.p.
	suggest that n. clause
	suggest n.p.
	say that n. clause
	state that n. clause
	show that n. clause
	show n.p.
	conclude that n. clause

Task 27 閱讀這篇報告摘要。將文章中出現先前語庫中的 verb chunks 畫線，並學習它們的用法。

The report shows that our previous estimates were wrong. It states clearly that our estimates were based on faulty information, although the report does not show the correct information. It also says that false information was supplied to us deliberately. The report recommends the collection of new data, and recommends that we carry out another assessment based on this new data. The report also suggests that we hire an outside consultant to do the assessment, and it suggests a few consultancies for us to contact.

The report concludes that the project still has possibilities, but that a new assessment is needed before a decision can be reached.

中譯

報告顯示我們先前的估計錯誤。它清楚地指出我們的估計乃基於錯誤資訊，雖然報告並未顯示正確資訊。它也指出有人蓄意提供錯誤訊息。報告建議我們蒐集新資料，並根據此新資料重新做評估。報告也建議我們雇請外部顧問來做此評估，它推薦了一些顧問來讓我們聯繫。

報告結論指出專案仍有可行性，但在達成決議之前必須先做好新的評估。

Task 28 現在請用 job、negotiations 或是 report 完成這些句子。

• After three weeks of no progress, the (1)＿＿＿＿ finally broke down.

• Also, the (2)＿＿＿＿ recommended that we close down one of the factories.

• Did the (3)＿＿＿＿ state that we need to improve working conditions?

• Did the (4)＿＿＿＿ suggest any improvements?

• Her new (5)＿＿＿＿ requires that she works really long hours, so I never get to spend any time with her.

• I wonder why the (6)＿＿＿＿ said that the employees were not happy.

• If the (7)＿＿＿＿ go well, I might get a promotion!

- It seems that the (8)_____ involve a lot of discussion about numbers.
- My (9)_____ involves too much waiting around. It's really boring.
- She told me that the (10)_____ involved looking at the figures from the last five years.
- The (11)_____ involves a lot foreign travel. Do you like travel?
- The (12)_____ are going badly. Neither side can agree.
- The (13)_____ are taking place right now.
- The (14)_____ continued after a break for lunch.
- The (15)_____ clearly shows that we are negligent here.
- The (16)_____ recommended several strong measures.
- The (17)_____ suggested that the factory was unsafe.
- Well, the (18)_____ shows no evidence of this.
- Why did the (19)_____ conclude that we should close down our plants?

請參看書末的解答核對你的答案。

現在我們要來學一些你可以與這些關鍵名詞一起搭配使用的形容詞。

Task 29 請將左欄形容詞與最常搭配的名詞配對。請看範例。（注意：名詞也有形容詞的功能。）

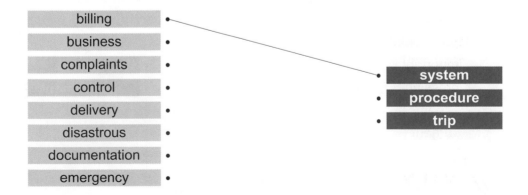

billing
business
complaints
control
delivery
disastrous
documentation
emergency

system
procedure
trip

enjoyable •	• system
inventory •	• procedure
standard operating •	• trip
weekend •	

 請參看書末的解答核對你的答案。「工具篇」附有中譯供參考。

Task 30 請將每個形容詞與最常搭配的名詞配對。

delicate •	
effective •	
excellent •	• negotiation
intensive •	• presentation
lengthy •	
ongoing •	
short •	

 請參看書末的解答核對你的答案。

Task 31 請將每個形容詞與最常搭配的名詞配對。皆可適用在這兩個名詞的形容詞至少有兩個。請找出是哪兩個。

board •	
departmental •	
important •	• meeting
pressing •	• appointment
team •	
urgent •	

 請參看書末的解答。

現在，我們來練習使用「形容詞＋名詞」詞組。

Task 32 記得在 task 29 至 task 31 學過的名詞嗎？現在來練習使用它們，請利用它們來完成下列句子。

- I had to take minutes at the board (1)_____ .
- I have a very important (2)_____ with him. Please let him know I have arrived.
- I have an urgent (3)_____ this afternoon. I have to leave now.
- I have to go on a business (4)_____ to Hong Kong next week.
- I like his (5)_____. They are always very short.
- I think we have problems with the inventory (6)_____. We have too much of one kind of stock, and not enough of the other.
- If a customer makes a complaint, you have to follow the complaints (7)_____.
- If there is a fire, please follow the emergency (8)_____.
- My wife and I are taking a weekend (9)_____ to Okinawa!
- Our control (10)_____ is not working well. There are many faulty products.
- Please make sure you follow the documentation (11)_____. Otherwise the documents will get mislaid.
- Standard operating (12)_____ is to report all workplace injuries within 24 hours.
- That was a disastrous (13)_____! The flight was delayed and then the hotel burned down!
- That was a very effective (14)_____. I liked your slides very much.
- The (15)_____ are very lengthy. We have a lot of points to cover.
- The delivery (16)_____ is working very well. We can track shipments all over the world.
- The intensive (17)_____ made everyone exhausted.
- The ongoing (18)_____ seem to be taking forever.
- We are conducting (19)_____ for a merger.

- We have a departmental (20)_____ this afternoon.
- We have a new billing (21)_____. The bill will be sent to you automatically.
- We need a team (22)_____ to discuss the project.
- What an enjoyable (23)_____! It was so relaxing and such fun!
- Your (24)_____ was excellent! Congratulations!

參看解答核對你的答案。

現在我們來學一些含有 presentation 這個名詞的複合名詞。

Task 33 請將這些複合名詞與下列句子代表的意義配對。

presentation skills	presentation handout
presentation slides	presentation package
presentation style	

1. All the contents of the presentation, including handouts, slides, and performance. _____

2. The papers you give to the audience at the end of the presentation. _____

3. The visuals you display to the audience during the presentation. _____

4. The way of doing a presentation. _____

5. Your ability to give a presentation. _____

Task 34 現在請你使用上一個 task 當中的複合名詞改寫以下句子，使句意不變。請先研讀範例。

例： He has excellent skills for giving presentations.
→ He has excellent presentation skills

1. I forgot the handouts for the presentation.

_____

2. The slides for the presentation were very well designed.

_____

3. The whole package of the presentation was very professional.

_____

4. I like his style of presentation. It's very clear and easy to follow.

_____

5. You need to work on your skills for giving presentations.

_____

 請參考解答核對你的答案。

⊙ 強化練習

好了，在我們結束這個單元之前，一起來加強一下我們學過的東西。看看你學到了多少。

Task 35 練習寫一封信給朋友，說明你的工作內容。盡量包含細節，並且盡可能地多多使用你在本單元學到的用語。

Dear Johnny,

I hope you are well there and everything is still OK at home. I have been in the U.S. for three weeks now, working at my new job, and so far I am really enjoying it! The people here are very nice, and very helpful. Everyone has been so kind helping me to settle in to the company.

I want to tell you a little bit about my job, 'cause it's all so new and exciting to me! Mostly my duties are to assist the manager of the accounting department. It's a very junior job, but I think it will get better after a few months. At the moment I am learning how to follow the procedures and implement the systems they have here. There are so many of them, sometimes I get confused. Also, I have been learning how to take minutes for meetings, and how to draw up agendas for the meetings. I don't actually participate in the meetings, just listen and take notes, but it's good training for my English. My boss tells me I am doing a great job, so I must be doing something right!

I also have to inform my manager about changes to his schedule, and make and confirm his appointments. He's very busy, so I have to write a lot of emails for him, cancelling and changing his schedule. It's good that I studied email writing so hard at home! He has to put together quite a lot of proposals, submit tons of reports, and also give presentations so I have been helping him with that, you know, collecting data and running around for him.

Last week he had to conduct important negotiations with a client, and he took me along with him to watch and learn. It was so interesting to see how all these people do business together. So different from our country!

Next week, things will be a bit easier as he is going on a business trip for a week. I hope to have more time to write more to you then. Meanwhile, give lots of love to Mum and Dad and squeeze Baby Alice for me.

Lots of love,

Jade

中譯

親愛的強尼：

我希望你在那邊一切安好，家中也一切無恙。我到美國已經三星期了，做著我的新工作，到目前為止我很享受這份工作。這邊的人都很好，也很樂於助人。每個人都很好心地幫助我在公司安定下來。

我想和你大概談談我的工作。因為它對我來說是如此新奇和刺激！我主要的職責是協助會計部門的經理。這是個非常初階的工作，但我想幾個月後情況會轉好。此刻我學著如何遵照他們這邊所使用的程序和系統執行。為數眾多，我有時都搞混了。此外，我也學著做會議記錄和如何設定會議議程。我通常不參與會議，只是旁聽和做筆記，但這對我的英文能力也是很好的訓練。老闆告訴我我做得很好，所以我一定是做對事了。

我也必須通知經理關於他的行程的變更，幫他預約會面和確認約會。他非常忙碌，所以我必須替他寫許多的電子郵件，取消和變更他的行程。還好我在家時很認真地學習電子郵件的寫作。他必須整合許多的提案、提交大量的報告和做簡報，所以我一直在幫他處理這些事，你知道的，蒐集資料、替他跑跑腿。

上星期他必須和客戶進行一場重要的談判，他帶著我去觀摩和學習。看著這些人如何一起做生意實在非常有趣，和我們國家非常不同。

下星期他要出差一週，所以應該會輕鬆一些。我希望到時會有更多時間寫信給你，同時，獻上諸多的愛給爸媽，幫我用力地抱抱寶貝愛麗絲。

非常愛你們，
潔

 請參看本書後面的解答，已為你標示出本章學過的重要用語。

好了，本單元到此結束。希望你學會了如何談論與寫出你的工作程序。在接下來的單元裡，你還會遇到許多在此單元中學過的字彙。屆時你將學習以不同的方式使用它們。

在進入下一個單元之前，請回到單元一開始的學習目標清單，檢視自己是否都達成目標了。

工具篇：本章重點語彙

1. system 的搭配詞組

control 控制	
billing 記帳	**system 系統**
delivery 運送	
inventory 存貨	

例 billing system = 記帳系統

2. procedure 的搭配詞組

complaints 抱怨	
documentation 文件證明	**procedure 程序**
emergency 緊急	
standard operating 標準化作業	

3. trip 的搭配詞組

disastrous 悲慘的	
enjoyable 愉快的	**trip 旅行**
weekend 週末的	
business 公務的	

4. negotiation 的搭配詞組

ongoing 進行中的	
lengthy 冗長的	**negotiation 談判**
intensive 密集的	
delicate 棘手的	

5. presentation 的搭配詞組

excellent 很棒的 effective 有效果的 short 簡短的	**presentation 簡報**

6. meeting 的搭配詞組

departmental 部門的 team 小組 board 董事會 important 重要的 urgent 緊急的	**meeting 會議**

7. appointment 的搭配詞組

pressing 緊急的 important 重要的 urgent 緊急的	**appointment 約會**

8. 關鍵字彙的搭配詞組

❖ draw up an agenda 設定議程
❖ put something on an agenda 將某事項列入議程
❖ approve an agenda 核准議程

❖ have an appointment 有約會
❖ confirm an appointment 確認約會
❖ miss an appointment 錯過約會

❖ report to your manager 向你的經理做報告
❖ inform your manager about something 通知你的經理某事
❖ act as manager 做為經理

- go to a meeting 參加會議
- arrange a meeting 安排一個會議
- chair a meeting 主持會議

- read through the minutes 讀過會議記錄
- take meeting minutes 做會議記錄
- sign meeting minutes 在會議記錄上簽名

- hold negotiations 召開談判
- conduct negotiations 進行談判
- open negotiations 開始談判

- give a presentation 做簡報
- attend a presentation 參加簡報
- see a presentation 觀看簡報

- read a proposal 閱讀提案
- write a proposal 寫提案
- put together a proposal 整合提案

- read a report 閱讀報告
- receive a report 收到報告
- submit a report 交報告

- introduce a procedure 引進程序
- carry out a procedure 實行程序
- follow a procedure 遵照程序

- implement a system 執行系統
- establish a system 建立系統
- develop a system 研發系統

- ❖ go on a trip 外出一趟
- ❖ arrange a trip 安排行程
- ❖ cut short a trip 縮短行程

- ❖ do a good job 工作做得很棒

9. 與 job 相關的字串

job 工作	involve n.p. 包含……
	involve Ving 包含……
	require that n. clause 需要……

10. 與 negotiation 相關的字串

negotiation 談判	take place 舉行
	go well 進行順利
	go badly 進行不順利
	continue 繼續
	involve n.p. 包含……
	involve Ving 包含……
	break down 破裂

11. 與 report 相關的字串

report 報告	recommend that n. clause 建議……
	recommend n.p. 建議……
	suggest that n. clause 建議……
	suggest n.p. 建議……
	say that n. clause 指出……
	state that n. clause 指出……
	show that n. clause 顯示……
	show n.p. 顯示……
	conclude that n. clause 結論指出……

Unit 2

商務對談 Business Talk

It's not what you say but how you say it.

Anonymous

agenda 議程	analysis 分析	challenge 挑戰
concern 顧慮	effect 效果	factor 因素
figures 數據	issue 議題	meeting 會議
opportunity 機會	option 意見	point 觀點
position 見解；處境	problem 問題	question 詢問；問題
recommendation 推薦	situation 情況	solution 解決方法
suggestion 建議		

這些都是我們在這個單元裡要學的關鍵名詞。這些字彙都屬於高頻使用率與總括性意義的字。意思是說，這些字彙的意思非常廣泛，你可以在任何產業與任何工作領域裡使用它們。是經常出現在商務對談中的字彙。

在這個單元裡我們的學習焦點在於，如何能在會議、簡報、談判與社交的各個場合裡使用這些字彙。在接下來的幾個單元，還會介紹更多關於這些字彙的其他用法。讀完本單元，你將達到以下的學習目標：

☐ 瞭解與關鍵字彙一起使用的主要搭配詞
☐ 瞭解一些能與關鍵字彙一起使用的同義字
☐ 運用關鍵字彙與它們的搭配詞，做一些聽力、口說與寫作的練習
☐ 能夠有信心地在商務對談中使用這些關鍵名詞

上手篇

首先，我們來學一些「動詞＋名詞」、「形容詞＋名詞」的搭配詞組。

Task 1 　將左欄動詞與最常搭配的名詞配對。請看範例。兩個名詞皆可搭配的動詞至少有兩個，請找出是哪兩個。

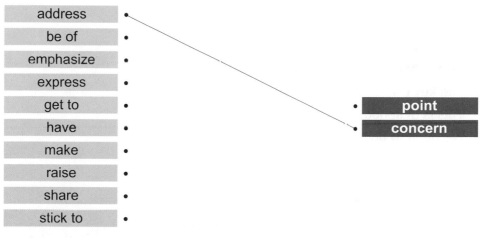

address	
be of	
emphasize	
express	
get to	**point**
have	**concern**
make	
raise	
share	
stick to	

 請參看本書後面的解答。「工具篇」附有中譯供參考。

Task 2 　將左欄形容詞與最常搭配的名詞配對。兩個名詞皆可搭配的形容詞至少有一個，請找出是哪一個。

controversial	
general	
key	
legitimate	**point**
main	**concern**
primary	
serious	

請參看本書後面的解答。

Task 3 從先前 task 裡選一個正確的名詞填入空格，完成下列的慣用語。

- Can you please get to the (1)＿＿＿＿＿?
- I have a number of (2)＿＿＿＿＿ with this.
- I have a number of key (3)＿＿＿＿＿ here.
- I have already expressed my main (4)＿＿＿＿＿.
- I would really like to emphasise this (5)＿＿＿＿＿.
- I'd like to share my (6)＿＿＿＿＿ with you.
- My general (7)＿＿＿＿＿ is …
- Please stick to the main (8)＿＿＿＿＿.
- The key (9)＿＿＿＿＿ I want to make here is …
- This is of serious (10)＿＿＿＿＿ to us.
- We need to address the primary (11)＿＿＿＿＿ of …
- You've raised a controversial (12)＿＿＿＿＿ there.
- You've raised a legitimate (13)＿＿＿＿＿.

 做完練習，別急著找答案，先繼續往 task 4 前進吧。

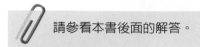 08

Task 4 聽取 CD 08 來核對 task 3 的答案。聽的時候，請一邊練習這些慣用語的念法。

如果需要，可以對照書末的錄音稿。把這些句子當成範例研讀搭配詞組的用法。

現在我們來看兩個字彙，它們分別都有兩個不同的意思： question 可以表示 inquiry「詢問」或 issue「爭論點、問題」；而 position 可以表示 opinion「見解、看法」或 situation「立場、處境」。做完下列練習，你會對這二個單字的用法有更清楚的概念。

Task 5 　將每個動詞與最常搭配的名詞意思配對。請看範例。

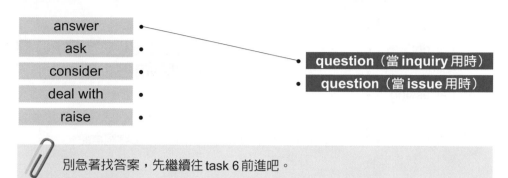

answer	
ask	
consider	**question**（當 **inquiry** 用時）
deal with	**question**（當 **issue** 用時）
raise	

 別急著找答案，先繼續往 task 6 前進吧。

Task 6 　將每個形容詞與最常搭配的名詞意思配對。

complex	
crucial	
good	**question**（當 **inquiry** 用時）
immediate	**question**（當 **issue** 用時）
tricky	

 現在可以參看書末的解答，留意 question 如何和動詞、形容詞搭配。

Task 7 　將每個動詞與最常搭配的名詞意思配對。

clarify	
explain	
find oneself in	**position**（當 **opinion** 用時）
outline	**position**（當 **situation** 用時）
put sb. in	
state	

別急著找答案，先繼續往 task 8 前進吧。

Task 8 將每個形容詞與最常搭配的名詞意思配對。

earlier	•
current	•
awkward	•
embarrassing	•

• **position**（當 opinion 用時）
• **position**（當 situation 用時）

 現在可以參看書末的解答，留意 position 如何和動詞、形容詞搭配。

Task 9 請以 question 或 position 填入空格，完成下列的慣用語。

- Can we please deal with the immediate (1)_____ of …?
- Can you clarify your current (2)_____ on this issue?
- Here I would just like to outline our earlier (3)_____.
- I apologize for putting you in an embarrassing (4)_____.
- I don't know how to answer that tricky (5)_____.
- I think I have already clearly stated my (6)_____ on this.
- I'd like to explain my (7)_____ on this.
- We need to consider two crucial (8)_____ now.
- Well, I find myself in an awkward (9)_____.
- You've asked a very good (10)_____.
- You've raised a complex (11)_____ there.

 做完練習，別急著找答案，先繼續往 task 10 前進吧。

🎧 09

Task 10 聽取 CD 09 來核對 task 9 的答案。聽的時候，請一邊練習這些慣用語的念法。

 如果需要，可以對照書末的錄音稿。把這些句子當成範例研讀搭配詞組的用法。

到目前為止，我們都在學習動詞與名詞（或動詞、形容詞與名詞）的詞組。在這些組合當中，動詞都出現在名詞前面。然而在從事商務活動的時候，有些關鍵字彙的動詞會出現在名詞後面。現在，我們來看看這些組合。

Task 11 將右欄動詞與最常搭配的名詞配對。請看範例。至少有一個動詞可以被使用兩次，請找出是哪一個。

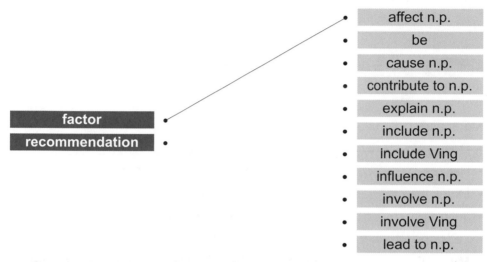

factor	affect n.p.
recommendation	be
	cause n.p.
	contribute to n.p.
	explain n.p.
	include n.p.
	include Ving
	influence n.p.
	involve n.p.
	involve Ving
	lead to n.p.

請參看本書後面的解答，如果還不甚理解這些詞組如何使用，不用擔心，在 task 13 中可以學到這些詞組的範例。

Task 12 將每個動詞與最常搭配的名詞配對。請看範例。至少有一個動詞可以被使用兩次，請找出是哪一個。

figures	confirm n.p.
analysis	confirm that n. clause
	demonstrate n.p.
	demonstrate that n. clause
	include n.p.

		indicate n.p.
		suggest that n. clause
figures	•	indicate that n. clause
analysis	•	provide n.p.
		represent n.p.
		suggest n.p.

請參看解答，如果還不甚理解這些詞組如何使用，在 task 13 中可以學到這些詞組的範例。

Task 13 從上二個 task 中選出一個正確的名詞填入空格，完成下列的慣用語。

- Dennis's (1)_____ do not involve any expense.
- Does your (2)_____ include redesigning the product?
- Her (3)_____ involves retraining all emergency personnel.
- I think the (4)_____ demonstrates that our strategy is the correct one.
- Julie's (5)_____ confirms that the market is indeed shrinking.
- Let's see whether the (6)_____ confirms this.
- My (7)_____ will demonstrate the effectiveness of these measures.
- My (8)_____ is at the back of the report.
- The (9)_____ provides clear evidence of a recession.
- The (10)_____ represent the situation last year.
- The (11)_____ in the report include cost analyses.
- There are many (12)_____ which influence a customer's decision to purchase something.
- There are three main (13)_____ affecting our margins at the moment.
- These (14)_____ may have contributed to the situation.
- These (15)_____ include all the data available up to the present time.
- This critical (16)_____ lead to the fire in the factory.
- This (17)_____ has caused problems for other companies before.
- This (18)_____ is important to take into consideration.

- The (19)＿＿＿＿＿ suggest a fall in consumer confidence.
- This (20)＿＿＿＿＿ still does not explain the cause of the decline.
- The (21)＿＿＿＿＿ suggests that it might be better to increase prices now.

請參看本書後面的解答，並學會這些詞組的用法。

⊕ 語言的提升

有一個方法可以使你的英文表達更豐富生動，那就是使用同義字。現在，我們就來學學可以與關鍵字彙 figures「數據」與 analysis「分析」搭配使用的同義字。在本書後面的幾個單元裡，我們還會學到更多的同義用法。

Task 14 請將這些 verb chunks 依照意義來歸類，意義相同者歸為一類。

- indicate n.p.
- show that n. clause
- reveal n.p.
- indicate that n. clause
- reveal that n. clause
- show n.p.

事實上，這些 verb chunks 相互皆為同義字！請看以下例句：
The figures show a drop in sales. 數據顯現出業績滑落。
The figures indicate a drop in sales. 數據指出業績滑落。
The figures reveal a drop in sales. 數據顯示出業績滑落。

要靈活運用這些同義字，就要熟悉 n. clause（名詞子句）和 n.p.（名詞片語）的用法。接下來的這個 task 會幫助你更加熟悉它們的使用方式。

Task 15 從下列找出最適合的 chunks 來完成句子。請看範例。

- a drop in sales
- the possibility of a recession

- the market is shrinking
- we need to increase our staff
- a rise in prices
- there are not enough sales staff

1. The figures show _a drop in sales_ .
2. The figures indicate _____ .
3. The figures reveal _____ .
4. The analysis shows that _____ .
5. The analysis indicates that _____ .
6. The analysis reveals that _____ .

 首先你必須分辨出上列的 chunk 是 n. clause 還是 n.p.。請參看本書後面的解答。

接著我們來學一些你在會議與簡報中可以使用的慣用語。

Task 16 研讀這些慣用語，然後從下面表格中選出一個字彙來完成句子。

agenda	effect	opportunity	recommendation
challenge	issue	option	situation
concern	meeting	problem	solution
			suggestion

- Anyone have any ideas about how to solve this (1)_____?
- Does anyone have any (2)_____ for this?
- During my presentation I'll be presenting a range of (3)_____ .
- I have a number of (4)_____ .
- I'd like to begin by briefing you on the current (5)_____ .
- I'd like to make a couple of (6)_____ at this point.
- I'd like to make a (7)_____ here, if I may.

- I'd like to move on to the next point on the (8)_____ now.
- I'd like to offer a (9)_____.
- I'd like to open this (10)_____ by …
- I'd like to take this (11)_____ to welcome …
- Let's just briefly review the present (12)_____.
- Let's look at the (13)_____ of this on our business.
- There is no easy (14)_____.
- We are facing a number of difficult (15)_____.
- We have a number of (16)_____ at this point.
- What are our (17)_____?
- Please stick to the (18)_____.
- The key (19)_____ is …

做完練習，別急著找答案，先繼續往 task 17 前進吧。

⌒ 10

Task 17 聽取 **CD 10** 來核對 **task 16** 的答案。聽的時候，請一邊練習這些慣用語的念法。

如果需要，可以對照書末的錄音稿。

⊙ 強化練習

好，現在我們來聽一場會議以強化和複習先前學過的語彙。

⌒ 11

Task 18 請聽會議的片斷。聽的時候，看看你是否能聽出本單元開頭介紹的關鍵字彙。注意它們在會議中如何被使用。然後回答下列問題：

⊙ 他們的計畫有什麼問題？
⊙ 山姆做了什麼建議？
⊙ 其他人對山姆的建議有什麼想法？

請參看錄音稿來核對你的答案。閱讀錄音稿時，除了在關鍵字彙下方畫線，也請注意先前學過的搭配詞與慣用語在這場會議中如何被使用。

接著，我們來聽一段簡報，學習將先前學過的用語套用在簡報中。

 12

Task 19 請聽這段簡報。聽的時候，看看是否能聽出本單元開頭介紹的關鍵字彙。注意它們在簡報中是如何被使用。然後回答這個問題：

▶ 這家公司在日本市場遇到哪兩個問題？

請參看錄音稿來核對你的答案。閱讀錄音稿時，除了在關鍵字彙下方畫線，也請注意先前學過的搭配詞與慣用語在這場簡報中如何被使用。

Task 20 請溫習本單元學過的用語。然後試著模擬一場會議或簡報，或是在你的下一場會議或簡報時使用這些用語。替自己錄音以便評估。

聽錄音時一邊想想下列問題：
• 你使用了多少本章的用語？
• 你是否使用正確？
• 使用它們對你而言容易嗎？
• 下一次使用時你要如何改善？

好了，本單元到此結束。在進入下一個單元之前，先回到本單元一開始的學習目標清單，檢視自己是否完全達成目標了。

工具篇：本章重點語彙

1. point 的搭配詞組

與動詞搭配

get to 進行到	
stick to 回到	
have 有	point 論點
raise 提出	
make 提出	
emphasize 強調	

例 get to the point = 快講重點（當某人講話言不及義時使用）

stick to the point = 回到重點（當某人講話離題時使用）

與形容詞搭配

general 一般的	
main 主要的	point 論點
key 重要的	
controversial 有爭議的	

2. concern 的搭配詞組

與動詞搭配

have 有	
raise 提出	
share 分享	concern 顧慮
address 提出	
express 表明	
be of 有	

例 be of concern = 有顧慮的（詳見下頁例句）

	concern 顧慮
main 主要的	
serious 嚴重的	
primary 主要的	
legitimate 合理的	

3. point 與 concern 的相關用語

❖ Can you please get to the point? 可不可以請你講重點？

❖ I have a number of concerns with this. 關於這件事我有幾點顧慮。

❖ I have a number of key points here. 我這邊有幾個重點要說明。

❖ I have already expressed my main concern. 我已經表明了我主要的顧慮。

❖ I would really like to emphasise this point. 我非常想強調這一點。

❖ I'd like to share my concerns with you. 我想要跟你分享我的顧慮。

❖ My general point is … 我主要的論點是……。

❖ Please stick to the main point. 請回到主要論點。

❖ The key point I want to make here is …
  我在這邊要說明的主要重點是……。

❖ This is of serious concern to us. 這是我們嚴重關切的事。

❖ We need to address the primary concern of …
  我們必須說明對於……的主要顧慮。

❖ You've raised a controversial point there. 你提出了一個頗具爭議的論點。

❖ You've raised a legitimate concern. 你提出了一個合理的顧慮。

4. question 的搭配詞組

當 inquiry「詢問」用時

動詞	形容詞	question 問題
ask 問	good 好的	
answer 回答	tricky 棘手的	

動詞	形容詞	
raise 提出	complex 複雜的	**question 議題**
consider 考慮	crucial 重要的	
deal with 處理	immediate 當前的	

5. position 的搭配詞組

當 opinion「觀點」用時

動詞	形容詞	
explain 解釋	earlier 早先的	**position 觀點**
outline 概述要點	current 目前的	
state 陳述		
clarify 釐清		

當 situation「處境」用時

動詞	形容詞	
find oneself in 發覺某人處於	awkward 為難的、棘手的	**position 處境**
put sb. in 使某人處於	embarrassing 尷尬的、窘迫的	

6. question 和 position 的相關用語

❖ Can we please deal with the immediate question of ...

我們可不可以處理當前……的議題？

❖ Can you clarify your current position on this issue?

您可不可以說明目前您在這項議題上的看法？

❖ Here I would just like to outline our earlier position.

在這裡我只是要略述我們早先的看法。

❖ I apologize for putting you in an embarrassing position.

我感到抱歉讓你陷入一個尷尬的處境。

❖ I don't know how to answer that tricky question.

我不知道如何回答那個棘手的提問。

❖ I think I have already clearly stated my position on this.

我想我已經清楚地說明了我對這件事的看法。

❖ I'd like to explain my position on this.

我想解釋我對這件事的看法。

❖ We need to consider two crucial questions now.

我們現在必須考慮兩件重要的議題。

❖ Well, I find myself in an awkward position.

嗯，我覺得自己身處窘境。

❖ You've asked a very good question.

你問了一個相當好的問題。

❖ You've raised a complex question there.

你提出了一個複雜的議題。

7. 與 factor 相關的字串

factor 因素	be 是……
	influence n.p. 影響……
	affect n.p. 影響……
	contribute to n.p. 造成……
	cause n.p. 造成……
	lead to n.p. 造成……
	explain n.p. 說明了……

8. 與 recommendation 相關的字串

recommendation 建議	be 是……
	involve Ving 包含……
	involve n.p. 包含……
	include n.p. 包含……
	include Ving 包含……

9. 與 figures 相關的字串

figures 數據	represent n.p. 代表……
	include n.p. 包含……
	suggest n.p. 說明……
	suggest that n. clause 說明……

10. 與 analysis 相關的字串

analysis 分析	demonstrate n.p. 顯示……
	demonstrate that n. clause 顯示……
	provide n.p. 提供……
	confirm n.p. 證實……
	confirm that n. clause 證實……
	suggest n.p. 指出……
	suggest that n. clause 指出……

Part 2 | 商務管理
Managing in Business

接下來的兩個單元裡，我們要來學一些在管理的時候你會用到的語言。先從專案管理開始，接著是策略管理。我們要學習如何使用這些關鍵字彙來「做」管理，以及在不同的情形下用這些字「談論」管理的話題。

Unit 3

專案管理 Project Management

The secret to managing is to keep the guys who hate you
away from the guys who are undecided.

Casey Stengel

agenda 議程	assessment 評估	budget 預算
cost 成本	challenge 挑戰	change 改變
delay 延遲	issue 議題	manager 經理
meeting 會議	minutes 會議記錄	problem 問題
project 專案	proposal 提案	recommendation 建言
report 報告	situation 情形、狀況	solution 解決方案
suggestion 建議		

這些是本單元我們要學的關鍵字彙。你將學習如何使用它們來說出與寫出你的專案管理。看完本單元,你將達到以下的學習目標:

☐ 瞭解何謂專案管理與如何做專案管理
☐ 瞭解與關鍵字彙一起使用的主要搭配詞
☐ 瞭解一些關鍵字彙的複合名詞
☐ 能夠運用同義字提升英文表達的豐富性
☐ 運用關鍵字彙與它們的搭配詞,做一些聽力與口說的練習
☐ 能夠有信心地使用關鍵名詞來談論與寫出專案管理

上手篇

一開始，我們先來瞭解更多關於專案管理的內容，以及練習在文段中找出關鍵字彙。

Task 1 請閱讀以下的短文，並找出當中的關鍵字彙。留意這些字彙在段落中如何被使用。

Tracy works for a software company. She has recently been assigned to be project manager for a software development project for a key customer. The first thing she does is assess the customer's situation in order to identify the key issues for the customers, and make sure she understands their needs.

Then, when she has carried out her assessment of the situation, she puts together a proposal. In her proposal she puts forward her recommendations for how to meet the client's needs. She estimates the cost of developing the program, and then prepares a budget for the whole project. She allocates tasks to her team members, and sets up procedures for dealing with delays which may occur.

When her proposal has been accepted, she starts to implement the project. If the team comes across problems, they try to look for the cheapest and most efficient solutions. Sometimes the client might make a change, then Tracy and her team have to find ways to overcome this challenge. Tracy manages the project by having regular meetings with her team. Tracy listens carefully when her team members come up with suggestions. She draws up agendas for the meetings, and keeps minutes. This way she can make sure the project is on time, and she can use the agendas and minutes to prepare her reports. She submits her reports to her manager and to the client, so that they know how the project is going.

中譯

崔西在一家軟體公司上班。最近她被指派為專案經理,負責一家主要客戶的軟體發展專案。她做的第一件事就是評估客戶的狀況,以便為客戶找出主要的議題,並確定瞭解他們的需求。

接著,當她評估完情形後,她會整合出一個提案。在她的提案中,她提出該如何滿足客戶需求的建議。她預估發展計畫所需的成本,然後為整個專案準備預算。她將任務分配給她的團隊成員,並訂定程序以因應可能發生的延遲。

她的提案被接受之後,她開始執行專案。如果團隊遇到問題,他們試著尋找最便宜且最有效率的解決方案。有時候客戶可能想做一些變更,崔西與她的團隊就必須找出方法來克服挑戰。崔西藉著與她的團隊定期開會來管理專案。當她的團隊成員提出建議時崔西都仔細聆聽。她為會議擬出議程,並做會議記錄。如此一來,她可以確定專案按時進行,並且利用議程與會議記錄準備她的報告。她向她的經理與客戶提出報告,好讓他們知道專案進行得如何。

⮕ 配對練習

接下來這個部分我們要把重心放在 6 個關鍵名詞。一開始先來學習與這些名詞一起搭配使用的動詞。

Task 2 請將左欄動詞與最常搭配的名詞配對。請看範例。

82

go through	•		•	meeting
have	•		•	agenda
read through	•		•	minutes
sign	•			
stick to	•			

 請參看本書後面的解答。有不認識的字彙，別擔心，「工具篇」附有完整中譯可供對照。

Task 3 請將左欄動詞與最常搭配的名詞配對。

brief sb. on	•			
coordinate	•		•	project
implement	•		•	situation
prepare	•		•	report
read	•			
resolve	•			
review	•			
run	•			
submit	•			

 參看解答核對你的答案。記住，在這些搭配詞組中，某些字可以搭配在一起使用，某些字不行。重要的是，把那些可以配對在一起的詞組學起來。把你在先前 task 裡配錯的組合記錄下來，加強研讀它們的正確組合。在接下來的單元裡你還會再次遇到這些字，屆時你將學到更多能與這些字一起搭配使用的字，如此，你就能夠利用這些簡單的字彙，變化出更多的搭配詞組，以應付商務活動中不同的任務。

下一個 task 要幫助你學會在句子中使用與這些關鍵名詞搭配的動詞。

請以前面那些 task 中的關鍵名詞完成這些句子。想想這些名詞應該使用單數還是複數，在答題過程中請留意這些名詞是與哪個動詞搭配使用。

- Because there are so many teams involved, it's difficult to coordinate this (1)_____.
- Did you read that (2)_____ on the IT sector?
- Hang on, I'm still reading through the (3)_____ of the last meeting.
- He did an excellent job of running the (4)_____.
- Hey, do we have an (5)_____ for this meeting?
- I am currently preparing a (6)_____. It will be ready tomorrow.
- I hope we can resolve the (7)_____ quickly so that we can all get back to work.
- I submitted my (8)_____ on Monday. I don't know if they have had time to read it yet.
- I'd like to go through the (9)_____ as quickly as possible please, so that we can finish the meeting quickly.
- I'm going to call a (10)_____ about the project.
- I'm sorry, but I can't accept these (11)_____. I don't think they reflect the meeting as I remember it.
- John, can you please chair this (12)_____?
- Let's review the (13)_____ in three months and see if there have been any changes.
- Mary, you forgot to sign the (14)_____ from the last meeting.
- OK, well, as the prototype is not ready, let's call off the (15)_____. There's no point talking about it if it's not ready.
- Please let's stick to the (16)_____, otherwise we will run out of time.
- Tracy, can you brief us on the (17)_____?
- We have spent a long time on planning, now it's time to implement the (18)_____.

請參閱解答。

現在我們來學習與關鍵字彙一起搭配使用的形容詞。

Task 5 將左欄形容詞與最常搭配的名詞配對。請看範例。

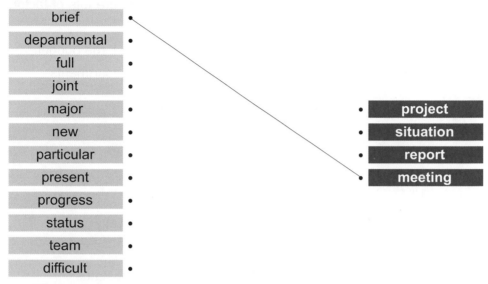

brief
departmental
full
joint
major
new
particular
present
progress
status
team
difficult

project
situation
report
meeting

請參閱解答。將答錯的組合抄下來，確實地研讀改正。你可以幾天後重新複習先前做過的 task，看看自己記得多少搭配詞組。

Task 6 請利用先前學過的關鍵名詞完成這些句子。想想這些名詞應該使用單數還是複數，在答題過程中請留意這些名詞和哪些形容詞搭配。

- Can you give us a quick status (1)_____? What's going on?
- He wasn't at the team (2)_____ yesterday, even though he is part of the team.
- I submitted a full (3)_____ last week. Didn't you read it yet?
- I'm working on a new (4)_____ at the moment. It involves lots of people.
- In this particular (5)_____ we need to be careful, otherwise it could get worse.
- It was a very brief (6)_____. He announced his resignation!
- It's a departmental (7)_____ , so we all need to be there, even if you're not involved in any projects.

- It's a difficult (8)_____ and I don't know how to resolve it.
- John, can you give us a quick progress (9)_____? How much have you completed?
- The present (10)_____ is very complicated. There are lots of factors we need to think about.
- This is a major (11)_____ with several teams and a large budget.
- This joint (12)_____ will involve teams from three departments.

參看解答核對你的答案。你可以把句子中的動詞與形容詞畫底線,幫助自己記憶這些搭配詞組。

接著我們來學習 project 這個字的複合名詞。

Task 7 請將表格中的字彙與正確的句意配對。請看範例。

project coordinator	project management	project status
project leader	project manager	project status review
	project proposal	project team

1. A meeting in which the current situation of a project is presented.

   _____

2. All the people working on a project. _____

3. An idea for a new project. _____

4. Someone who makes sure all the teams involved in a project are communicating with each other. _____

5. Someone who takes overall responsibility for the project.
   *project leader*_____

6. The current situation of a project. _____

7. The process of managing the project. _____

參看解答核對你的答案。

Task 8 請先研讀這兩個句子。然後使用前一個 task 中的複合名詞，依照相同的方式改寫下列句子。

例： He is the leader of the project.
→ He is the project leader.

1. The management of a project can be quite tricky sometimes.

_____

2. The person who coordinates the project needs to be able to communicate very well in English.

_____

3. The team for this project has some excellent people.

_____

4. I'd now like to tell you about the status of the project.

_____

5. We are having a review of the status of the project next week.

_____

6. The manager of the project does not know what she is doing.

_____

7. This is my first time to be a leader of a project.

_____

8. I outlined the problems in the proposal for the project.

_____

對照完解答，請將句子多研讀幾次，以熟悉這些詞彙的用法。

➔ 語言的提升

在接下來的部分，我們要來做 recommendation、proposal 與 suggestion 這三個字的同義字練習。在商業英文裡，a proposal「一份提案」通常是一份正式的書面文件，可能包含改進商務程序的建議（recommendation），或是新計畫的提議（suggestion）。在此階段先不用擔心這些字彙間的差異，因為差異通常取決於它們與哪些字詞搭配使用。

Task 9 將左欄動詞與它們最常搭配的名詞配對。當中有些動詞與三個關鍵名詞皆可以搭配。請看範例。

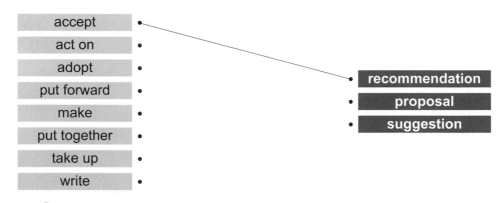

 請核對答案。不熟悉當中的某些字彙，不用擔心，「工具篇」提供了完整的中譯供參考。

Task 10 現在請將意思最相近的同義動詞兩兩一組配對。
例：**put forward - make**。

 請核對答案。熟悉同義詞的替換使用，可以豐富英文表達的多樣性。

現在我們用形容詞來做同樣的練習。

Task 11 將左欄形容詞與最常搭配的名詞配對。請看範例。

constructive •
draft •
firm •
preliminary •
sensible •
strong •

• **recommendation**
• **proposal**
• **suggestion**

 請核對答案。

Task 12 現在請將意思最相近的同義形容詞兩兩一組配對。

例： **firm - strong**。

核對完答案，接著就火練習使用這些同義字彙。能夠活用這些同義字，對於提升英文說、寫的程度有很大助益。

Task 13 請使用前面學過的同義動詞與形容詞重寫下列句子，使兩個句子意思不變。請看範例。

例： I'd like to put forward a proposal.
→ I'd like to make a proposal.

1. We have decided to adopt your recommendation.

_____

2. I'm putting together a proposal at the moment.

_____

3. We like your suggestion and we are going to act on it.

_____

4. He made a firm recommendation for a bigger budget.

_____

5. It's just a preliminary proposal. I'm still working on the details.

_____

6. Does anyone have any sensible suggestions?

_____

 如果你覺得這個練習很困難,多花點時間比較和熟悉每組句子,直到了解透徹為止。

接著我們來做一些聽力練習,除了學會前述語彙的使用方式,能夠聽、說這些語彙也很重要。

🎧 13、14

Task 14　瑪芮爾是一名商業顧問。她指導高階經理應付商業管理中許多不同層面的問題。在這裡她發表一則關於專案經理的談話。聽聽這兩部分的談話,將你聽到在本單元學過的關鍵字彙記下來。並回答這些問題:

⊙ 專案的兩個主要階段是什麼?
⊙ 你的專案提案裡需要包含什麼?
⊙ 在提案執行的階段你需要處理哪些事?

 在做完聽力練習前,不要先看錄音稿喔。如果你覺得很難聽懂,持續前進練習下一個 task,屆時你會覺得容易一些。

🎧 13、14

Task 15　請先看看這則談話的要點,然後再聽一次瑪芮爾的談話。聽的時候按照這些要點的順序。建議你將關鍵名詞與它們的動詞畫底線,幫助自己跟上談話進度。

Phase 1: Planning the Project

<u>Writing a proposal</u>

→ Describe the situation.

→ Do some assessment of the market situation and the financial situation of the company.

→ Make recommendations, and put forward suggestions.

→ Identify the problem, put forward some solutions.

→ Highlight some issues. For example, avoiding delays, managing changes to the product, dealing with changes to the circumstances. Other challenges?

→ Estimate the costs to the company of implementing the project.

→ Set a budget, and plan a timeline.

Phase 2: Implementing the Project

- Keep within budget by making sure costs don't go up.
- Make up delays.
- Implement changes smoothly and efficiently.
- Schedule meetings, have agendas, keep minutes.
- Inform your manager of the project status.
- Write frequent reports

中譯

第一階段：規劃專案

寫提案

→ 描述情形。

→ 對市場情形與公司的財務狀況做一些評估。

→ 給建言，提出建議。

→ 指出問題，提出一些解決方案。

→ 強調一些議題。例如，避免延遲，管理產品的變更，應付環境的改變。其他挑戰？

→替公司預估執行專案的成本。

→訂定預算，安排時間表。

第二階段：執行專案

• 確保成本不升高，保持在預算之內。

- 彌補延遲。
- 順暢且有效率地的執行變更。
- 安排會議、擬定議程、做會議記錄。
- 告知你的經理專案狀況。
- 經常寫報告。

🎧 13、14

Task 16 請再仔細聽一遍這兩部分談話,聽的時候,從下方表格挑出正確的形容詞來填入空格。聽聽看瑪芮爾用了哪些形容詞。

accurate 正確的 background 背景的 clear 清楚的 current 目前的 detailed 細節的	main 主要的 major 重大的 necessary 必要的 new 新的 possible 可能的	practical 實用的 present 現今的 realistic 實際的 regular 定期的 specific 特定的	sudden 突然的 tight 緊縮的 unexpected 不預期的 unnecessary 不必要的

Phase 1: Planning the Project

Writing a proposal for a (1)_____ project:

→ Describe the (2)_____ situation.

→ Do some (3)_____ assessments of the (4)_____ market situation, and the (5)_____ financial situation of the company.

→ Make (6)_____ recommendations, and put forward (7)_____ suggestions.

→ If the proposal is for solving a problem, identify the (8)_____ problem that you want to tackle, then put forward some (9)_____ solutions.

→ Identify and highlight some (10)_____ issues which might arise during the project. For example, avoiding (11)_____ delays. How do you intend to manage (12)_____ changes to the product or deal with (13)＿＿＿＿ changes to the circumstances of the project. What other (14)＿＿＿＿ challenges do you think you might meet?

→ Estimate the costs to the company of implementing the project.

→ Set a (15)＿＿＿＿ budget, and plan a timeline.

Phase 2: Implementing the Project

- During the implementation of the project, keep within budget by making sure costs don't go up.

- If you experience (16)＿＿＿＿ delays, try to make up the time later in the process.

- If you need to make (17)＿＿＿＿ changes, implement them as smoothly and as efficiently as possible.

- Schedule (18)＿＿＿＿ team meetings, and make sure you have agendas for your meetings. Keep (19)＿＿＿＿ minutes of all the meetings.

- Inform your manager of the project status by writing frequent status or progress reports.

核對完答案，你也可以看看這二段談話的錄音稿。閱讀時，你可以把關鍵名詞的搭配詞組畫底線以加強印象。

➔ 強化練習

Task 17 請利用上一個 task 的要點來練習發表一段談話。替自己錄音。

聽聽自己的錄音。檢視先前學過的搭配詞組用得正不正確？如果覺得自己說得不夠正確，試著再練習一遍。然後比較兩段錄音看看自己是否有進步。

Tracy works for a software company. She has recently been assigned to be project (1)_____ for a software development project for a key customer. The first thing she does is assess the customer's (2)_____, in order to identify the key (3)_____ for the customers, and make sure she understands their needs.

Then, when she has carried out her (4)_____ of the situation, she puts together a (5)_____. In her proposal she puts forward her (6)_____ for how to met the client's needs. She estimates the (7)_____ of developing the program, and then prepares a (8)_____ for the whole project. She allocates tasks to her team members, and sets up procedures for dealing with (9)_____ which may occur.

When her proposal has been accepted, she starts to implement the (10)_____. If the team comes across (11)_____, they try to look for the cheapest and most efficient solutions. Sometimes the client might make a (12)_____, then Tracy and her team have to find ways to overcome this (13)_____. Tracy manages the project by having regular (14)_____ with her team. Tracy listens carefully when her team members come up with (15)_____. She draws up (16)_____ for the meetings, and keeps (17)_____. This way she can make sure the project is on time, and she can use the agendas and minutes to prepare her (18)_____. She submits her (19)_____ to her manager and to the client, so that they know how the project is going.

是否覺得這段文章似曾相識？！請再次閱讀本章 task 1 的文章來核對你的答案，也可藉此評量你學會了多少本章所教的語彙。

好了，本單元到此結束。希望你學會了如何使用談論與寫作專案管理的語言。在你繼續下一個單元之前，請回到單元一開始的學習目標清單，檢視自己是否都達成目標了。

工具篇：本章重點語彙

1. meeting 的搭配詞組

與動詞搭配

call 召開	
chair 主持	**meeting 會議**
call off 取消	

例 call a meeting = 召開會議

與形容詞搭配

brief 簡短的	
team 小組的	**meeting 會議**
departmental 部門的	

2. agenda 的搭配詞組

與動詞搭配

go through 看過	
stick to 回到	**agenda 議程**
have 有	

3. minutes 的搭配詞組

與動詞搭配

read through 讀過	
sign 在……上簽名	**minutes 會議記錄**
accept 接受	

4. project 的搭配詞組

與動詞搭配

run 執行	
coordinate 協調運作	**project 專案**
implement 執行	

與形容詞搭配

new 新的	
major 主要的	**project 專案**
joint 聯合的	

複合名詞

project coordinator 專案協調員

project leader 專案領導者

project management 專案管理

project manager 專案經理

project proposal 專案提案

project status 專案進展狀況

project status review 專案進度審視

project team 專案小組

5. situation 的搭配詞組

與動詞搭配

review 審視	
brief sb. on 向某人概述	**situation 情況**
resolve 解決	

與形容詞搭配

present 目前的	
difficult 困難的	**situation 情況**
particular 特別的	

6. report 的搭配詞組

與動詞搭配

prepare 準備	
read 讀	**report 報告**
submit 提交	

與形容詞搭配

status 進度	
progress 進展	**report 報告**
full 完整的	

7. recommendation 的搭配詞組

與動詞搭配

adopt 採用	
accept 接受	
put forward 提出	**recommendation 建議**
make 提出	

與形容詞搭配

firm 強烈的	**recommendation 建議**
strong 強烈的	

8. proposal 的搭配詞組

與動詞搭配

put together 整合	
write 寫	
put forward 提出	**proposal 提案**
make 做	

與形容詞搭配

draft 草稿的	**proposal 提案**
preliminary 初步的	

9. suggestion 的搭配詞組

與動詞搭配

act on 按照……行事	
take up 採納	**suggestion 建議**
put forward 提出	
make 提出	

與形容詞搭配

constructive 有建設性的	**suggestion 建議**
sensible 合理的	

Unit 4

策略管理
Strategic Management

Successful enterprises are usually led by a proven chief executive who is a competent benevolent dictator.

Richard Pratt

alliance 聯盟	analysis 分析	assessment 評估
business 事業	challenge 挑戰	change 改變、變異
company 公司	development 發展	economy 經濟
effect 影響	factor 因素	finance 財務
growth 成長	investment 投資	issue 議題
level 層次	loss 損失	management 管理
manager 經理	market 市場	marketing 行銷
merger 合併	negotiation 協商	opportunity 機會
option 選擇方案	problem 問題	profit 獲利
prospects 遠景	research 研究	risk 風險
situation 情形、狀況	solution 解決方案	strategy 策略

這個單元我們要來學習這些關鍵名詞。你將學習如何使用它們來說出與寫出你的策略管理。看完本單元，你將達到以下的學習目標：

☐ 更瞭解何謂策略管理
☐ 瞭解與關鍵字彙一起使用的主要搭配詞
☐ 瞭解一些關鍵字彙的複合名詞
☐ 能夠運用同義字提升英文表達的豐富性
☐ 運用關鍵字彙與它們的搭配詞，做一些聽力與口說的練習
☐ 能夠更有信心地使用關鍵字彙來談論與寫作策略管理

上手篇

首先，我們來瞭解更多關於策略管理的內容，以及練習閱讀文段中的關鍵字彙。

Task 1 請閱讀以下的短文，並找出當中的關鍵字彙。注意這些字彙在文中如何被運用。

What Is Strategic Management?

Strategic management is the job of setting the overall direction of the company. This job is usually done by the CEO, or the managing director. The CEO does this by deciding the main objective of the company, and then devising strategies for achieving this objective. There are various factors which can have an effect on the decision making process.

First, the CEO has to make an assessment of the economic situation of the country or countries in which the company operates. If the local economy is growing, this means the local markets will expand, as more people will want to buy goods and services. The CEO in this case not only has to be on the look out for opportunities to expand the business, but also has to constantly assess the short term and long term prospects for the economy. If the company operates in more than one market, the CEO has to conduct research into each of those markets.

Secondly, the CEO has to achieve a certain level of growth, and encourage development of the company's activities. However, if the company grows too fast, the risks increase. The CEO therefore has to constantly assess risk. Every opportunity has a cost, and the CEO has to maximize profits and reduce losses. The CEO may look at a number of options to achieve growth. He may try to form an alliance with partners such as suppliers and distributors. This will help to cut costs. He may also consider a merger with a competitor in order to expand the company's market share. Or he may make additional investments in new products or machinery.

Thirdly, the CEO has to manage change. In a highly volatile global market, change is happening all the time, posing new challenges and raising new and complex issues. The CEO has to be able to detect potential problems before they happen, and find sensible solutions to them quickly and easily.

The CEO does his job by working closely with his senior managers. He has to understand finance and marketing, he has to be able to handle negotiations, and he has to be constantly performing analyses of the company's strengths and weaknesses, and of the wider economy.

中譯

何謂策略管理？

策略管理是建立一家公司大方向的工作。這個工作通常是由總裁或是管理董事來擔任。總裁決定公司的主要目標，然後擬定策略以達到目標。在做決定的過程中有許多因素會產生影響。

第一，總裁必須對公司營運所在地的國家做經濟情況的評估。如果當地的經濟成長，這表示當地的市場會擴展，因為會有更多的人想買商品或服務。在這種情形下，總裁不僅得尋找機會擴大事業，還必須持續地評估短期與長期的經濟展望。如果公司營運的市場不只一個，總裁必須對這些市場逐一進行研究。

第二，總裁必須為公司達到一定程度的成長，並鼓勵公司活動的發展。然而，如果公司成長太快，風險會增高。於是總裁必須經常評估風險。每一個機會都有成

本，總裁必須獲取最大的利益並減少損失。總裁為達到成長可能會審視幾個選擇方案。他可以試著與合作伙伴形成聯盟，例如供應商與經銷商。如此將有助於減少成本。他也可以考慮與競爭者合併以擴大公司的市場佔有率。或者，他可以額外投資在新的產品或機器上。

第三，總裁必須能夠應付變動。在高度善變的全球市場中，變動隨時發生，因此掀起新的挑戰，並引起新的複雜議題。總裁必須能夠在潛在問題發生前就偵察出來，並快速且輕易地找出合理的解決方案。

總裁藉由與他的高階經理們密切合作來完成工作。他必須瞭解財務與行銷，他必須要能夠進行協商，他必須要經常地分析公司的競爭優勢與劣勢，以及更廣的經濟面。

⊙ 配對練習

一開始我們要把學習焦點放在與這些關鍵名詞一起搭配使用的動詞。

Task 2 請將左欄動詞與最常搭配的名詞配對。請看範例。

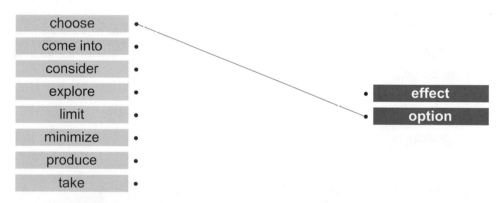

choose
come into
consider
explore
limit
minimize
produce
take

effect
option

請核對答案。記住，搭配詞組並沒有一定的法則說明某些字可以搭配在一起，某些字不行。重要的是，把正確的搭配詞組學起來。將你搭配錯誤的組合記錄下來，加強研讀它們的正確型式。

Task 3　將左欄動詞與最常搭配的名詞配對。

address ·
clarify ·
decide ·
face ·　　　　　　　　　　　　　　　· **challenge**
meet ·　　　　　　　　　　　　　　　· **issue**
pose ·
raise ·
resist ·

 請參看本書後面的解答。若不了解這些詞組的意義，「工具篇」附有中譯可供對照。

Task 4　將左欄動詞與最常搭配的名詞配對。

await ·
bring about ·
encourage ·
make ·　　　　　　　　　　　　　　　· **change**
manage ·　　　　　　　　　　　　　　· **development**
resist ·
stimulate ·
support ·

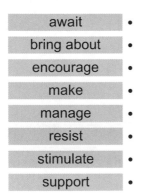 請核對答案，在 task 7 我們會進一步練習這些搭配詞組的用法。

Task 5　將左欄動詞與最常搭配的名詞配對。

act as ·　　　　　　　　　　　　　　· **manager**
appoint ·　　　　　　　　　　　　　· **management**

be promoted to	•			
become	•			
improve	•		•	**manager**
oversee	•		•	**management**
provide	•			
simplify	•			

 請核對答案,並加強研讀答錯部分的正確型式。

Task 6 將左欄動詞與最常搭配的名詞配對。

break off	•			
cancel	•			
complete	•		•	**merger**
establish	•		•	**alliance**
propose	•			
seek	•			

 請參照書末的「解答」。對前面幾個 task 的搭配詞組還是一知半解?!不用擔心,接下來,我們就來練習使用這些詞組。

現在先回頭溫習一下先前學過的搭配詞組,熟悉它們的意義。因為接下來,我們就要來練習如何在句子中使用它們。

Task 7 請以前面 task 中的關鍵名詞完成這些句子。想想這些名詞應該使用單數還是複數。

• Can we do anything to minimize the (1)_____ of these regulations?
• I am acting as (2)_____ for John, who is on personal leave.
• I await (3)_____. I can't make a decision until I know how things are going to develop.

- I don't want to limit our (4)_____. Let's keep an open mind to all ideas.
- I hope the new measures will stimulate the (5)_____ of the local economy.
- I want to improve (6)_____. We need to make it more efficient.
- I was promoted to (7)_____ at the age of 26.
- I'll raise this (8)_____ with the board at our next meeting.
- If we can establish an (9)_____ with them, that will help us with our distribution problems.
- It was not me who proposed the (10)_____. It was my predecessor who thought joining the companies together would be a good idea.
- It's foolish to resist (11)_____. You can't stop it.
- Let's consider our (12)_____ here. Maybe we can find a better alternative.
- My main job as CEO is to manage (13)_____.
- New market conditions pose the biggest (14)_____.
- The new regulations will come into (15)_____ next month.
- They were not fulfilling their part of the deal, so we broke off the (16)_____.
- This restructuring will simplify (17)_____.
- Together we can meet this (18)_____ and make the company better and stronger.
- We need to clarify the (19)_____. Can you go over them again for us?
- When we complete the (20)_____, many employees will lose their jobs.

請參看本書後面的「解答」。你可以把這些句子裡的動詞畫底線，幫助自己記憶「動詞＋名詞」的搭配詞組。

這些關鍵字彙可和哪些形容詞一起搭配使用呢？我們接著就來學習與形容詞搭配的組合吧。

Task 8 將左欄形容詞與最常搭配的名詞配對。

alternative •	
best •	
direct •	• effect
negative •	• option
positive •	
realistic •	
significant •	
viable •	

 請核對答案。將答錯的組合記錄下來，確實地研讀改正。最好幾天後能夠再次複習配對練習的單元，評量自己還記得多少。

Task 9 將左欄形容詞與最常搭配的名詞配對。

complicated •	
considerable •	
controversial •	• challenge
exciting •	• issue
real •	
serious •	

 請參看書末的「解答」。「工具篇」附有這些搭配詞組的中譯可供查閱。

Task 10 將左欄形容詞與最常搭配的名詞配對。

business •	
fundamental •	• change
major •	• development
product •	

slow •

structural •

sustainable •

uneven •

• change

• development

請參看書末的「解答」。

Task 11 將左欄形容詞與最常搭配的名詞配對。

assistant •

day-to-day •

line •

risk •

• manager

• management

請核對答案。在 task 13 會進一步示範這些詞組在句子中的用法。

Task 12 將左欄形容詞與最常搭配的名詞配對。

company •

department •

strategic •

strong •

• merger

• alliance

請參看書末的「解答」。

現在先回頭溫習一下剛學過的搭配詞組，熟悉它們的意義。因為接下來，我們就要來練習如何在句子中使用它們。

Task 13 請用前面 task 中的關鍵名詞完成這些句子。想想這些名詞應該使用單數還是複數，在答題的過程中將搭配的形容詞畫底線。

- A company (1)＿＿＿＿＿ is always a risky business.
- Although I am the manager, my assistant oversees most of the day-to-day (2)＿＿＿＿＿.
- A department (3)＿＿＿＿＿ is one way to save money.
- If you have problems with this, you should inform your line (4)＿＿＿＿＿. She will be able to help you.
- It's a controversial (5)＿＿＿＿＿, which I think we should discuss later.
- Meeting these targets will be a considerable (6)＿＿＿＿＿.
- My job is to focus on business (7)＿＿＿＿＿. I have to make the business grow.
- Risk (8)＿＿＿＿＿ is the key to a successful insurance business.
- Running a business this size is a serious (9)＿＿＿＿＿.
- Sustainable (10)＿＿＿＿＿ is important, otherwise the business could grow too fast.
- Thanks for your suggestion, but it's not really a viable (11)＿＿＿＿＿.
- The best (12)＿＿＿＿＿ is to withdraw from the market. There's no other way.
- The new image had a very positive (13)＿＿＿＿＿ on our sales.
- The new regulations will have a direct (14)＿＿＿＿＿ on our business.
- The real (15)＿＿＿＿＿ is what we can do to improve revenue.
- We are going to make fundamental (16)＿＿＿＿＿ to the business next year.
- We formed a strategic (17)＿＿＿＿＿ with one of our suppliers.
- We have established a strong (18)＿＿＿＿＿ with our main distributor.
- We have seen a slow (19)＿＿＿＿＿ in the business environment over the last five years.
- We need to appoint an assistant (20)＿＿＿＿＿.

請參看本書解答核對你的答案。將句子裡的搭配詞組畫底線，幫助自己記憶。

接著我要來進一步說明business這個關鍵字彙，它有兩個非常不同的意思與用法。

Task 14 請比較這兩個句子中business的用法，並將它們分別與下列的說明配對，屬於a的說明在括弧內填上a；屬於b的則填上b。

a) We do good business in Japan.

b) I have managed to develop a thriving business.

1. This use of the word is countable. (　　)
2. This meaning of the word is: process. (　　)
3. A synonym for this word is trade. (　　)
4. This use of the word is uncountable. (　　)
5. This meaning of the word is: thing. (　　)
6. A synonym for this word is company. (　　)

請參考解答核對答案。題目的中譯如下：
1. 這個字是可數的。
2. 這個字的意思指的是「過程」。
3. 這個字的同義字是 trade「貿易」。
4. 這個字是不可數的。
5. 這個字的意思指的是「事情」。
6. 這個字的同義字是 company「公司商行」。

現在我們來看看哪些動詞與形容詞分別可以和business的兩個用法搭配。

Task 15 將左欄動詞與最常搭配的名詞配對。請看範例。

attract ●

be bad for ●　　　　　　　　　● **business**（當 **process** 用時）

be good for ●　　　　　　　　　● **business**（當 **thing** 用時）

build ●

conduct	•			
develop	•			
discuss	•			
do	•			
establish	•		•	**business**（當 **process** 用時）
expand	•		•	**business**（當 **thing** 用時）
manage	•			
operate	•			
run	•			
start	•			

請參看「解答」。

Task 16 將左欄形容詞與最常搭配的名詞配對。當中至少有一個形容詞與 **business** 的兩個用法都可搭配。

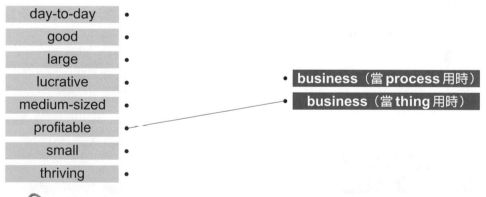

day-to-day	•			
good	•			
large	•			
lucrative	•		•	**business**（當 **process** 用時）
medium-sized	•		•	**business**（當 **thing** 用時）
profitable	•			
small	•			
thriving	•			

請核對答案。在 task 17 可以學到這些 business 詞組在句子中的使用方式。

Task 17 請用前面表格中的動詞或形容詞完成下列的句子。注意動詞的時態要正確。

• I like (1)＿＿＿＿＿ business there. It's a nice place, and I always do (2)＿＿＿＿＿ business there.

- It took me many years to (3)_____ the business.
- Product recalls (4)_____ business. It damages the company's reputation.
- It's difficult to (5)_____ a business in this market. Small business regulations are very tight.
- We were (6)_____ business over lunch. He's good to talk to.
- I am trying to (7)_____ the business. We are looking for steady growth.
- If we can (8)_____ more business, we will increase our revenue.
- They (9)_____ the business over 20 years ago. It's now a (10)_____ business, and very successful.

 請參看「解答」。請將這些句子當成範例研讀。

我們接著來學習 business 二個意義的複合名詞。

Task 18 請將名詞配對。分別將 **business** 這個字彙的兩個用法與最常搭配的名詞配對。請看以下範例。

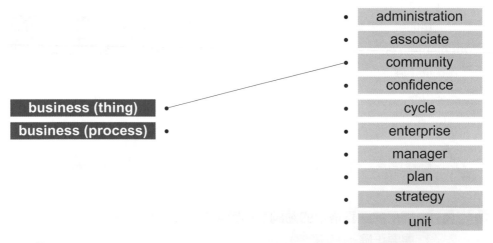

- administration
- associate
- community
- confidence
- cycle
- enterprise
- manager
- plan
- strategy
- unit

business (thing)
business (process)

請參看「解答」。如果需要,可對照「工具篇」中譯幫助了解。我們在下一個 task 會練習它們的用法。

Task 19 請研讀範例的兩個句子。然後使用前一個 **task** 裡的複合名詞，按照相同的方式重寫下列句子。

例：He is one of my associates in my business.
→ He is one of my business associates.

1. I am the manager of a business.

   _____

2. I have a good plan for the business.

   _____

3. I have a strategy for the business which will give us a lot of growth.

   _____

4. I studied the administration of business.

   _____

5. Confidence in business was boosted after the election.

   _____

6. The cycle of the business follows the same pattern every year.

   _____

7. The community of foreign business people in Taiwan is quite small.

   _____

 請核對答案。

現在我們將利用更多的關鍵字彙來做同樣的複合名詞搭配練習。

Task 20 將每個字彙與最常搭配的名詞配對。請看範例。

development	•	•	buy-out
company	•———————————•		car
management	•	•	consultancy

	director
	headquarters
	logo
	plan
	policy
	program
	project
	spokesperson
	strategy
	style
	structure
	team

development •

company •

management •

 核對完答案，請多研讀幾次這些複合名詞。如果需要，可以參考「工具篇」的中譯。

Task 21 請研讀範例的二個句子。然後使用前一個 task 裡的複合名詞，按照相同的方式重寫其他句子。

> 例：I have a good plan for development. Want to hear it?
> → I have a good development plan. Want to hear it?

1. His style of management is very different from mine.

_____

2. I used to work for a company that consulted on management issues.

_____

3. I lost my job in a buy-out by the management.

_____

4. The policy of the company is to invest 35% of all profits back into the company.

_____

5. The spokesperson for the company said they were not going to build here.

_____

6. The structure of management in this company is very complex. I want to simplify it.

_____

7. This is part of a wider project for development. We are working hard to improve the area.

_____

8. You will be given a car by the company as part of your package.

_____

 將你的答案與本書後面提供的解答做一番比較，並多練習幾次正確的用法。

⊙ 語言的提升

在接下來的部分，我們要來做同義字練習並增強你的英文聽力。我們把學習焦點放在 business（當 thing 使用時）與 company 這兩個同義字上面。

Task 22 將這些同義動詞與最常搭配的名詞配對。當中有些動詞與 **business**、**company** 這兩個關鍵名詞都可以搭配。請看範例。

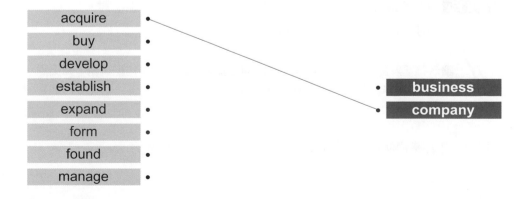

acquire •
buy •
develop •
establish •
expand •
form •
found •
manage •

business
company

run •	• business
start •	• company

 Task 23 現在請將上一個 task 中意思最相近的同義動詞兩兩一組配對。

例： **start - establish**

請參看「解答」核對 task 22、23 的答案，並研讀這些搭配詞組。

現在我們用形容詞來做同樣的練習。

Task 24 將這些同義的形容詞與最常搭配的名詞配對。請看範例。

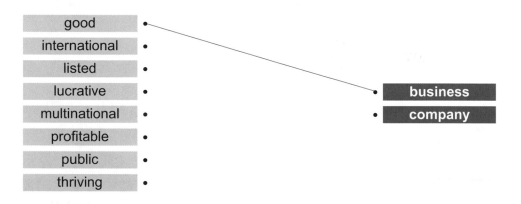

good
international
listed
lucrative
multinational
profitable
public
thriving

business
company

 Task 25 請將 task 24 中意思最相近的同義形容詞兩兩一組配對。

例： **lucrative - profitable**

請參看「解答」核對 task 24、25 的答案，並研讀這些搭配詞組。如果需要，可以參考「工具篇」的中譯。

現在我們來練習使用這些同義詞。

Task 26 請使用前面學過的同義動詞與形容詞重寫下列句子，使兩個句子意思相同。請看範例。

例： The business was founded 20 years ago.
→ The company was formed 20 years ago.

1. It's already a good business, but I'm trying to expand it so that it becomes really profitable.

_____

2. I started the business 20 years ago and ran it for 10 years.

_____

3. We have just bought a listed company. It was very expensive, so I hope this will give us growth.

_____

4. He is the CEO of a huge multinational company.

_____

 如果你覺得這個練習很困難，多花點時間比較每組句了直到了解透徹為止。

現在我們來做一些聽力練習，幫助你聽出正在學的這些語言。

🎧 15

Task 27 麥克是一家中型企業的執行長兼老闆。他向他的高階經理團隊發表一篇演說。仔細聽取內容並回答下列問題。

⊙ 從麥克的演說，你對他的公司瞭解到什麼？
⊙ 他對未來提出兩個關於什麼主題的提案？
⊙ 關於部門合併他有什麼意見？

Task 28 請再仔細聽一次這篇演說。聽的時候，將你聽到的關鍵字彙打 ✔ 。

the company	(	)
business	(	)
challenge	(	)
development	(	)
options	(	)
merger	(	)
alliance	(	)
issues	(	)
changes	(	)
management	(	)
effect	(	)
manager	(	)

🎧 15

Task 29 請再聽一次這篇演說。這次聽的時候，請將你聽到的搭配詞組填入表格。請看範例。

started	the company
develop the thriving	business
	business
	challenge
	development
	options
	merger
	alliance
	issues
	changes
	management
	effect
	manager

你可以參看「錄音稿」和「解答」來核對 task 27-29 的答案。閱讀錄音稿時，請將搭配詞組畫線幫助自己留意它們的用法。

⊛ 強化練習

Task 30 現在，想像你是麥克，使用 task 29 表格中的搭配詞組擬一篇演說。接著，發表演說並替自己錄音，聽聽自己的搭配詞組用法是否正確。

聽自己的錄音。聽聽看先前學過的搭配詞組用得正不正確？如果覺得自己說得不夠正確，試著再練習一遍。然後比較兩段錄音看看自己是否有進步。

Task 31 試著使用在本單元學到的用語寫一篇提案，關於你的公司所面臨的策略議題。

完成提案之後，將自己使用的搭配詞組畫線，看看用法是否正確。

Task 32 請用本單元學過的詞彙填入這篇文章裡的空格。

What Is Strategic Management?

Strategic (1)_____ is the job of setting the overall direction of the company. This job is usually done by the CEO, or the managing director. The CEO does this by deciding the main objective of the company, and then devising (2)_____ for achieving this objective. There are various (3)_____ which can have an (4)_____ on the decision making process.

First, the CEO has to make an (5)_____ of the economic (6)_____ of the country or countries in which the company

---

operates. If the local (7)＿＿＿＿＿ is growing, this means the local (8)＿＿＿＿＿ will expand, as more people will want to buy goods and services. The CEO in this case not only has to be on the look out for (9)＿＿＿＿＿ to expand the (10)＿＿＿＿＿, but also has to constantly assess the short term and long term (11)＿＿＿＿＿ for the economy. If the (12)＿＿＿＿＿ operates in more than one market, the CEO has to conduct research into each of those markets.

Secondly, the CEO has to achieve a certain (13)＿＿＿＿＿ of growth, and encourage (14)＿＿＿＿＿ of the company's activities. However, if the company grows too fast, the risks increase. The CEO therefore has to constantly assess (15)＿＿＿＿＿. Every opportunity has a cost, and the CEO has to maximize (16)＿＿＿＿＿ and reduce (17)＿＿＿＿＿. The CEO may look at a number of (18)＿＿＿＿＿ to achieve (19)＿＿＿＿＿. He may try to form an (20)＿＿＿＿＿ with partners such as suppliers and distributors. This will help to cut costs. He may also consider a (21)＿＿＿＿＿ with a competitor in order to expand the company's market share. Or he may make additional (22)＿＿＿＿＿ in new products or machinery.

Thirdly, the CEO has to manage (23)＿＿＿＿＿. In a highly volatile global market, change is happening all the time, posing new (24)＿＿＿＿＿ and raising new and complex (25)＿＿＿＿＿. The CEO has to be able to detect potential (26)＿＿＿＿＿ before they happen, and find sensible (27)＿＿＿＿＿ to them quickly and easily.

The CEO does his job by working closely with his senior (28)＿＿＿＿＿. He has to understand (29)＿＿＿＿＿ and (30)＿＿＿＿＿, he has to be able to handle (31)＿＿＿＿＿, and he has to be constantly performing (32)＿＿＿＿＿ of the company's strengths and weaknesses, and of the wider economy.

是否覺得這段文章似曾相識？！請再次閱讀本章 task 1 的文章來核對你的答案，也可藉此評量你學會了多少本章所教的語彙。

好了，本單元到此結束。希望你學會了如何使用談論與寫作策略管理的語言。在你繼續進行下一個單元之前，回到一開始的學習目標清單，檢視自己是否都達成目標了。

工具篇：本章重點語彙

1. effect 的搭配詞組

與動詞搭配

come into 產生	
minimize 使……減至最小	**effect 影響**
produce 產生	
take 產生	

與形容詞搭配

direct 直接的	
negative 負面的	**effect 影響**
positive 正面的	
significant 重大的	

2. option 的搭配詞組

與動詞搭配

choose 選擇	
consider 考慮	**option 選擇方案**
explore 細察	
limit 限定	

與形容詞搭配

alternative 替代的	
best 最好的	**option 選擇方案**
realistic 實際的	
viable 可行的	

3. challenge 的搭配詞組

face 面對	
meet 遇到	challenge 挑戰
pose 引起、帶來	
resist 拒絕	

considerable 相當多的	
exciting 刺激的	challenge 挑戰
serious 重大的	

4. issue 的搭配詞組

address 提出	
clarify 釐清	issue 議題
decide 決定	
raise 提出	

complicated 複雜的	
controversial 引起爭論的	issue 議題
real 真正的	

5. change 的搭配詞組

bring about 造成	
make 做	change 變更
manage 管理	
resist 拒絕	

fundamental 基本的 major 主要的 slow 緩慢的 structural 結構上的	**change 變更**

6. development 的搭配詞組

與動詞搭配

await 等待 encourage 鼓勵 stimulate 刺激 support 支持	**development 發展**

與形容詞搭配

business 企業 product 產品 sustainable 可持續的 uneven 不均衡的	**development 發展**

複合名詞

development plan 發展計畫

development program 發展計畫

development project 發展專案

7. manager 的搭配詞組

與動詞搭配

act as 做為 appoint 任命 become 成為 be promoted to 被提升為	**manager 經理**

assistant 輔助的	manager 經理
line 產品線	

8. management 的搭配詞組

與動詞搭配

provide 提供	management 管理
improve 改善	
oversee 監督	
simplify 簡化	

與形容詞搭配

day-to-day 日常	management 管理
risk 風險	

複合名詞

management buy-out 管理層收購

management consultancy 管理顧問

management team 管理團隊

management style 管理風格

management strategy 管理策略

management structure 管理結構

9. merger 的搭配詞組

與動詞搭配

cancel 取消	merger 合併
complete 完成	
propose 提議	

與形容詞搭配

company 公司	merger 合併
department 部門	

10. alliance 的搭配詞組

與動詞搭配

break off 解除	
establish 建立	**alliance** 聯盟
seek 尋求	

與形容詞搭配

strategic 策略的	
strong 有力的	**alliance** 聯盟

11. business 的搭配詞組（當 process 用時）

與動詞搭配

attract 吸引	
be bad for 對……有害	
be good for 對……有益	**business**
conduct 處理	業務、生意
discuss 討論	
do 處理	

與形容詞搭配

good 好的	**business**
day-to-day 日常	業務、生意

複合名詞

business administration 企業管理

business associate 業務伙伴

business confidence 企業信心

business cycle 景氣循環

business strategy 經營策略

12. business 的搭配詞組（當 thing 用時）

與動詞搭配

build 建立	
develop 發展	
establish 建立	
expand 擴展	business 事業
manage 管理	
operate 經營	
run 經營	
start 開始	

與形容詞搭配

good 好的	
thriving 興盛的	
profitable 有獲利的	
lucrative 可獲利的	business 事業
large 大的	
medium-sized 中型的	
small 小的	

複合名詞

business community 企業團體　　business enterprise 企業單位

business manager 企業經理人　　business plan 商業計畫

business unit 事業單位

13. company 的複合名詞

company director 公司董事

company car 公司用車

company spokesperson 公司發言人

company policy 公司政策

company headquarters 公司總部

company logo 公司商標

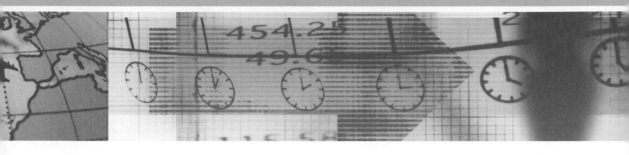

Part 3 | 核心商務活動
Talking about Core Business Activities

在接下來四個單元裡，我們要來談論四種相互關連的核心商務活動：行銷、業務、生產與財務。在這四項主題領域裡，你將會學到許多關鍵名詞的搭配詞組。你還會學到如何使用同義詞來提升你的英語表達。

Unit 5

行銷 Marketing

Marketing is the art of identifying and understanding customer needs and creating solutions that deliver satisfaction to the customers, profits to the producers, and benefits for the stakeholders.

Philip Kotler

ad 廣告	advertising 廣告	analysis 分析
assessment 評估	brand 品牌	budget 預算
campaign 宣傳活動	data 資訊、情報	economy 經濟
feature 特色	market 市場	marketing 行銷
opportunity 機會	price 價錢	product 產品
research 研究	situation 情形	strategy 策略

這些是本單元要學的關鍵名詞。你將學習如何使用這些字彙來說寫行銷議題。閱讀完本單元，你將達到以下的學習目標：

- [ ] 更加瞭解何謂行銷
- [ ] 瞭解與關鍵字彙一起使用的主要搭配詞
- [ ] 瞭解一些關鍵字彙的複合名詞
- [ ] 能夠運用同義字提升英文表達的豐富性
- [ ] 運用關鍵字彙與它們的搭配詞，做一些聽力與口說的練習
- [ ] 能夠有信心地使用關鍵名詞來談論與寫作行銷議題

上手篇

一開始我們先來瞭解更多關於行銷的內容，以及練習閱讀文段中的關鍵字彙。

Task 1 請閱讀、理解以下短文，並找出當中的關鍵字彙。注意這些字彙在文中如何被運用。

What is Marketing?

Marketing is the process of creating demand for a company's products or services. Sales is the process of meeting that demand. Marketers employ several methods to create demand. First, they conduct research into the local market. They try to understand the distinguishing features of the market, for example: what the local economy is like, what the income level of consumers is, what their needs and desires are. They often use a research house to collect market data, and they perform in-depth analysis on this data. When this detailed assessment of the market is complete, they develop different marketing strategies. These might include advertising campaigns, using TV, radio, or magazine ads.

Marketers also try to develop the company's brands. Great advertising is very important in this. Marketers also set the price of the company's products depending on the local market situation. Some products can be sold for a higher price in some markets. Marketers are also usually on the look out for unexpected opportunities that may arise for helping them to increase demand.

Because the marketing department is very important to the company's success, they usually have very big budgets.

何謂行銷？

行銷是為公司產品或服務創造需求的過程。銷售則是滿足此需求的過程。行銷人員用了許多方法創造需求。首先，他們在當地市場做研究。他們要試著瞭解市場的突出特色，例如：當地的經濟是什麼樣子，顧客的收入層級在哪，他們的需要與想望是什麼。他們通常利用研究室收集市場情報，並且對情報進行深入的分析。詳細的市場評估完成後，他們便發展出不同的行銷策略。可能包括廣告宣傳活動，利用電視、廣播或是雜誌廣告。

行銷人員也試著發展公司品牌。好的廣告對此非常重要。行銷人員根據當地市場狀況訂定公司產品的價格。某些產品在某些市場可以賣得較高的價錢。行銷人員也總在尋找意料外的機會，幫助他們增加需求。

由於行銷部門對公司能否成功很重要，他們通常擁有很大的預算。

⊙ 配對練習

一開始我們要把學習重點放在與關鍵字彙搭配使用的動詞上。熟悉這些搭配詞組，對於活用關鍵字彙有極大的幫助。

Task 2 將左欄動詞與最常搭配的名詞配對。請看範例。

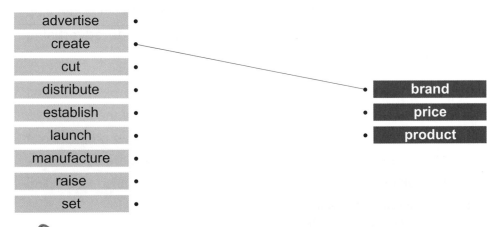

參看「解答」核對你的答案。「工具篇」附有完整中譯可供參考。

Task 3 請將左欄動詞與最常搭配的名詞配對。

allocate •
begin •
develop •
go over •
implement •
launch •

• campaign
• budget
• strategy

 參看「解答」核對你的答案。

Task 4 請將左欄動詞與最常搭配的名詞配對。

assess •
come across •
grasp •
handle •
include •

• situation
• opportunity
• feature

 核對完答案，記得多研讀幾次正確的搭配詞組，以熟悉用法。

Task 5 請將左欄動詞與最常搭配的名詞配對。

affect •
enter •
establish •
flood •
manage •
stimulate •

• economy
• market

 參看「解答」核對你的答案。

Task 6　請將左欄動詞與最常搭配的名詞配對。

create •
develop •
do •
dominate •
expand •
get •
improve •
make •
manage •
run •
take out •
use •

　　　　• ad
　　　　• advertising
　　　　• market
　　　　• marketing

參看「解答」核對答案。記住,這些搭配詞組並沒有一定的法則說明某些字可以一起使用,某些字不行。重要的是,把正確的搭配詞型式學習起來即可。把你在前面幾個 task 裡答錯的組合記錄下來,然後加強研讀它們的正確型式。

下一個 task 要幫助你學會在文段中使用與關鍵名詞搭配的動詞。

Task 7　請用下面表格中的動詞完成這篇 task 1 的文章摘要。請留意動詞的時態。

set	develop	conduct	establish

Marketing is the process of creating demand for a company's products or services. Marketers employ several methods to create demand, including (1)＿＿＿＿＿ research into the local market and consumers, and (2)＿＿＿＿＿ different marketing strategies. Marketers also try to (3)＿＿＿＿＿ the company's brands and (4)＿＿＿＿＿ the price of the company's products.

行銷是為公司產品和服務創造需求的過程。行銷人員採用數種方式創造需求,包含針對當地市場和消費者進行研究,和制定不同的行銷策略。行銷人員也試著發展公司品牌,並訂定公司產品的價格。

 參看「解答」核對你的答案。

接著我們來學習與關鍵字彙一起搭配使用的形容詞。學會這些搭配詞組,可以讓你的英語表達更有張力。

Task 8 將左欄形容詞與最常搭配的名詞配對。請看範例。

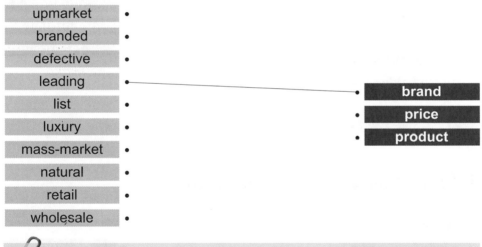

upmarket	
branded	
defective	
leading	brand
list	price
luxury	product
mass-market	
natural	
retail	
wholesale	

 參看「解答」核對你的答案。「工具篇」附有完整中譯供參考。

Task 9 請將左欄形容詞與最常搭配的名詞配對。

annual	campaign
business	budget
innovative	strategy
long-term	

national	
new	campaign
public relations	budget
shoestring	strategy
training	

 參看「解答」核對你的答案。

Task 10 請將左欄形容詞與最常搭配的名詞配對。

complicated	
current	situation
distinguishing	opportunity
golden	feature
standard	
unexpected	

 核對完答案，記得多研讀幾次正確的搭配詞組，以熟悉用法。

Task 11 請將左欄形容詞與最常搭配的名詞配對。

developed	
overseas	economy
small	market
stable	

 參看「解答」核對你的答案。

Task 12 請將左欄形容詞與最常搭配的名詞配對。

aggressive •
competitive •
free •
large •
misleading •
national •
successful •

• ad
• advertising
• market
• marketing

 參看「解答」核對你的答案。將前面幾個 task 裡答錯的組合記錄下來,確實研讀其正確型式。你可以幾天後重新複習「配對練習」單元,看看自己還記得多少。

下一個 task 要幫助你從文段中學會使用與這些關鍵名詞搭配的形容詞。

Task 13 請用下面表格中的字彙完成這篇文章摘要。

innovative	local	unexpected	wholesale

Marketing is the process of creating demand for a company's products or services. Marketers employ several methods to create demand, including conducting research into the (1)_____ market and consumers, and develop (2)_____ strategies. Marketers look for (3)_____ opportunities which might occur. They also set the (4)_____ price of the company's products.

 參看「解答」核對你的答案。

Market 與 marketing 這兩個字有許多實用的搭配詞組,例如: marketing activity「行銷活動」與 market analysis「市場分析」。注意, marketing 和 market 雖然是名詞,但在此則是做為形容詞的功能。

Task 14 將 market 和 marketing 與最常搭配的字彙配對。請看範例。

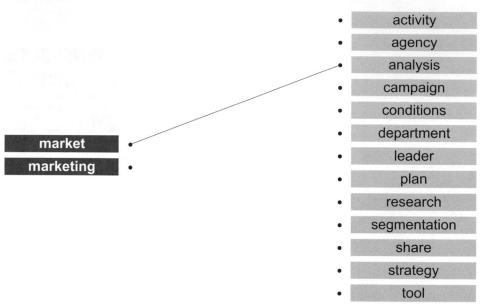

- activity
- agency
- analysis
- campaign
- conditions
- department
- leader
- plan
- research
- segmentation
- share
- strategy
- tool

market

marketing

 參看本書「解答」核對你的答案。同樣地,將答錯的組合確實地研讀改正。

現在,我們來嘗試將 market 和 marketing 的搭配詞組使用在句子中。

Task 15 請研讀這兩個句子。然後使用前一個 task 中的複合名詞,按照相同的方式重寫下列句子。

例:We will need to hire an agency for marketing to help us with this.
→ We will need to hire a marketing agency to help us with this.

1. We are using a range of tools for marketing right now.

_____

2. We are the leader of the market.

_____

3. We are doing a lot of very interesting activities with our marketing right now.

_____

4. The share of the market is too small.

_____

5. The segmentation of the market is very important for helping us to reach the right consumers.

_____

6. The research into the market shows we are still behind.

_____

7. The plan for the marketing is ready. Want to take a look?

_____

8. The department of marketing is too small for this project.

_____

9. The conditions of the market are hard.

_____

10. I am doing some analysis of the market.

_____

11. A good strategy for marketing will help us to increase sales.

_____

➔ 語言的提升

在這個部分，我們要來學習如何使用同義字來提升你的英文能力。

商業英文中，research、assessment 與 analysis 這三個字通常互為同義字。看看下列例句就能明白我的意思。

> 例： Our **assessment** shows that now is a good time to enter the market.
> Our **analysis** shows that now is a good time to enter the market.
> Our **research** shows that now is a good time to enter the market.
> 我們的評估／分析／研究顯示現在是進入市場的好時機。

雖然這三個字互爲同義字，但它們在使用的時候，仍然有些微的文法差異，例如：research into、assessment of 與 analysis of。還有，research 爲不可數，而 assessment 與 analysis 爲可數。

Task 16 請用 research、assessment 或 analysis 來完成下列句子。

1. We have done extensive _____ into the needs of the consumer.
2. I have never seen such a detailed _____ .
3. What's your _____ of the situation?

 請參看「解答」核對你的答案。

大部分與這三個字彙其中之一個搭配使用的動詞和形容詞也可以與其他兩個搭配，但並非全部。另外，許多搭配的動詞與形容詞彼此也互爲同義字。

Task 17 請將這些字彙歸類放進下列正確的同義群組裡。

carry out	extensive	reveal
comprehensive	indicate	rough
demonstrate	preliminary	undertake

1. careful, detailed, extensive, _____
2. initial, _____
3. general, _____
4. do, perform, _____, _____
5. show, _____, _____, _____

 請參看「解答」核對你的答案。在下一個 task，我們會學習這些字詞在句子裡的使用方式。

Task 18　使用 task 17 裡的同義字重寫這些句子。請看範例。

例：We need to perform more detailed analysis.
　　→ We need to undertake more careful analysis.

1. We did extensive research into the situation and found no evidence of wrongdoing.

_____

2. The analysis we carried out showed that the product is overpriced.

_____

3. This is only a rough assessment.

_____

4. The preliminary research shows consumers like the product.

_____

5. A comprehensive analysis showed that the product needs more functionality.

_____

　請參看「解答」核對你的答案。把答案當成例句研讀這些字詞的用法。

現在我們來做一些聽力訓練，看看你能不能藉由這段行銷人員的訪談，聽出關鍵字彙與它們的搭配詞組，以增強你的聽力。一開始我們先全面性地略聽，接著再做進一步、詳細的聽力訓練。

🎧 16、17

Task 19　Zoe Chen 是一家快速流動性商品公司的行銷經理。她的公司販售美容健康產品。請聽 CD 16、17 這兩部分的訪談，測試自己能理解多少內容。先別對照錄音稿喔！

Task 20　請再仔細聽一次 CD 16。聽的時候，請將你聽到的字彙打 ✔。

company's products	(	)
two brands	(	)
brand	(	)
research	(	)
market situation	(	)
market data	(	)
market analysis	(	)
good marketing	(	)
careful assessment	(	)
marketing strategy	(	)
plan	(	)
market	(	)
promotional campaign	(	)

Task 21　請再聽一次 CD 16。這次聽的時候，請將你在訪談中聽到的搭配詞組填入表格。你需要填入的有可能會是二個以上的字。請看範例。

marketing	company's products
	two brands
	brand
	research
	market situation
	market data
market analysis	
	good marketing
	careful assessment
	marketing strategy
	plan
	market
	promotional campaign

如果你覺得這兩個聽力練習很困難，多聽幾次直到你能完成全部表格為止。做完之後，再閱讀書末的錄音稿。讀的時候，可以一邊將搭配詞組畫底線，幫助自己留意它們的用法。

🎧 17

Task 22 請再仔細聽一次 CD 17。聽的時候，請將你聽到的字彙打 ✔。

promotional campaign   (   )
TV and media advertising   (   )
ads   (   )
TV commercials   (   )
advertising budget   (   )
big budget   (   )
tight budget   (   )
economy   (   )
feature   (   )
sensitive   (   )
great opportunities   (   )

🎧 17

Task 23 現在請再聽一次 CD 17。這次聽的時候，請將你在訪談中聽到的搭配詞組填入表格。你需要填入的有可能會是二個以上的字。請看範例。

plan and organize	promotional campaign
	TV and media advertising
	ads
	ads
	TV commercials
	advertising budget
	big budget
	a tight budget

	economy	
		economy
		feature
		sensitive
		great opportunities

如果聽完第一次，無法找出所有搭配詞組，就再多聽幾次直到你能完成全部表格為止。除非真的需要，否則盡量不要對照後面的錄音稿。閱讀錄音稿時，建議你將搭配詞組畫底線，幫助你提高對語言的敏銳度。

Task 24 以下是訪談中的一些問題。想像你是 **Zoe Chen**，利用 **task 21** 和 **task 23** 中的搭配詞組來練習回答這些問題。

Part 1

1. Can you begin by telling us a little bit about your job. What does it involve for you?
2. So how do you promote your brands?
3. Why is market analysis important?
4. Do you have to develop the marketing strategy yourself?

Part 2

1. Can you tell us a little bit more about how you plan and organize promotional campaigns? How does that work?
2. Do you use international celebrities to endorse your products?
3. Tell us a little bit about the two markets you work in. Are they quite different or are they quite similar?
4. What does "price sensitive" mean?

如果發覺自己不熟悉這些搭配詞組的用法，建議各位可到「工具篇」多研讀幾次這些詞組。

➔ 強化練習

Task 25 請用本單元學過的詞彙填入這篇文章裡的空格。

What is Marketing?

(1)_____ is the process of creating (2)_____ for a company's products or services. Sales is the process of meeting that demand. Marketers employ several methods to create demand. First, they conduct (3)_____ into the local (4)_____. They try to understand the distinguishing (5)_____ of the market, for example: what the local (6)_____ is like, what the income level of consumers is, what their needs and desires are. They often use a research house to collect market (7)_____, and they perform in-depth (8)_____ on this data. When this detailed (9)_____ of the market is complete, they develop different marketing (10)_____. These might include advertising (11)_____, using TV, radio or magazine (12)_____.

Marketers also try to develop the company's (13)_____. Great (14)_____ is very important in this. Marketers also set the (15)_____ of the company's products depending on the local market (16)_____. Some products can be sold for a higher price in some markets. Marketers are also usually on the look out for unexpected (17)_____ that may arise for helping them to increase demand.

Because the marketing department is very important to the company's success, they usually have very big (18)_____.

 有沒有覺得這篇文章似曾相識？！你可以再次閱讀 task 1 的文章來核對你的答案。

Task 26 現在請根據 task 1 的文章寫一篇或報告一篇摘要。記得使用本章學過的搭配詞組。

在最後這個 task 裡，你可以練習寫作或是口說（當然，最好是兩個都做！）。如果你要練習寫作，那麼完成後與 CD 16、17 的錄音稿比較一下，看看是否寫得很相近。如果要練習口說，記得錄下你的報告，然後聽錄音並與 CD 16、17 比較一下是否相近。重點在於你是否運用了前面學到的搭配詞組。多練習幾次，直到流利順暢為止。

好了，本單元到此結束。在你繼續進行下一個單元之前，回到單元一開始的學習目標清單，檢視自己是否都達成目標了。

希望你瞭解了更多行銷議題，也學會了更多可以在這個領域中使用的語言。記得，盡量在你的工作中尋找機會使用學到的新語言，如此，英文水平才能顯著提升。

工具篇：本章重點語彙

1. brand 的搭配詞組

與動詞搭配

create 創造 establish 建立 launch 展開	**brand** 品牌

與形容詞搭配

leading 領導的 luxury 高級的 mass-market 大眾市場的	**brand** 品牌

2. price 的搭配詞組

與動詞搭配

cut 減低 raise 提高 set 訂定	**price** 價格

與形容詞搭配

list 標示的 retail 零售的 wholesale 批發的	**price** 價格

3. product 的搭配詞組

與動詞搭配

manufacture 製造 advertise 為……做廣告 distribute 分發	**product** 產品

branded 自有品牌的	**product 產品**
defective 瑕疵的	
natural 天然的	

4. campaign 的搭配詞組

與動詞搭配

begin 開始	**campaign 宣傳活動**
launch 展開	

與形容詞搭配

national 全國性的	**campaign 宣傳活動**
public relations 公關的	
new 新的	

5. budget 的搭配詞組

與動詞搭配

allocate 分配	**budget 預算**
go over 超過	

與形容詞搭配

annual 年度的	**budget 預算**
training 訓練的	
shoestring 不足的	

6. strategy 的搭配詞組

與動詞搭配

develop 發展	**strategy 策略**
implement 實行	

business 商業	
innovative 創新的	**strategy 策略**
long-term 長期的	

7. situation 的搭配詞組

與動詞搭配

assess 評估	**situation 情況**
handle 處理	

與形容詞搭配

complicated 複雜的	**situation 情況**
current 目前的	

8. opportunity 的搭配詞組

與動詞搭配

come across 遇到	**opportunity 機會**
grasp 抓住	

與形容詞搭配

golden 千載難逢的	**opportunity 機會**
unexpected 意外的	

9. feature 的搭配詞組

與動詞搭配

include 包含	**feature 特色**

與形容詞搭配

distinguishing 特殊的	**feature 特色**
standard 標準的	

10. economy 的搭配詞組

與動詞搭配

affect 影響 manage 操縱 stimulate 刺激	**economy 經濟**

與形容詞搭配

developed 已發展的 stable 穩定的	**economy 經濟**

11. market 的搭配詞組

與動詞搭配

enter 進入 establish 建立 flood 大量湧入 develop 發展 dominate 支配 expand 擴展	**market 市場**

與形容詞搭配

overseas 海外的 small 小的	**market 市場**

複合名詞

market analysis 市場分析

market conditions 市場情況

market leader 市場領導者

market research 市場研究

market share 市場佔有率

market segmentation 市場區隔

12. ad 的搭配詞組

與動詞搭配

take out 登 make 做 run 播	**ad 廣告**

與形容詞搭配

misleading 不實的	**ad 廣告**

13. advertising 的搭配詞組

與動詞搭配

create 創造 get 取得 use 使用	**advertising 廣告**

與形容詞搭配

national 全國性的 free 免費的	**advertising 廣告**

14. marketing 的搭配詞組

與動詞搭配

improve 改善 do 做 manage 管理	**marketing 行銷**

與形容詞搭配

aggressive 積極的 successful 成功的	**marketing 行銷**

marketing activity 行銷活動

marketing agency 行銷代理商

marketing campaign 行銷宣傳活動

marketing department 行銷部門

marketing plan 行銷計畫

marketing strategy 行銷策略

marketing tool 行銷工具

Unit 6

銷售業務 Sales

Business is not financial science; it's about trading, buying and selling. It's about creating a product or service so good that people will pay for it.

Anita Roddick

cash 現金	client 客戶	consignment 運送的貨品
contract 合約	credit 信用貸款	customer 顧客
deal 交易	delay 延遲	delivery 運送
discount 折扣	feature 特徵	invoice 發票、發貨單
negotiation 協商	offer 供應、出價	order 訂單
payment 付款	price 價錢	product 產品
sale 特價	service 服務	strategy 策略
target 目標		

這些是本單元要學的關鍵名詞。你將學習如何使用這些字彙來說、寫有關
業務的議題。看完本單元，你將達到以下的學習目標：

- [ ] 更加瞭解何謂銷售
- [ ] 瞭解與關鍵字彙一起使用的主要搭配詞
- [ ] 瞭解一些關鍵字彙的複合名詞
- [ ] 能夠運用同義字提升英文表達的豐富性
- [ ] 運用關鍵字彙與它們的搭配詞，做一些聽力與口說的練習
- [ ] 能夠有信心地使用關鍵名詞來談論與寫作銷售議題

上手篇

一開始我們先來瞭解更多關於銷售的具體內容。

Task 1 請閱讀以下關於蓋瑞與喬依斯的敘述，並回答問題。

▶ 你比較希望做哪一項工作？

▶ 為什麼？

找出文章中的關鍵字彙，注意這些字彙在文中如何被運用。

Gerry is a sales rep for a company that produces surgical instruments. He travels around the country visiting hospitals and talking to doctors. His job is to identify prospective customers, visit them, introduce his products to them, including all the unique and important features, and enter into negotiations with the purchasing managers of the hospitals. He has some flexibility in setting the prices, and he is allowed to make generous offers, and give special discounts on large orders, and extend credit. His objective is to try to get a good deal for his company. He employs different sales strategies to make the sale.

When he receives an order from the hospital, he makes arrangements to receive payment, issues a sales invoice, and then arranges delivery of the order. Sometimes, if there is a shipment delay, he has to track the consignment to find out where it is, but this doesn't happen very often.

It's a high-pressure job, because he has strict monthly sales targets which he has to meet.

Joyce is a financial consultant for a private wealth management company. She has a lot of private clients who are at very high income levels. These kinds of clients usually have a lot of surplus cash, which Joyce manages for them. She provides a highly professional and confidential consultancy service based on her knowledge and experience of the changing conditions of the global financial markets.

Her job is quite stressful because she has to ensure satisfactory growth for her clients' money. If they are not satisfied with her performance, they will not renew their contracts, and her income suffers as a result.

中譯

葛瑞是一家生產外科儀器公司的銷售業務代表。他在國內四處旅行，拜訪醫院並與醫生談話。他的工作是找出可能成為買主的顧客、拜訪他們、向他們介紹他的產品所包括的各種獨特且重要的特色，然後與醫院的採購經理協商談判。他有決定價錢的一些空間，他也能夠做出優惠的提案，然後針對大量的訂單給予特別的折扣，並且延長信用貸款期限。他的目標是替他的公司取得一筆好交易。為了達成銷售業務他採用了不同的銷售策略。

當他接到醫院的訂單，他就安排接收付款，開出銷售發貨單，然後安排送貨。有時候，如果船運延遲，他必須追蹤運送的貨品位於何處，但這並不常發生。

這是一個壓力大的工作，因為他每個月都有嚴格的業績目標得達成。

喬依斯是一家私人財富管理公司的財務顧問。她有許多高收入的私人客戶。這種客戶通常有大量的多餘現金需要喬依斯替他們管理。她憑藉著她對於變動的全球財務市場狀況的知識與經驗，提供高度專業且機密的顧問服務。

她的工作壓力相當大，因為她必須確保她客戶的錢有令人滿意的成長。如果他們不滿意她的表現，他們就不會延續他們與她的合約，她的收入就會因此受到影響。

➔ 配對練習

接下來，我們要把學習焦點放在與關鍵字彙搭配使用的動詞上。

Task 2 請將左欄動詞與最常搭配的名詞配對。請看範例。

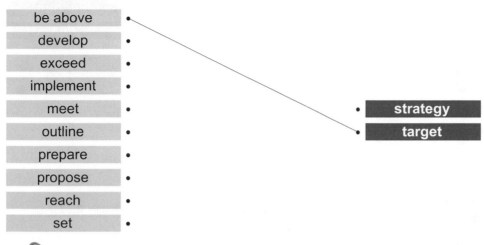

be above
develop
exceed
implement
meet
outline
prepare
propose
reach
set

strategy
target

 請參看書末「解答」核對你的答案。「工具篇」附有完整中譯供參考。

Task 3 請將左欄動詞與最常搭配的名詞配對。

accept
arrange
avoid
be
expect
experience
guarantee
reduce

delay
delivery

 請參看「解答」核對你的答案。

Task 4 請將左欄動詞與最常搭配的名詞配對。

accept
conclude
consider

offer
discount
deal

give	•		•	**offer**
offer	•		•	**discount**
secure	•		•	**deal**

記住，在搭配詞組裡並沒有一定的法則說明某些字可以搭配使用，某些字不行。重要的是，把那些搭配在一起的詞組學習起來即可。把你在前面 task 裡配錯的組合記錄下來，然後加強研讀它們的正確型式。

下一個 task 會示範在文段中如何使用與關鍵名詞搭配的動詞。

Task 5 請用下面表格中的動詞完成這篇文章。注意動詞的時態要正確。

arrange	consider	meet	reduce
conclude	develop	offer	set
	implement		

My boss (1)_____ the sales strategy, and then we have to (2)_____ it. He makes the decisions, and we have to put them into practice. He also (3)_____ our sales targets, and it's our job to (4)_____ them. Sometimes, in order to (5)_____ the deal, I have to (6)_____ a discount. I always give my customers time to (7)_____ my offer, because it's important not to rush a sale. Sometimes, I have to (8)_____ delivery of the products, and do my best to (9)_____ delays.

請參看「解答」核對你的答案。將文章當成詞組的使用範例，多研讀幾次。

現在我們來學一些與關鍵字彙搭配使用的形容詞。

Task 6 請將左欄形容詞與最常搭配的名詞配對。請看範例。

| annual | • | | • | **strategy** |
| detailed | • | | • | **target** |

innovative	•	
monthly	•	
overall	•	• **strategy**
quarterly	•	• **target**
regional	•	
revenue	•	

 請參看「解答」核對答案，也可參考「工具篇」的中譯。

Task 7 請將左欄形容詞與最常搭配的名詞配對。

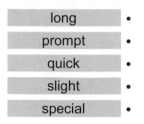

long	•	
prompt	•	• **delay**
quick	•	• **delivery**
slight	•	
special	•	

 請參看「解答」核對你的答案。

Task 8 請將左欄形容詞與最常搭配的名詞配對。

better	•	
big	•	
conditional	•	• **offer**
initial	•	• **discount**
substantial	•	• **deal**
the terms of the	•	

 請核對答案。把前面 task 裡答錯的組合記錄下來，確實地研讀改正。你可以過幾天重新複習「配對練習」單元，看看自己還記得多少。

下一個 task 要幫助你學會在文段中使用與關鍵名詞搭配的形容詞。

Task 9　請用下面表格中的字彙完成這篇文章摘要。

better	prompt	revenue	the terms of the
overall	regional	substantial	

The (1)＿＿＿＿＿ (2)＿＿＿＿＿ strategy is set by the head office abroad, and we have to work out the details locally. So long as we meet our (3)＿＿＿＿＿ targets and make lots of money for the company, they are not too fussy about how we do it. Last week my customer got a (4)＿＿＿＿＿ offer from our competitor, so I had to give her a (5)＿＿＿＿＿ discount in order to get the deal. (6)＿＿＿＿＿ deal are that we guarantee (7)＿＿＿＿＿ delivery. I hope there won't be any delays.

請參看「解答」核對答案。將文章當成詞組的使用範例，多研讀幾次。

學完與關鍵字彙搭配的動詞、形容詞，接下來我們要學習的是從關鍵字彙擴展出的複合名詞。熟悉這些複合名詞，字彙量自然也會倍增。

Task 10　請將關鍵字彙與右欄的字彙配對組成有意義的複合名詞。
請看範例。

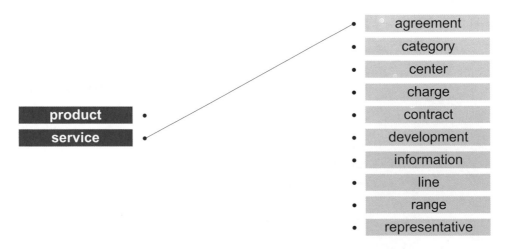

- agreement
- category
- center
- charge
- contract
- development
- information
- line
- range
- representative

product
service

請參看「解答」核對答案，也可參考「工具篇」的中譯。

Task 11 請將關鍵字彙與右欄的字彙配對組成有意義的複合名詞。

- address
- book
- charge
- date
- forecast
- form
- note
- number
- pitch
- promotion
- rep
- schedule
- tax
- volume

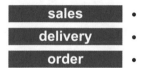

sales
delivery
order

 請參看「解答」核對答案。

Task 12 請將關鍵字彙與右欄的字彙配對組成有意義的複合名詞。

- card
- freeze
- hike
- list
- price
- voucher
- war

discount
price

請參看「解答」核對答案。

請將關鍵字彙與右欄的字彙配對組成有意義的複合名詞。

- agreement
- card
- cow
- crunch
- discount
- dispenser
- **cash** • flow
- **credit** • inflow
- injection
- limit
- outflow
- rating
- reserve
- risk

參看「解答」核對你的答案。將前面幾個 task 裡答錯的組合記錄下來，確實研讀其正確型式。你可以過幾天重新複習「配對練習」單元，看看自己還記得多少。

Task 14 請研讀這兩個句子。然後使用先前 task 裡的複合名詞，按照相同的方式重寫下列句子。

例：We must present the information about the product clearly so that people know how to use it.

→ We must present the product information clearly so that people know how to use it.

1. Can you let me see the list of prices?

_____

2. Do you have a card for discounts?

_____

3. I have reached the limit of my credit.

_____

4. Please check the address for delivery.

_____

5. The charge for service is too high. Can you reduce it a bit?

_____

6. The date of delivery is wrong. It should have arrived yesterday.

_____

7. The number of the order is NTV20056.

_____

8. The outflow of cash is greater than the inflow of cash.

_____

9. The volume of sales is not high enough.

_____

10. We are doing a promotion to increase sales right now.

_____

11. We are in the stage in which we are developing the product. It will be ready in a few months.

_____

12. We have a brand new center for services. You should pay us a visit soon.

_____

13. We need an injection of cash: revenue is down.

_____

完成了配對練習的單元，你現在對於如何活用這些關鍵字彙，應該有更進一步的概念了。

➔ 語言的提升

接著來做更多字彙擴展的練習吧。一開始我們先來看這些搭配詞組的差異。

Task 15 請用表格中的字彙填入下列句中的空格。有些字彙你可以使用不只一次。

client	customer	potential	private
corporate	major	prospective	regular

1. A _____ is someone who buys a product.
2. A _____ is someone who buys a service.
3. A _____ customer/client is a company that buys a product or a service.
4. A _____ customer/client is a private individual who buys a product or a service.
5. A _____ client/customer is someone who makes very big purchases.
6. A _____ client/customer is someone who makes very frequent purchases.
7. A _____ client/customer is someone who might make a purchase in the future.

請參看「解答」核對答案。

現在我們來做一些同義字練習。使用同義字可以提升英文表達的多樣化。一開始我們先練習詞組配對。

請將左欄動詞與最常搭配的名詞組成有意義的搭配詞組。

accept •
collect •
dispatch •
ensure •
guarantee •
receive •
send •
take •

• consignment
• delivery

Task 17 現在請將 task 16 中意思最相近的同義動詞兩兩一組配對。例：
take - accept。

 請參看「解答」核對答案。

接下來我們用形容詞來做相同的練習。

Task 18 請將左欄形容詞與最常搭配的名詞配對。請看範例。

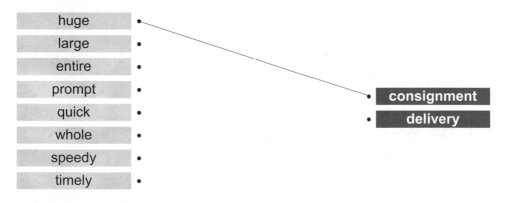

huge •
large •
entire •
prompt •
quick •
whole •
speedy •
timely •

• consignment
• delivery

Task 19 現在請將 task 18 中意思最相近的同義形容詞兩兩一組配對。例：
large - huge

 請參看「解答」核對答案。

現在我們來學習同義字要如何互換使用，以增加英文表達的豐富性。

Task 20 請使用先前 **task** 裡的同義動詞與形容詞重寫下列句子，使兩個句子意思相同。請看範例。

例：We sent the whole consignment of these goods last week.
→ We dispatched the entire consignment last week.

1. Can you guarantee quick delivery?

_____

2. Please be ready to take timely delivery.

_____

3. Did you receive that large consignment of goods I sent you last week?

_____

4. The entire consignment you dispatched last week was rotten.

_____

 請參看「解答」核對答案。如果你覺得這個練習很困難，多花點時間比較每組句子，直到了解透徹為止。

現在我們來學更多與銷售關鍵字彙搭配的同義字，這些關鍵字彙是：offer、service、target、deal 與 discount。

Task 21 請用下列表格中的同義字重寫以下句子，使句子意思不變。請看範例。

achieve	finalize	receive	special
complete	great	refuse	strike
exceed	offer	reject	substantial

例：I cant believe they rejected my best offer!
→ I can't believe they refused my special offer!

1. We provide an excellent service.

_____

2. We need to work harder if we are going to reach our targets this quarter.

_____

3. I am negotiating the deal with them at the moment.

_____

4. I got a generous discount on this purchase.

_____

5. Let's go for a drink to celebrate when we conclude the deal.

_____

6. My sales results are above the monthly target!

_____

7. I have no choice but to refuse this offer.

_____

8. I'll make a deal with you, OK?

_____

請參看「解答」核對答案。

接下來我們來做搭配詞組的練習。

Task 22 將這些搭配詞組按照銷售進行的階段排出正確順序。請看範例。

(   )   accept payment
(   )   agree on a price
(*1*)   approach a prospective customer
(   )   close the sale
(   )   conduct a negotiation
(   )   dispatch the order

(   )   draw up and sign the contract
(   )   introduce the product
(   )   issue a sales invoice
(   )   provide after-sales service
(   )   quote a price
(   )   show the product features
(   )   track the consignment

請參看「解答」核對答案。

做完上一個練習，你應該完全掌握搭配詞組的意義了。接著來做些聽力練習，看看你能否在一段對話中聽出這些詞組。

🎧 18

Task 23 請聽喬治與瑪麗談論他們的一天。然後回答以下的問題。

▸ 是誰過了美好的一天？
▸ 是誰過了糟糕透頂的一天？
▸ 為什麼？

🎧 18

Task 24 現在請再仔細聽一次這段談話。聽的時候，在下列的表格中將你聽到的搭配詞組打 ✔，並且留意是喬治還是瑪麗說的。請看範例。

George		Mary
	achieve my sales targets	
	agree on the price	
	ask for a discount	
	be a defective product	
	collect the consignment	
	complete the negotiation	
	complete the sales invoice correctly	
	dispatch a big bulk order	

	extend credit	
	finalize the terms of the deal	
	provide great after-sales service	
	guarantee next-day delivery	
	have a new customer	✔
	make a great offer	
✔	make my first sale	
	pay cash	
	provide service	
	show all the features	
	sign the contract	
	use a new sales strategy	
	visit a prospective client	
	withhold payment	

如果你覺得這個 task 很困難，再多聽幾次直到你能完成全部表格為止。完成練習之後，閱讀錄音稿，建議你將這些搭配詞組畫底線，幫助自己留意它們的用法。

Task 25 想像你是喬治或瑪麗。寫一封信給朋友，告訴他你今天過了很糟糕的一天或很美好的一天。請使用 task 24 的搭配詞組來寫；或者，找一位伙伴一同練習對話。一人扮演喬治，另一個為瑪麗。練習運用 task 24 的搭配詞組來說。

在這個 task 裡，你可以練習寫作或是口說（當然，最好是兩個都做！）。如果你要練習寫作，完成後與 CD 18 的錄音稿比較一下你寫的信，看看用語是否相近。如果要練習口說，記得錄下你們的對話，然後聽錄音並與 CD 18 比較一下是否相近。重點在於你是否運用了前面學到的搭配詞組。多練習幾次，直到流利順暢為止。

➔ 強化練習

在本單元的最後部分，爲了強化在這個單元所學到的搭配詞組，我們再來看一次銷售程序。

Task 26 請將左欄的動詞與右欄的名詞片語配對，組成可以用來描述銷售程序的搭配詞組。請看範例。

accept	*approach*	a prospective customer
agree on		the product
~~approach~~		the product features
close		a price
conduct		a negotiation
dispatch		a price
draw up and sign		the sale
introduce		the contract
issue		the order
provide		the consignment
quote		payment
show		a sales invoice
track		after-sales service

 你可以參看 task 22 的解答來核對你的答案。

最後，我們來練習將這些搭配詞組運用在段落當中。

Task 27 請用本單元學過的詞彙填入這篇文章裡的空格。

Gerry is a sales rep for a company that produces surgical instruments. He travels around the country visiting hospitals and talking to doctors. His job is to identify prospective (1)＿＿＿＿＿＿, visit them, introduce his (2)_____ to them, including all the unique and important (3)_____, and enter into (4)_____ with the purchasing managers of the hospitals. He has some flexibility in setting the (5)_____, and he is allowed to make generous (6)_____, and give special (7)_____ on large orders, and extend (8)_____. His objective is to try to get a good (9)_____ for his company. He employs different sales (10)_____ to make the (11)_____.

When he receives an (12)_____ from the hospital, he makes arrangements to receive (13)_____, issues a sales (14)_____, and then arranges (15)_____ of the order. Sometimes, if there is a shipment (16)_____, he has to track the (17)_____ to find out where it is, but this doesn't happen very often.

It's a high-pressure job, because he has strict monthly sales (18) _____ which he has to meet.

Joyce is a financial consultant for a private wealth management company. She has a lot of private (19)_____ who are at very high income levels. These kinds of clients usually have a lot of surplus (20)_____, which Joyce manages for them. She provides a highly professional and confidential consultancy (21)_____ based on her knowledge and experience of the changing conditions of the global financial markets.

Her job is quite stressful because she has to ensure satisfactory growth for her clients' money. If they are not satisfied with her performance, they will not renew their (22)_____, and her income suffers as a result.

有沒有覺得這篇文章似曾相識？！你可以再次閱讀 task 1 的文章來核對你的答案。

好了，本單元到此結束。希望你對於銷售業務有更進一步的了解，也學到更多你可以在這個領域使用的語言。現在請回到單元一開始的學習目標清單，檢視自己是否都達成目標了。

記得，盡量在你的工作中尋找機會使用你學到的新詞彙。

工具篇：本章重點語彙

1. strategy 的搭配詞組

與動詞搭配

develop 發展 prepare 準備 outline 草擬 propose 提出 implement 實施	strategy 策略

與形容詞搭配

detailed 詳細的 innovative 革新的 overall 全面的 regional 區域性的	strategy 策略

2. target 的搭配詞組

與動詞搭配

set 設定 meet 達到 reach 達到 exceed 超過 be above 超過	target 目標

與形容詞搭配

annual 年度的 monthly 每月的 quarterly 每季的 revenue 盈收	target 目標

3. delivery 的搭配詞組

accept 接受
arrange 安排
expect 期待
ensure 確保
guarantee 保證

delivery 送貨

prompt 立即的
timely 及時的
quick 快速的
speedy 快速的
special 特別的

delivery 送貨

delivery address 送貨地址

delivery charge 送貨費用

delivery date 送貨日期

delivery note 送貨通知

delivery schedule 送貨時程

4. delay 的搭配詞組

avoid 避免
be 有
reduce 減少
experience 經歷

delay 延遲

例 There will **be a delay**. 將會有延遲。

long 長時間的	**delay** 延遲
slight 輕微的	

5. offer 的搭配詞組

與動詞搭配

accept 接受	**offer** 出價
consider 考慮	

與形容詞搭配

better 更好的	**offer** 出價
conditional 有條件的	
initial 最初的	

6. deal 的搭配詞組

與動詞搭配

conclude 完成	**deal** 交易
secure 確保	

與形容詞搭配

the terms of the ……的條件	**deal** 交易
better 更好的	

7. discount 的搭配詞組

與動詞搭配

give 給	**discount** 折扣
offer 提供	

與形容詞搭配

big 大的	**discount** 折扣
substantial 大量的	

discount voucher 折扣券

discount card 折扣卡

discount price 折扣價

8. consignment 的搭配詞組

與動詞搭配

collect 收	
receive 收	**consignment**
dispatch 急送	託運貨品
send 寄	

與形容詞搭配

large 大的	
huge 大的	**consignment**
whole 全部的	託運貨品
entire 全部的	

9. product 的複合名詞

❖ product category 產品種類

❖ product development 產品發展

❖ product information 產品資訊

❖ product line 產品線

❖ product range 產品範圍

10. service 的複合名詞

❖ service agreement 服務協定

❖ service center 服務中心

❖ service charge 服務費用

❖ service contract 服務合約

❖ service representative 服務代表

11. sales 的複合名詞

* sales forecast 銷售預測
* sales pitch 推銷話術
* sales promotion 促銷
* sales rep 業務代表
* sales tax 銷售稅
* sales volume 銷售額

12. order 的複合名詞

* order book 訂貨簿
* order form 訂貨表格
* order number 訂貨號碼

13. price 的複合名詞

* price list 價格表
* price hike 價格飛漲
* price freeze 價格凍結
* price war 價格戰

14. cash 的複合名詞

* cash card 現金卡
* cash cow 帶來財源的生意
* cash discount 現金折扣
* cash dispenser 自動提款機
* cash flow 現金流通
* cash inflow 現金流入
* cash injection 單次的現金注入
* cash limit 現金限額
* cash outflow 現金流出
* cash reserve 現金準備

15. credit 的複合名詞

- ❖ credit agreement 信用協定
- ❖ credit card 信用卡
- ❖ credit crunch 信用緊縮
- ❖ credit limit 信用限額
- ❖ credit rating 信用評比
- ❖ credit risk 信用風險

16. 銷售用語

- ❖ approach a prospective customer 接洽可能客戶
- ❖ introduce the product 介紹產品
- ❖ show the product features 展示產品特色
- ❖ quote a price 報價
- ❖ conduct a negotiation 進行談判
- ❖ agree on a price 同意價格
- ❖ close the sale 完成交易
- ❖ draw up and sign the contract 草擬和簽署合約
- ❖ dispatch the order 依訂單送貨
- ❖ track the consignment 追縱運送貨品
- ❖ accept payment 收款
- ❖ issue a sales invoice 開銷售發票
- ❖ provide after-sales service 提供售後服務

Unit 7

生產 Production

The production of too many useful things results in too many useless people.

Karl Marx

consignment 運送的貨物	contract 合約	control 控制
cost 成本	delay 延遲	delivery 運送
function 功能	manufacturer 製造商	problem 問題
product 產品	production 生產	solution 解決方案
supplier 供應商		

這些是本單元我們要學的關鍵名詞。你將學習如何使用這些字彙來說、寫關於生產的議題。看完本單元，你將達到以下的學習目標：

- ☐ 更加瞭解何謂生產
- ☐ 瞭解與關鍵字彙一起使用的主要搭配詞
- ☐ 瞭解一些關鍵字彙的複合名詞
- ☐ 能夠運用同義字提升英文表達的豐富性
- ☐ 運用關鍵字彙與它們的搭配詞，做一些聽力與口說的練習
- ☐ 能夠有信心地使用關鍵名詞來談論和寫作生產的議題

上手篇

一開始我們先來瞭解更多關於生產的具體內容，以及練習閱讀文段中的關鍵字彙。

Task 1 請閱讀以下這篇關於生產外包之全球趨勢的短文。找出當中的關鍵字彙，並注意這些字彙在文中如何被使用。

Production is the process of manufacturing and assembling the products of a company.

There is an increasing trend now in business for companies to locate their production lines in developing countries where labor and operating costs are cheaper. The parent company can either own the factory or outsource their production to an OEM or ODM company. In this kind of business model, the manufacturer fulfills the function of the production arm of the parent company, working closely with them on all aspects of production.

Outsourcing production overseas can cause some problems. First, it's difficult to guarantee quality. Quality controls are difficult to maintain, and finding reliable suppliers of raw materials is not easy. Secondly, it's difficult to guarantee timely delivery of raw materials, component parts and finished products; consignments may be delayed. Delays might arise due to many unforeseen factors, such as weather conditions or political circumstances.

It's not easy to find clever solutions to these problems. Although contracts can cover some of the terms of the relationship between the two parties, they cannot cover everything. More important is trust.

生產是一家公司製造與組裝產品的過程。

現在商業裡有一個趨勢,越來越多的公司將他們的生產線設立在勞力與營運成本比較便宜的發展中國家。總公司可以擁有工廠或將他們的生產外包給原產委託製造加工或原始委託設計加工公司。在這種商業模式裡,製造者履行總公司生產部門的功能,並與他們在生產的各個面向密切合作。

外包海外生產可能帶來一些問題。首先,要保證品質很困難。品質控管難以維持,找到值得信賴的原料供應商不容易。其次是,難以保證原料、零組件與完成品的及時運送,貨品可能會延遲。延遲可能是由於許多不可預期的因素,例如天氣狀況或政治環境。

要找到解決這些問題的聰明方法並不容易。雖然合約可以包含兩方關係的一些條款,但無法涵蓋所有事。更重要的是信任。

➔ 配對練習

在接下來的部分我們要來做一些配對練習,焦點放在與關鍵字彙搭配使用的動詞。

Task 2 將左欄動詞與最常搭配的名詞配對。請看範例。

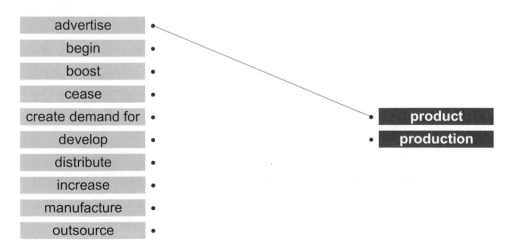

advertise ·
begin ·
boost ·
cease ·
create demand for ·
develop ·
distribute ·
increase ·
manufacture ·
outsource ·

· **product**
· **production**

請參看書末「解答」核對答案。「工具篇」附有中譯可供參考。

Task 3　請將左欄動詞與最常搭配的名詞配對。

accompany　•

arrange　•

collect　•

deliver　•

dispatch　•　　　　　　　　　　　•　**delivery**

expect　•　　　　　　　　　　　•　**consignment**

guarantee　•

make　•

receive　•

take　•

請參看「解答」核對答案。

Task 4　請將左欄動詞與最常搭配的名詞配對。

exercise　•

fulfill　•

have　•

implement　•　　　　　　　　　　•　**control**

maintain　•　　　　　　　　　　•　**function**

perform　•

provide　•

put in place　•

請核對答案。記住，搭配詞組並沒有一定的法則說明某些字可以搭配使用，某些字不行。重要的是，把那些搭配在一起的詞組學起來，當成固定用語來使用。把你在前面 task 裡配錯的組合記錄下來，然後加強研讀它們的正確型式。

下一個 task 要幫助你學會在文段中使用與關鍵名詞搭配的動詞。

Task 5 請利用下面表格中的動詞完成這篇文章摘要。注意動詞的時態要正確。

ensure	outsource	ship
manufacture	provide	put in place

Nowadays, there is a trend towards (1)_____ production overseas. Many companies (2)_____ their products in countries where labor is cheaper. This can cause problems. Companies have to (3)_____ quality controls. It's also difficult to (4)_____ prompt delivery, and (5)_____ consignments to international markets can be costly. Many shipping companies now (6)_____ a tracking function, so consignments don't get lost.

 請參看「解答」核對答案。

學完動詞,現在我們要把焦點轉到與關鍵字彙搭配使用的形容詞。

Task 6 將左欄形容詞與最常搭配的名詞配對。請看範例。

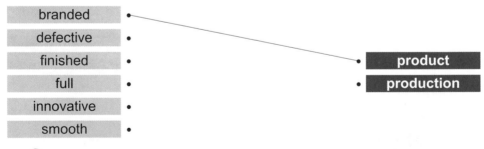

branded
defective
finished
full
innovative
smooth

product
production

 請參看書末「解答」核對答案。「工具篇」附有中譯可供參考。

Task 7　請將左欄形容詞與最常搭配的名詞配對。

early	•
fast	•
large	•
particular	•
recorded	•
single	•
special	•
whole	•

• **delivery**

• **consignment**

　請參看「解答」核對答案。

Task 8　請將左欄形容詞與最常搭配的名詞配對。

administrative	•
basic	•
cost	•
effective	•
main	•
strict	•
tight	•
useful	•

• **control**

• **function**

　請核對答案。將先前 task 裡答錯的組合記錄下來，確實地改正並研讀正確詞組。你可以過幾天後重新複習「配對練習」單元，看看自己還記得多少。

下一個 task 要幫助你學會在文段中使用與關鍵名詞搭配的形容詞。

Task 9　請用下面表格中的字彙完成這篇文章摘要。

defective	primary	speedy	valuable
large	smooth	strict	

Maintaining (1)＿＿＿＿＿ quality controls are essential if companies want to avoid manufacturing (2)＿＿＿＿＿ products, and to ensure (3)＿＿＿＿＿ production. Also, logistics are important. (4)＿＿＿＿＿ consignments may be extremely (5)＿＿＿＿＿, and (6)＿＿＿＿＿ delivery is essential to maintaining market share. The company's quality control and logistics departments are therefore a (7)＿＿＿＿＿ function of the whole manufacturing process.

請參看「解答」核對答案。

學完與關鍵字彙搭配的動詞、形容詞，接下來我們要學習的是從關鍵字彙擴展出的複合名詞。熟悉這些複合名詞，活用關鍵字彙的能力也會倍增。

Task 10　將名詞配對成有意義的複合名詞。請看範例。

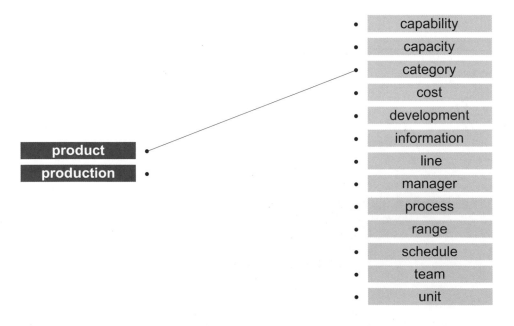

請核對答案。同樣地，請針對你答錯的組合，專心地研讀改正。

Task 11 請研讀這兩個句子。然後使用先前 **task** 裡的複合名詞，按照相同的方式重寫下列句子。

> 例：Most of the goods for this category of product are quite cheap, so they don't make much money.
> → Most of the goods for this product category are quite cheap, so they don't make much money.

1. The cost of production is too high. We need to try to reduce it.

_____

2. The line of this product includes shampoo, conditioner, hairspray, and gel.

_____

3. The process of production was developed in our German factory.

_____

4. The schedule of production is already delayed.

_____

5. The team handling production consists of three people.

_____

6. We produce a full range of products for the company.

_____

 請參看「解答」核對答案。

➔ 語言的提升

在接下來的部分，我們要做一些練習以進一步提升語言表達的能力，包括運用同義字與增進聽力技巧。

請用表格中的字彙填入下列句中的空格。有些字彙你可以使用不只一次。

capability	line	range
category	capacity	

1. A product _____ is all the products which come under one brand name.

2. A product _____ is all the different branded products produced by one company.

3. A product _____ refers to the type of product. For example, skincare products and ready-to-drink coffee products are not the same kind of products.

4. A production _____ is the machinery and the process of manufacturing a product in a factory.

5. Production _____ is the different kinds of products a factory is able to make without too much alteration to the machinery and the process of production.

6. Production _____ is the amount of products a factory is able to produce.

請參看「解答」核對答案。

現在我們來學一些可與 problem 與 solution 搭配使用的同義動詞。這兩個字彙在商務英文中出現極為頻繁，特別是在談論有關生產的議題。因此花時間把這些字彙與它們的搭配詞組學好是值得的。

Task 13 請將左欄動詞與最常搭配的名詞配對。請看範例。

cause	•		•	**problem**
encounter	•		•	**solution**
hit upon	•			

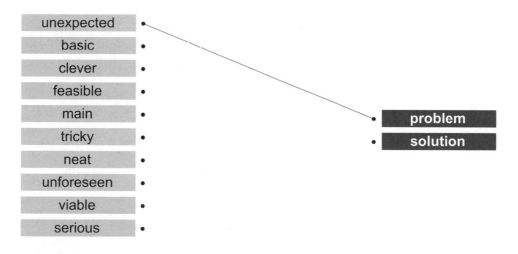

rule out •
solve •
reject •
come up against •
sort out •
find •
pose •

• **problem**
• **solution**

unexpected •
basic •
clever •
feasible •
main •
tricky •
neat •
unforeseen •
viable •
serious •

• **problem**
• **solution**

Task 14 現在請將上一個 task 中意思最相近的動詞兩兩一組配對。

例： **cause - pose** 。

請參看「解答」核對答案。

學完動詞,接下來我們用形容詞來做相同的練習。

Task 15 請將左欄形容詞與最常搭配的名詞配對。請看範例。

Task 16 現在請將上一個 task 中意思最相近的形容詞兩兩一組配對。

例： **tricky - serious** 。

請參看「解答」核對答案。

知道哪些字詞可以替換使用後,接著就來示範如何把它們運用在句子中。

Task 17 請使用先前 task 裡的同義動詞與形容詞重寫下列句子,使兩個句子意思相同。請看範例。

例: This could cause a serious problem for us.
→ This could pose a tricky problem for us.

1. We need to solve the main problem before we proceed.

_____

2. We have encountered an unexpected problem.

_____

3. The production team has found a neat solution.

_____

4. We rejected this solution last time. It's just not feasible.

_____

 請核對答案。如果你覺得這個練習很困難,多花點時間比較每組句子,直到了解透徹為止。

現在我們來學更多與生產字彙搭配的同義字,這些字彙是: contract、supplier、cost、delay 與 manufacturer。

Task 18 從下列表格裡選出正確的同義字彙重寫以下句子。請看範例。

arise	follow	long	specify
be	have	produce	switch
extra	largest	reduce	terminate
fall		reliable	

例: We might have to cancel the contract if you don't honor it.
→ We might have to terminate the contract if you don't follow it.

1. The contract stipulates the terms of our agreement.

2. I think we should change suppliers. We need a more dependable one.

3. You will incur additional costs if you want special delivery of the raw material.

4. We found a way to cut production costs, and now they are going down.

5. You might experience considerable delays if you choose this shipping method.

6. Unexpected production delays have occurred, for which we apologize.

7. We are the leading manufacturer of this type of product.

8. Manufacturers made too much of this product. Now there is a surplus and the price has dropped.

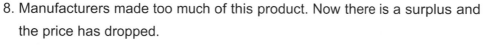

 請核對答案。如果無法完全答對,多花點時間比較每組句子,直到了解透徹為止。

接著我們來練習從文段中聽出關鍵字彙。能夠聽出使用中的關鍵字彙,熟悉它們的發音和語調,自然能更有信心地使用這些字彙。

Task 19 請聽 CD 19 這場會議。生產部經理麥可正在解釋生產團隊目前所面臨的問題。

⊙ 他們面臨了什麼問題？
⊙ 建議的解決方案是什麼？

麥可對他的供應商有兩個抱怨：零件配送與零件品質。有人建議強制執行與供應商的合約，但是這個方案試過後並沒有成功。會議中沒有人可以建議其他的解決方案。聽的時候試著不要對照錄音稿。如果你覺得這個 task 很困難，再多聽幾次直到你能聽出答案為止。

🎧 19

Task 20 現在請再仔細聽一次這段談話。聽的時候，請將你聽到的字彙打 ✔。

problems	( )
supplier	( )
manufacturer	( )
delays	( )
consignments	( )
delivery	( )
costs	( )
products	( )
controls	( )
production process	( )
contract	( )
solution	( )

🎧 19

Task 21 請再聽一次 CD 19，並完成表格中的搭配詞組，如範例。注意談話者使用了哪幾個搭配詞組。

run into seriou	problems	
	supplier	
	manufacturer	
	delays	
	consignments	
	delivery	
	costs	
	products	
	controls	*have risen*
	production process	
	contract	
	contract	
	solution	

 請參看「解答」，也可以閱讀這場會議的錄音稿。閱讀時，可將搭配詞組畫底線，幫助自己更能注意它們的用法。

➔ 強化練習

Task 22 請使用 task 21 中的搭配詞組，練習談論關於麥可所面臨的問題。

 幫自己錄音。然後聽錄音，檢視你是否能流利地説出這些搭配詞組。

Task 23 請用本單元學過的詞彙填入這篇文章裡的空格。

(1)＿＿＿＿＿ is the process of manufacturing and assembling the
(2)＿＿＿＿＿ of a company.

There is an increasing trend now in business for companies to locate their production lines in developing countries where labor and operating (3)_____ are cheaper. The parent company can either own the factory or outsource their production to an OEM or ODM company. In this kind of business model, the (4)_____ fulfills the (5)_____ of the production arm of the parent company, working closely with them on all aspects of production.

Outsourcing production overseas can cause some (6)_____. First, it's difficult to guarantee quality. Quality (7)_____ are difficult to maintain, and finding reliable (8)_____ of raw materials is not easy. Secondly, it's difficult to guarantee timely (9)_____ of raw materials, component parts and finished products; (10)_____ may be delayed. (11)_____ might arise due to many unforeseen factors, such as weather conditions or political circumstances.

It's not easy to find clever (12)_____ to these problems. Although (13)_____ can cover some of the terms of the relationship between the two parties, they cannot cover everything. More important is trust.

有沒有覺得這篇文章似曾相識？！你可以再次閱讀 task 1 的文章來核對你的答案。

好了，本單元到此結束。希望你現在能夠運用這些談論和寫作生產議題的用語了。如果你在生產部門工作，可以使用你在本單元學到的技巧，來學習工作時接觸到的新字彙，並且盡量把握機會在工作中使用學到的新字彙。在你繼續進行下一個單元之前，回到一開始的學習目標清單，檢視自己是否都達成目標了。

工具篇：本章重點語彙

1. product 的搭配詞組

與動詞搭配

advertise 為……做廣告
create demand for 為……創造需求
develop 發展
distribute 流通、分發
manufacture 製造

product 產品

與形容詞搭配

branded 自有品牌的
defective 有瑕疵的
finished 完成的
innovative 創新的

product 產品

複合名詞

product category 產品種類

product development 產品發展

product information 產品資訊

product line 產品線

product range 產品範圍

2. production 的搭配詞組

與動詞搭配

begin 開始
boost 增加
cease 停止
increase 增加
outsource 外包

production 生產

full 全面的	**production 生產**
smooth 順利的	

複合名詞

production capability 生產能力

production capacity 能夠生產的最大量（產能）

production cost 生產成本

production line 生產線

production manager 生產經理

production process 生產流程

production schedule 生產時程

production team 生產團隊

production unit 生產單位

3. delivery 的搭配詞組

與動詞搭配

arrange 安排	
expect 等待	
guarantee 保證	**delivery 送貨**
make 處理	
take 接收	

與形容詞搭配

early 早的	
fast 快速的	
recorded 掛號的	**delivery 送貨**
special 特別的	

4. consignment 的搭配詞組

與動詞搭配

accompany 伴隨
collect 收
deliver 運送
dispatch 急送
receive 收

consignment
運送的貨品

與形容詞搭配

large 大的
particular 特別的
single 單一的
whole 全部的

consignment
運送的貨品

5. control 的搭配詞組

與動詞搭配

exercise 行使
have 有
implement 執行
maintain 維持
put in place 執行

control 控管

例 put in place the cost control = 執行成本控管

與形容詞搭配

cost 成本
effective 有效的
strict 嚴格的
tight 嚴密的

control 控管

6. function 的搭配詞組

與動詞搭配

exercise 行使	
fulfill 完成、履行	
have 有	**function 功能**
perform 執行	
provide 提供	

與形容詞搭配

administrative 管理的	
basic 基本的	
main 主要的	**function 功能**
useful 實用的	

7. problem 的搭配詞組

與動詞搭配

encounter 遇到	
come up against 遇到	
solve 解決	
sort out 解決	**problem 問題**
pose 引起	
cause 造成	

與形容詞搭配

unexpected 意外的	
unforeseen 意外的	
basic 基本的	
main 主要的	**problem 問題**
tricky 棘手的	
serious 嚴重的	

8. solution 的搭配詞組

與動詞搭配

hit upon 發現	
find 找到	solution 解決之道
reject 駁回、否決	
rule out 排除	

與形容詞搭配

clever 聰明的	
neat 巧妙的	solution 解決之道
feasible 可行的	
viable 可行的	

Unit 8

財務 Finance

A corporation's primary goal is to make money. Government's primary role is to take a big chunk of that money and give it to others.

Larry Ellison

analysis 分析	assessment 評估	bank 銀行
budget 預算	capital 資金	cash 現金
control 控制	cost 成本	credit 信用借貸
data 資訊、情報	economy 經濟	figures 數據
financing 融資	growth 成長	investment 投資
invoice 交易發貨單	loss 虧損	market 市場
payment 付款	profit 盈利	prospects 遠景
research 研究	return 報酬	risk 風險
situation 狀況	strategy 策略	

這些是本單元我們要學的關鍵名詞。你將學習如何使用這些字彙來說、寫關於財務的議題。看完本單元,你將達到以下的學習目標:

- [ ] 更加瞭解何謂財務
- [ ] 瞭解與關鍵字彙一起使用的主要搭配詞
- [ ] 瞭解一些以關鍵字彙組成的複合名詞
- [ ] 能夠運用同義字彙提升英文表達的豐富性
- [ ] 運用關鍵字彙與它們的搭配詞,做一些聽力與口說的練習
- [ ] 能有信心地使用關鍵名詞來談論和寫作生產議題

上手篇

一開始我們先來瞭解更多關於財務的具體內容，以及練習閱讀文段中的關鍵字彙。

Task 1 請閱讀下面這篇短文。找出當中的關鍵字彙，並注意這些字彙在文中如何被使用。

What is Finance?

It's well known that a corporation exists to make money. There are three main ways a corporation can make money. The first way, of course, is by selling its products. In order to make a profit by doing this, companies have to minimize costs by setting tight budgets and exercising controls on spending. They have to be very strict about collecting payment for goods or services, and must not extend credit to customers, because that is expensive for the company. Sales people have to be very careful about checking invoices, and keeping careful financial records for the tax office. Usually, in the first few years of a company's life, the company incurs losses.

The second way of making money is to manage the profits generated by sales. The CFO (Chief Financial Officer) does this by carrying out research into the domestic and international financial markets, and then investing in funds which have good prospects.

In order to help the CFO plan financial strategy, he or she has to be very good at conducting analyses of financial data, at assessing the economic situation. Some CFO's of very large multinational corporations also make short-term investments in different currency markets.

The third way of making money is by raising capital. There are a number of ways to do this. If a company needs to raise a small amount of cash quickly, they can borrow money from a bank. If they need larger amounts, they can attract investment from private or corporate investors, or they can sell shares and obtain financing that way. However, because most investors are looking for low risks and high returns, the company has to be in good financial shape before selling shares, and should be able to sustain continued growth. The economy also has to be stable. The CFO has to release his company's financial figures on a regular basis to help investors make an accurate assessment of the company's performance.

中譯

何謂財務

眾所皆知的，一家公司的存在就是要賺錢。一家公司要賺錢有三個主要方法。第一個方法當然是販售他們的產品。如此做是為了要賺取盈利，公司必須藉由精打細算的預算與花費控制使成本降到最小。他們對於收取商品或服務的款項必須非常嚴格，不能讓顧客延長信貸，因為這對公司而言代價高昂。銷售人員必須非常謹慎地核對交易發貨單，並保持詳細的財務記錄給賦稅局。在一家公司壽命的頭幾年裡，公司通常會有虧損。

第二種賺錢的方法是管理經由銷售產生的利潤。財務主管在國內與國際金融市場進行研究，然後將利潤投資在有遠景的基金上。

為了幫助財務主管策畫財政策略，他或她對於執行金融情報分析與評估經濟狀況必須非常在行。有一些大型跨國企業的財務主管也在不同的貨幣市場裡作短期的投資。

第三種賺錢的方式是籌措資本。有許多方法可以辦到。如果一家公司需要快速張羅小額現金，他們可以跟銀行借款。如果他們需要更大筆的金額，他們可以吸引私人或企業投資者投資，或者他們可以賣掉持股，並以此方式獲得融資。然而，因為大部分的投資者尋求低風險與高報酬，公司在賣掉持股之前必須擁有好的財務狀況，並且要能持續成長。經濟也必須穩定。財務主管必須定期發布公司的財務數據，幫助投資者對公司的表現做出正確的評估。

➔ 配對練習

在接下來的部分我們要來做一些配對練習，焦點放在與關鍵字彙搭配使用的動詞上。

Task 2　將左欄動詞與最常搭配的名詞配對。請看範例。

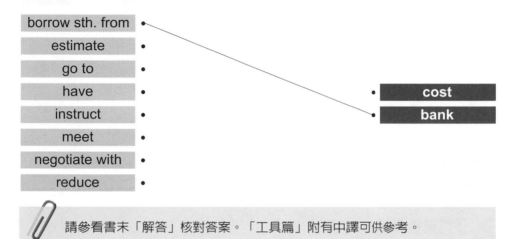

請參看書末「解答」核對答案。「工具篇」附有中譯可供參考。

Task 3　請將左欄動詞與最常搭配的名詞配對。

請參看「解答」核對答案。

avoid   •

earn   •

get   •

involve   •   • **risk**

maximize   •   • **return**

minimize   •

take   •

yield   •

請參看「解答」核對答案。

Task 5 請將左欄動詞與最常搭配的名詞配對。

adjust   •

arrive at   •

compare   •

examine   •   • **data**

look at   •   • **figures**

process   •

see   •

store   •

請參看「解答」核對答案。

Task 6 請將左欄動詞與最常搭配的名詞配對。

achieve   •

assess   •   • **prospects**

damage   •   • **growth**

enhance   •

experience	•
improve	•
see	•
stimulate	•

•	**prospects**
•	**growth**

 請參看「解答」核對答案。

Task 7 請將左欄動詞與最常搭配的名詞配對。

arrange	•
borrow	•
increase	•
invest	•
obtain	•
protect	•
provide	•
raise	•
recoup	•
repay	•

•	**financing**
•	**capital**
•	**investment**

 請核對答案。記住,搭配詞組並沒有一定的法則說明某些字可以搭配使用,某些字不行。重要的是,把那些搭配在一起的詞組學起來,當成固定用語來使用。把你在前面 task 裡配錯的組合記錄下來,然後加強研讀它們的正確型式。

下一個 task 要幫助你學會在文段中使用與關鍵名詞搭配的動詞。

Task 8 請用下面表格中的字彙完成這篇 task 1 的文章摘要。注意動詞的時態要正確。

assess	examine	maximize
borrow	invest	minimize
		reduce

There are several ways a company can make money. The first is by (1)＿＿＿＿＿ costs and making sure sales are high.

The second is by investing the company's profits so as to increase them. When investors are making decisions about where to (2)＿＿＿＿＿ their capital, they try to (3)＿＿＿＿＿ the risk and (4)＿＿＿＿＿ the return. They have to (5)＿＿＿＿＿ the data and (6)＿＿＿＿＿ the prospects of the company or fund they want to invest in.

The third method is by (7)＿＿＿＿＿ from the bank, or by issuing shares.

請參看「解答」核對答案。

學完動詞，現在我們要把焦點轉到與關鍵字彙搭配使用的形容詞。

Task 9 將左欄形容詞與最常搭配的名詞配對。請看範例。

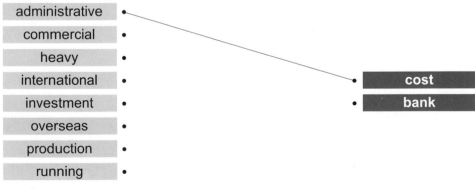

administrative •
commercial •
heavy •
international •
investment •
overseas •
production •
running •

cost
bank

請參看書末「解答」核對答案。「工具篇」附有中譯可供參考。

Task 10 請將左欄形容詞與最常搭配的名詞配對。

interest •

late •

monthly •

original •   • **invoice**

overtime •   • **payment**

sales •

tax •

VAT •

請參看「解答」核對答案。

Task 11 請將左欄形容詞與最常搭配的名詞配對。

annual •

calculated •

guaranteed •   • **risk**

maximum •   • **return**

minimal •

serious •

請參看「解答」核對答案。

Task 12 請將左欄形容詞與最常搭配的名詞配對。

comprehensive •

detailed •

financial •   • **data**

key •   • **figures**

official •

raw •

sales •	• data
trading •	• figures

 請參看「解答」核對答案。

Task 13 請將左欄形容詞與最常搭配的名詞配對。

continued •	
economic •	
exciting •	
gloomy •	• prospects
growth •	• growth
quick •	
steady •	
sustainable •	

 請參看「解答」核對答案。

Task 14 請將左欄形容詞與最常搭配的名詞配對。

corporate •	
foreign •	
initial •	
personal •	• finance
share •	• capital
sound •	• investment
venture •	
working •	

請核對答案。將前面 task 裡答錯的組合記錄下來，確實地改正並研讀正確詞組。你可以過幾天後重新複習「配對練習」單元，看看自己還記得多少。

接下來要練習在文段中使用與關鍵名詞搭配的形容詞。

Task 15 請用下面表格中的字彙完成這篇文章摘要。

calculated	financial	growth	investment
		guaranteed	running

There are several ways a company can make money. The first is by reducing (1)＿＿＿＿＿＿ costs and making sure sales are high.

The second is by investing the company's profits so as to increase them. When investors are making a decision about where to invest their capital, they know they are taking a (2)＿＿＿＿＿＿ risk, but they are hoping to get a (3)＿＿＿＿＿＿ return. They have to examine the (4)＿＿＿＿＿＿ data and assess the (5)＿＿＿＿＿＿ prospects of the company or fund they want to invest in.

The third method is by borrowing from an (6)＿＿＿＿＿＿ bank, or by issuing shares.

請參看「解答」核對答案。

學完與關鍵字彙搭配的動詞、形容詞，接下來我們要學習的是從關鍵字彙擴展出的複合名詞。熟悉這些複合名詞，活用關鍵字彙的能力也會倍增。

Task 16 請將名詞配對成有意義的複合名詞。請看範例。

capital	appreciation
investment	expenditure
growth	forecast
	fund
	gains
	inflow

	•	investment
	•	markets
capital •	•	opportunity
investment •	•	outflow
growth •	•	rate
	•	strategy
	•	target

請核對答案。「工具篇」附有中譯供參考。

Task 17 請將每個字彙與最常搭配的名詞配對。請看範例。

	•	assessment
	•	factor
	•	forecast
profit •	•	growth
risk •	•	management
	•	margin
	•	rating
	•	share

請核對答案。同樣地,請針對你答錯的組合,專心地研讀改正。

Task 18 請研讀這兩個句子。然後使用先前 **task** 裡的複合名詞,按照相同的方式重寫下列句子。

例: It's a great opportunity for investment.
→ It's a great investment opportunity.

1. It's a fund for investment. I have invested quite a lot in it already.

2. Our inflow of capital has been good this year.

_____

3. We tried to raise some money on the markets for capital, but our stock price didn't reach the target price.

_____

4. We had a high expenditure of capital because we built a new factory.

_____

5. The forecast for growth of the economy was too optimistic.

_____

6. The share of the profit we gave to shareholders was fair.

_____

7. There is a high factor of risk involved in this kind of speculation.

_____

請參看「解答」核對答案。

➔ 語言的提升

在接下來的部分，我們要做一些練習以進一步提升語言表達的能力，包括運用同義字與增進聽力技巧。

Task 19 請用表格中的字彙填入下列句中的空格。

account	card	loan
balance	charges	statement
		transfer

1. A bank _____ is where you keep your money. You can have several of these.
2. A bank _____ is when you borrow money from the bank.

3. A bank _____ is when you electronically send money from one account to another.
4. Bank _____ are what you pay for the services the bank gives you.
5. Every month, the bank sends you a bank _____ showing all the transactions on your accounts.
6. Your bank _____ is how much money you have in your account.
7. Your bank _____ is a piece of plastic that you can use to withdraw cash from your account.

請參看「解答」核對答案。可以把這些句子當成例句研讀，以熟悉這些字彙的用法。

在這個部分我們一開始要來學與財務關鍵字彙搭配使用的同義字，包括：budget、return、investment 與 growth。

Task 20 請從下列表格選一個正確的同義字重寫下列句子，使二個句子意思相同。請看範例。

achieve	earn	manage	quick
attract	experience	need	reduce
better	have	substantial	shoestring
exceed	higher	promote	sustained

例：Due to financial difficulties, we have had to cut your spending budget.
→ Due to financial difficulties, we have had to reduce your spending budget.

1. I control a large budget.

_____

2. We are on a very tight budget for this project.

_____

3. I have strict instructions not to allow anyone to go over their budget.

_____

4. This investment should yield a better return.

_____

5. I want to produce a better return on investment this time.

_____

6. We need to encourage some more investment in the company.

_____

7. This new project will require a massive investment.

_____

8. Last year the company saw a steady growth of 3%.

_____

9. We need to stimulate rapid growth in this market if we can.

_____

請核對答案。如果你覺得這個練習很困難，多花點時間比較每組句子，直到了解透徹為止。

學會了使用同義字可以提升英文表達的豐富性。現在我們來練習把同義字配對。

Task 21 請將左欄動詞與最常搭配的名詞配對。有些動詞與 profit 和 loss 皆可搭配。請看範例。

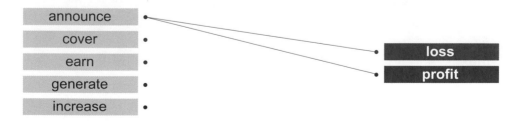

announce •
cover •
earn •
generate •
increase •

loss
profit

Task 22 請將意思最相近的同義動詞兩兩一組配對。

例：**announce - report**。

 參看「解答」核對你的答案。

接下來我們用形容詞來做相同的練習。

Task 23 請將左欄形容詞與最常搭配的名詞配對。有些形容詞與 **profit** 和 **loss** 皆可搭配。請看範例。

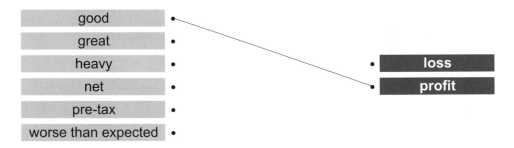

Task 24 請將意思最相近的形容詞兩兩一組配對。例：**good - great**。

 參看「解答」核對你的答案。

知道哪些字詞可以替換使用後，接著就來示範如何把它們運用在句子中。

Task 25 請使用先前 task 裡的同義動詞與形容詞重寫下列句子，使兩個句子意思相同。請看範例。

例：Last year we made a good profit on this product.
→ Last year we earned a great profit on this product.

1. We need to increase profits.

---

2. The whole group suffered heavy losses.

---

3. The fund announced half-yearly net profits of NT$30 million.

---

4. I hope we can make up the loss next year.

---

5. We invest the profits we make in overseas funds.

請核對答案。如果你覺得這個練習很困難，多花點時間比較每組句子，直到了解徹底為止。

接著我們來練習從文段中聽出關鍵字彙。能夠聽出使用中的關鍵字彙，熟悉它們的發音和語調，自然能更有信心地使用這些字彙。

🎧 20

Task 26 潔妮斯與保羅正在談論一場她與一家投資銀行開的會議。請聽聽他們之間的談話，然後回答以下的問題。

▷ 這家公司過去 5 年來的表現如何？
▷ 他們需要這筆資金做什麼？
▷ 你相信他們嗎？

聽的時候試著不要對照錄音稿。如果你覺得這個 task 很困難，再多聽幾次直到你能聽出答案為止。

Task 27 請再仔細地聽一次這場會議。聽的時候，在下列的表格中將你聽到的字彙 打 ✓ 。

bank　　　　　　（　　　）

capital　　　　　（　　　）

loss　　　　　　（　　　）

profits　　　　　（　　　）

prospects　　　　（　　　）

growth　　　　　（　　　）

figures　　　　　（　　　）

risk　　　　　　（　　　）

return　　　　　（　　　）

capital　　　　　（　　　）

investments　　　（　　　）

Task 28 請再聽一次，並完成表格中的搭配詞組，如範例所示。

	private investment	bank	
		capital	
		loss	
		profits	
		profits	
		prospects	
		growth	
		figures	
		risk	
		return	
		capital	
		investments	

 請參看「解答」，也可以閱讀對話的錄音稿。閱讀時，可將搭配詞組畫底線，幫助自己更注意它們的用法。

➔ 強化練習

Task 29 請利用 task 28 的搭配詞組，練習描述潔妮斯與保羅的談話內容。

 幫自己錄音。然後聽錄音，檢視你是否能流利地說出這些搭配詞組。

Task 30 請利用本單元學過的詞彙填入這篇文章裡的空格。

What is Finance?

It's well known that a corporation exists to make money. There are three main ways a corporation can make money. The first way, of course, is by selling its products. In order to make a (1)_____ by doing this, companies have to minimize (2)_____ by setting tight (3)_____ and exercising (4)_____ on spending. They have to be very strict about collecting (5)_____ for goods or services, and must not extend (6)_____ to customers, because that is expensive for the company. Sales people have to be very careful about checking (7)_____, and keeping careful financial records for the tax office. Usually, in the first few years of a company's life, the company incurs (8)_____.

The second way of making money is to manage the profits generated by sales. The CFO (Chief Financial Officer) does this by carrying out (9)_____ into the domestic and international financial (10)_____, and then investing in funds which have good (11)_____.

In order to help the CFO plan financial (12)_____, he or she has to be very good at conducting (13)_____ of financial (14)_____, at assessing the economic (15)_____. Some CFO's of very large

---

multinational corporations also make short-term investments in different currency markets.

The third way of making money is by raising (16)_____. There are a number of ways to do this. If a company needs to raise a small amount of (17)_____ quickly, they can borrow money from a (18)_____. If they need larger amounts, they can attract (19)_____ from private or corporate investors, or they can sell shares and obtain (20)_____ that way. However, because most investors are looking for low (21)_____ and high (22)_____, the company has to be in good financial shape before selling shares, and should be able to sustain continued (23)_____. The (24)_____ also has to be stable. The CFO has to release his company's financial (25)_____ on a regular basis to help investors make an accurate (26)_____ of the company's performance.

有沒有覺得這篇文章似曾相識？！你可以再次閱讀 task 1 的文章來核對你的答案。

好了，本單元到此結束。希望你學會如何談論和寫作關於財務議題的用語。如果你在財務部門工作，建議你使用本單元所學到的技巧與策略，來記錄與學習工作中遇到的新字彙，並且盡量把握機會在工作中使用你學到的新字彙。在繼續進行下一個單元之前，先回到單元一開始的學習目標清單，檢視自己是否都達成目標了。

工具篇：本章重點語彙

1. cost 的搭配詞組

與動詞搭配

estimate 估計
have 有
meet 達到
reduce 減少

cost 成本

與形容詞搭配

administrative 管理的
heavy 沈重的
production 生產
running 營運的

cost 成本

2. bank 的搭配詞組

與動詞搭配

borrow sth. from 從……借某物
go to 去
instruct 指示……做
negotiate with 與……談判

bank 銀行

例 instruct a bank = 指示銀行做……

與形容詞搭配

commercial 商業的
international 國際的
investment 投資
overseas 海外的

bank 銀行

3. invoice 的搭配詞組

與動詞搭配

issue 開	
get 拿到	**invoice 發票**
process 處理	
submit 提出	

與形容詞搭配

original 正本的	
sales 銷售	**invoice 發票**
tax 稅	
VAT 增值稅	

4. payment 的搭配詞組

與動詞搭配

suspend 中止	
remit 匯（寄）	**payment 付款**
withhold 扣留	
spread 延長……的期間	

與形容詞搭配

interest 利息的	
late 延遲的	**payment 付款**
monthly 每月的	
overtime 加班的	

5. risk 的搭配詞組

與動詞搭配

avoid 避免	
involve 包含	**risk 風險**
minimize 使……減至最小	
take 承擔	

calculated 經過預測的	**risk 風險**
minimal 最小的	
serious 嚴重的	

複合名詞

risk factor 風險因素

risk rating 風險評比

risk assessment 風險評估

risk management 風險管理

6. return 的搭配詞組

與動詞搭配

earn 賺取	**return 收益**
get 得到	
maximize 最大化	
yield 帶來	

與形容詞搭配

annual 年度的	**return 收益**
guaranteed 保證的	
maximum 最大的	

7. data 的搭配詞組

與動詞搭配

examine 檢視	**data 資料**
look at 看	
process 處理	
store 儲存	

comprehensive 全面的	
detailed 詳細的	**data 資料**
financial 財務的	
raw 原始的	

8. figures 的搭配詞組

與動詞搭配

adjust 調整	
arrive at 達到	**figures 數據**
compare 比較	
see 看	

與形容詞搭配

key 主要的	
official 正式的、官方的	**figures 數據**
sales 業績	
trading 貿易	

9. prospects 的搭配詞組

與動詞搭配

assess 評估	
damage 損害	**prospects 前景**
enhance 改善	
improve 改善	

與形容詞搭配

economic 經濟的	
exciting 讓人興奮的	**prospects 前景**
gloomy 黯淡的	
growth 成長	

10. growth 的搭配詞組

與動詞搭配

achieve 達到	
experience 經歷	growth 成長
see 看到	
stimulate 刺激	

與形容詞搭配

continued 持續的	
sustainable 持續的	growth 成長
quick 快速的	
steady 穩定的	

複合名詞

growth rate 成長率

growth forecast 成長預測

growth target 成長目標

11. financing 的搭配詞組

與動詞搭配

arrange 安排	
obtain 獲得	financing 融資
provide 提供	

12. finance 的搭配詞組

與形容詞搭配

corporate 公司的	finance 財務
personal 個人的	

13. capital 的搭配詞組

與動詞搭配

borrow 借
invest 投資
raise 籌措
repay 償還

capital 資本

與形容詞搭配

share 股份
venture 創業的
working 營運的

capital 資本

複合名詞

capital appreciation 資本增值

capital expenditure 資本費用

capital gains 資本收益

capital investment 資本投資

capital market 資本市場

capital outflow 資本流出

capital inflow 資本流入

14. investment 的搭配詞組

與動詞搭配

increase 增加
protect 保護
recoup 回收……的錢

investment 投資

與形容詞搭配

foreign 外國的
initial 最初的
sound 安全的

investment 投資

investment opportunity 投資機會

investment strategy 投資策略

investment fund 投資基金

15. profit 的搭配詞組

announce 宣告	
report 報告	
make 創造	
earn 賺取	profit 獲利
generate 產生	
increase 增加	
maximize 最大化	

net 淨	
pre-tax 稅前	
great 大的	profit 獲利
good 好的	

profit margin 邊際獲利

profit forecast 獲利預測

profit growth 獲利成長

profit share（分得的）一份利潤

16. loss 的搭配詞組

與動詞搭配

suffer 遭受	
incur 蒙受	
make up 補足	
cover 足敷（損失等）	loss 損失
announce 宣布	
report 報告	
make 產生	

與形容詞搭配

heavy 重大的	
worse than expected 比預期還嚴重的	
net 淨	loss 損失
pre-tax 稅前的	

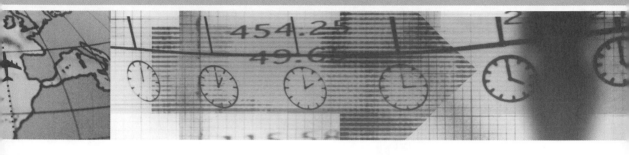

Part 4 | 支援性商務活動
Talking about Supporting Business Activities

在本書最後兩個單元裡，我們要來學一些你可以用在談論資訊工程與人力資源這兩個商務支援活動的用語。這兩個部門對大型企業而言非常重要，他們被稱為商務支援中心，由於不同於行銷、銷售、生產與財務這些部門，資訊工程與人力資源並非是公司生財的來源，而是作為支援公司生財來源的中心。這兩單元中有些字彙可能在前面學過，但是在這裡我們要看這些字如何運用在談論、寫作資訊工程與人力資源的議題上。

Unit 9

資訊工程 IT

Information technology and business are becoming inextricably interwoven. I don't think anybody can talk meaningfully about one without talking about the other.

Bill Gates

data 資料、情報

function 功能

information 資訊

network 網路

problem 問題

program 程式

project 專案

solution 解決方法

suggestion 建議

system 系統

這些是本單元要學的關鍵名詞。你將學習如何使用這些字彙來說、寫關於資訊工程的議題。看完本單元，你將達到以下的學習目標：

☐ 瞭解與關鍵字彙一起使用的主要搭配詞
☐ 瞭解一些關鍵字彙組成的複合名詞
☐ 能夠運用同義字彙提升英文表達的豐富性
☐ 運用關鍵字彙與它們的搭配詞，做一些聽力與口說的練習
☐ 能夠有信心地使用關鍵名詞來談論與寫作資訊工程的議題

上手篇

一開始我們先來練習閱讀文段中的關鍵字彙。

Task 1　請閱讀以下這篇短文討論關於資訊工程與商務之間的關係。找出當中的關鍵字彙，並注意這些字彙在文中如何被使用。

Two or three generations ago, the words "Information technology" were new. Business was conducted by paper and pen, and all financial and transaction records were made by hand and stored in paper files; calculations were done by simple pocket calculators; strategic decisions were often made on a hunch; and communications took time as documents were sent by air around the globe. Now, of course, the IT department is an indispensable part of every large company and receives a huge chunk of the company's budget.

Business people know that analyzing data on sales, customers, and markets can lead to more effective strategic decisions. A lot of emphasis is placed on gathering and storing information about sales, customers, and markets, and such information can often be bought and sold for millions of dollars. Software engineers, either hired as freelancers or employed full time, can design programs that can process data at incredible speeds and that can perform all kinds of functions to enable decisions to be made quickly and accurately.

As a result of the growth of IT, many business departments are more integrated than ever before. For example, the creation of new delivery, inventory control, and billing systems means that the sales, logistics, and accounting departments can be more integrated. This makes business more efficient and results in bigger margins and more revenue. There are programs which can help managers to plan and implement projects, and also to predict what kind of returns projects will generate. Another area which has been completely revolutionized by IT is communications. Now information can be sent all over the world at the touch of a button. Branches of a multinational company which might be located in different countries can now be connected to each other by means of a wide area network, creating an enormous virtual office which covers the globe.

Of course, this dependence on IT also has some disadvantages. Most business people do not have the very specialized skills to detect and solve the problems which a completely integrated IT system can pose. For this reason, IT departments often have to spend large portions of their budgets hiring specialists who can look for and put forward solutions to these problems, and make suggestions to increase the security and stability of a company's computers, networks, and systems.

中譯

兩三個世代之前，「資訊工程」還是個新字。生意都是由紙筆完成，所有的財務與交易記錄是手動完成，然後以紙張檔案儲存。計算是由簡單的口袋計算機完成，而策略性決定則通常是靠直覺判斷。溝通相當耗時，因為文件得靠空運送達全球。現今，資訊工程是每個大公司不可或缺的部門，並且佔有公司預算很大的一部分。

商務人士認為分析銷售、顧客與市場的資料可以促成更有效的策略性決定。蒐集與儲存關於銷售、顧客與市場的資訊受到很大的重視，而且這種資訊通常可以數百萬元來買賣。不論是以自由工作者被雇用或是全職，軟體工程師能夠設計程式來十分迅速地處理資訊，並且執行各種功能，以協助做出快速且正確的決定。

由於資訊工程的成長，許多商務部門比以往更密切地整合。舉例來說，新運送方

式、庫存控制和記帳系統的發明，代表銷售、後勤與會計部門可以更密切地整合。這使得商務更有效率，造成更大的盈餘與收益。有的程式可以幫助經理們計畫與執行專案，以及預測專案會產出哪一種報酬。另一個經由資訊工程而完全革新的領域是通訊。現在只要按下一個按鍵，就可以將訊息傳到全世界。跨國公司的分部或許位在不同的國家，現在則可以藉由寬域網路相互連結在一起，創造出一個遍布全球的巨大虛擬辦公室。

當然，仰賴資訊工程也有一些缺點。大部分商務人士沒有非常專業的技能來偵測與解決完全整合的資訊工程系統會造成的問題。為了這個原因，資訊工程部門通常必須花費他們很大一部分的預算來聘請專業人士，找到與提出這些問題的解決方案，作出建議來提高一家公司的電腦、網路與系統的安全與穩定。

⊙ 配對練習

在這個部分我們要先來學習 6 個關鍵名詞。把焦點放在與這些關鍵名詞搭配使用的動詞上。

Task 2 請將左欄動詞與最常搭配的名詞配對。請看範例。

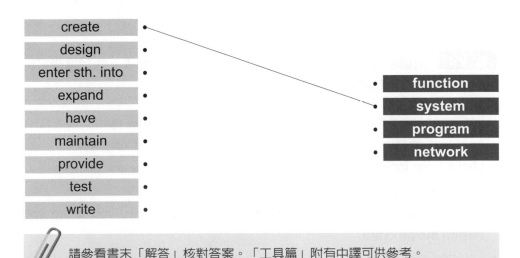

請參看書末「解答」核對答案。「工具篇」附有中譯可供參考。

Task 3 請將左欄動詞與最常搭配的名詞配對。

divulge •

examine •

have •

look at •   • **data**

process •   • **information**

provide •

record •

withhold •

 請核對答案。記住，搭配詞組並沒有一定的法則說明某些字可以搭配使用，某些字不行。重要的是，把那些搭配在一起的詞組學起來，當成固定用語來使用。把你在前面 task 裡配錯的組合記錄下來，然後加強研讀它們的正確型式。

有些字彙在前幾個單元已經學過，不過在本單元可以學到更多由這些字彙衍生出的搭配詞組，適用在商務活動的不同任務中。下一個 task 會幫助你練習在文段中使用與關鍵名詞搭配的動詞。

Task 4 請以前面那些 task 當中的關鍵名詞完成這些句子。想想這些名詞應該使用單數還是複數。

- I am creating a new (1)_____ for storing customer data.
- I am testing the (2)_____ now. So far it's working very well.
- I have been looking at the (3)_____, but I can't see any patterns in it.
- I have been up all night writing a new (4)_____.
- I have some (5)_____ which might be useful to you when you design the program.
- I started designing (6)_____ in college as a hobby. Now I get paid for it!
- If we examine the (7)_____ carefully, we will be able to see some patterns.

- It's a criminal offence to divulge personal (8)_____ without the customer's permission.
- Someone forgot to record the (9)_____, so it's full of gaps.
- The company doesn't provide very good (10)_____ about its products.
- The main part of my job is to maintain the (11)_____. You know, I make sure there are no problems with it.
- The program is processing the (12)_____ now. We need to wait a few minutes.
- This program has many different (13)_____. It's very useful.
- When we get a new customer, you must enter the customer data into the (14)_____.
- In the next version of the program, can you provide more (15)_____? It would be great if it could do more.
- You must not withhold (16)_____ that could help us to solve the problem.
- Your job over the next few weeks is to expand the (17)_____ to include 20 new computers.

請核對答案。你可以把句子裡的動詞畫底線，幫助自己記憶 verb-noun 詞組的用法。

學完動詞，現在我們要把焦點轉到與關鍵字彙搭配使用的形容詞。

Task 5 請將左欄形容詞與最常搭配的名詞配對。請看範例。

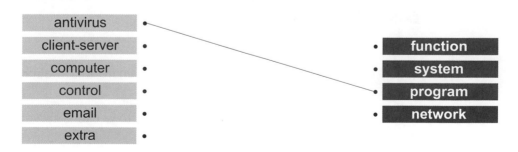

information	•
local area	•
operating	•
peer-to-peer	•
search	•
shareware	•
spreadsheet	•
wireless local area	•
word processing	•

•	function
•	system
•	program
•	network

 請參看書末「解答」核對答案。「工具篇」附有中譯可供參考。

Task 6 請將左欄形容詞與最常搭配的名詞配對。

additional	•
background	•
inside	•
personal	•
raw	•
supporting	•

•	data
•	information

 請核對答案。將前面 task 裡答錯的組合記錄下來，確實地改正並研讀正確詞組。你可以過幾天後重新複習「配對練習」單元，看看自己還記得多少。

Task 7 請以前面那些 task 當中的關鍵名詞完成這些句子。想想這些名詞應該使用單數還是複數。

- Additional (1)_____ goes in this field here.
- As IT manager, I am responsible for the company's entire information (2)_____.
- As the company expands, we might need to change to a client-server (3)_____.

- Can you give me some background (4)_____ on this? I want to understand it more fully.
- I think there might be something wrong with the operating (5)_____.
- I write computer (6)_____ for a living. It's not a very social job.
- In this department we analyze raw (7)_____ for the other departments.
- It's good talking to him. He always knows a lot of inside (8)_____.
- The accident happened because there are no control (9)_____ built into the computer.
- The email (10)_____ is malfunctioning. I can't access my inbox.
- The network topology used in this company is a peer-to-peer (11)_____.
- The new program has lots of extra (12)_____.
- The search (13)_____ doesn't work very well. Can we improve it?
- The supporting (14)_____ shows that not many people buy this product.
- The whole local area (15)_____ is down. There must be a problem with a cable somewhere.
- This new word processing (16)_____ is amazing. Do you want to try it?
- We forgot to update our antivirus (17)_____ so now we are infected with many different viruses.
- We use a wireless local area (18)_____. This makes it easier for visitors to access the Internet.
- Why don't we design the new product as a shareware (19)_____? We might generate more income that way.
- Excel is by far the most common spreadsheet (20)_____.
- You enter the user's personal (21)_____ into this field here.

請核對答案。你可以把句子裡的形容詞畫底線,幫助自己記憶這些詞組的用法。

學完與關鍵字彙搭配的動詞、形容詞，接下來我們要學習的是從關鍵字彙擴展出的複合名詞。熟悉這些複合名詞，活用關鍵字彙的能力也會倍增。

Task 8 請將左欄字彙與最常搭配的字彙配對。請看範例。

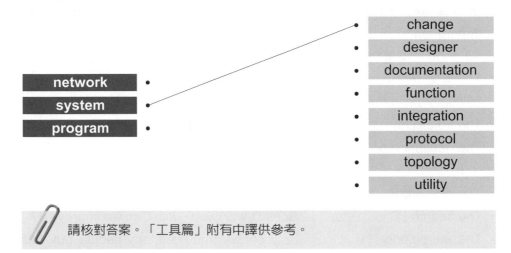

請核對答案。「工具篇」附有中譯供參考。

Task 9 請將左欄名詞與最常搭配的字彙配對。兩個名詞皆可搭配的字彙至少有一個，請找出是哪一個。

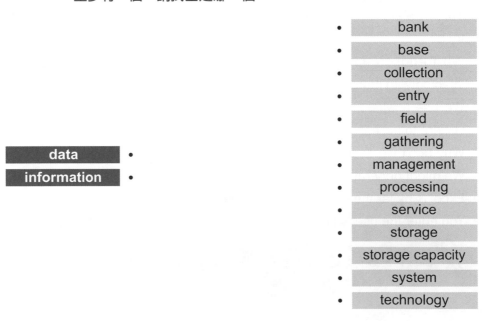

請核對答案。同樣地，請針對你答錯的組合，專心地研讀改正。

Task 10 請將複合名詞與下列句意相同的句子配合在一起。

data entry	information system	program designer
data field	network protocol	program documentation
data storage capacity	network topology	system integration
information service		system utility

1. A communication standard for computers in a network. _____
2. A detailed description of how a program works. _____
3. A person who uses computer code to write programs. _____
4. A service that you can contact to ask for information. _____
5. A small program included with an operating system, for example, a device driver. _____
6. The amount of space available for storing data in a database. _____
7. The process of linking together different parts of a system, or different systems. _____
8. The process of putting data into a data base. _____
9. The shape of a network: for example, computers connected like a star, or a ring. _____
10. The smallest subdivision of stored data that can be accessed, for example, the date or the time. _____
11. The system of people, data, records, and activities that process information in an organization. _____

請參看「解答」核對答案。

Task 11 請研讀這兩個句子。然後使用先前 **task** 裡的複合名詞，按照相同的方式重寫下列句子。

例：None of my utilities in the system are working.
→ None of my system utilities are working.

1. Entering data is probably the most boring job in IT.

_____

2. You must make sure you enter the information into the correct field for that data.

_____

3. Our capacity for storing data is too low.

_____

4. We offer a service that provides information for new users.

_____

5. The system of information here is very complex.

_____

6. The protocol for the network we use in this company is Ethernet.

_____

7. The topology for the network cannot really deal with the number of computers we have. We probably need to change it.

_____

8. Let's ask the designer of the program. Maybe he can help us.

_____

9. If we had the documentation for the program, we would be able to understand how it works.

_____

10. The integration of the system is almost complete.

_____

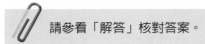 請參看「解答」核對答案。

⊙ 語言的提升

在接下來的部分，我們要做一些練習以進一步提升語言表達的能力，包括運用同義字與增進聽力技巧。

Task 12 左欄動詞可與 **network** 與 **system** 搭配使用。請將意思最相近的同義字兩兩一組配對。例：**upgrade - improve**。

build develop improve maintain manage upgrade	**network** **system**

1. _____

2. _____

參看「解答」核對你的答案。

Task 13 右欄動詞可與 **system** 與 **program** 搭配使用。請將意思最相近的動詞兩兩一組配對。

program **system**	work offer allow run enable provide

1. _____

2. _____

3. _____

參看「解答」核對答案。

接下來我們用同義字來做練習。

Task 14 請比較這兩個句子，然後使用前面兩個 task 裡的同義字重寫下列句子，使句意相同。

例：I am currently building a bigger network for the company.
→ I am currently developing a bigger network for the company.

1. How long will it take to upgrade the network?

_____

2. It's a difficult system to manage.

_____

3. My job is to maintain the network. It's a big network, so it takes up all my time.

_____

4. Over the years we have developed an excellent system for the company.

_____

5. The program enables you to save your work in different formats.

_____

6. The program works really well now.

_____

7. The system allows anyone to access it from anywhere in the building.

_____

8. The system is not working very smoothly.

_____

9. The system provides a platform for further growth.

_____

10. We need to spend some money on improving the system.

_____

11. What other functions does the program offer?

_____

 請核對答案。如果你覺得這個練習很困難，多花點時間比較每組句子，直到了解透徹為止。

接著我們來練習從文段中聽出關鍵字彙。能夠聽出使用中的關鍵字彙，熟悉它們的發音和語調，自然能更有信心地使用這些字彙。

🎧 21、22

Task 15 林傑克是一家台灣製造公司的資訊工程經理。他接受訪問談到他的工作。請聽這兩部分的訪談，在聽的過程中，將你聽到在本單元學過的關鍵字彙打 ✓ ，然後回答下列問題：

⊙ 傑克在這個工作中的主要任務是什麼？
⊙ 他目前正在進行什麼專案？
⊙ 他的工作中還要負責什麼其他的任務？

data	( )	program	( )
function	( )	project	( )
information	( )	solution	( )
network	( )	suggestion	( )
problem	( )	system	( )

 建議你聽的時候先不要對照錄音稿喔。如果無法一次就聽懂，可以多聽幾次直到更能掌握訪談內容。在做接下來的 task 時你會覺得容易一些。

Task 16 請再聽一次第一部分的訪談，這一次請找出傑克用了哪些與關鍵名詞搭配的動詞與形容詞，把你聽到的填入下面表格。如範例。

manage		system
	detailed	information
	-	system
		data
		information
		program
		program
		functions
		functions

請參看「解答」，也可以閱讀對話的錄音稿。閱讀時，可將搭配詞組畫底線，幫助自己更注意它們的用法。

Task 17 請再聽一次第二部分的訪談，這一次請找出傑克用了哪些與關鍵名詞搭配的動詞與形容詞，把你聽到的填入下面的表格。如範例。

running a		project
	easy	solution
		network
		project
	-	networks
	-	suggestions
		problems
		problems
		solution
		suggestions

請參看「解答」，也可以閱讀對話的錄音稿。閱讀時，可將搭配詞組畫底線，幫助自己更注意它們的用法。

➔ 強化練習

Task 18 下列有一些關於訪談的問題。想像你是林傑克，使用 task 16 與 task 17 中的搭配詞組來回答問題。記得替自己錄音。

Part 1

1. So Jack, why don't you tell us about the kinds of things you do everyday?
2. What's an information system?
3. Why is all this information necessary?
4. So how do you analyze all this data?
5. How long did it take you to write the program?

Part 2

1. So what are you working on at the moment?
2. Tell us more about this big project.
3. And what's your role in this project?
4. Anything else you have to do in your job?
5. Do you have to help other staff members with their IT problems often?

 聽取你替自己錄音的內容。聽聽你是否把搭配詞組說對了。如果你覺得說得不夠正確，試著再練習一次。然後比較兩次的錄音看看自己是否進步了。

Task 19 請利用本單元學過的詞彙填入這篇文章的空格。有些字可以重複使用。

Two or three generations ago, the words "(1)＿＿＿＿＿ technology" were new. Business was conducted by paper and pen, and all financial and transaction records were made by hand and stored in paper files; calculations were done by simple pocket calculators; strategic decisions were often made on a hunch; and communications took time as documents were sent by air around the globe. Now, of course, the

IT department is an indispensable part of every large company and receives a huge chunk of the company's budget.

Business people know that analyzing (2)_____ on sales, customers, and markets can lead to more effective strategic decisions. A lot of emphasis is placed on gathering and storing (3)_____ about sales, customers, and markets, and such information can often be bought and sold for millions of dollars. Software engineers, either hired as freelancers or employed full time, can design (4)_____ that can process data at incredible speeds and that can perform all kinds of (5)_____ to enable decisions to be made quickly and accurately.

As a result of the growth of IT, many business departments are more integrated than ever before. For example, the creation of new delivery, inventory control, and billing (6)_____ means that the sales, logistics, and accounting departments can be more integrated. This makes business more efficient and results in bigger margins and more revenue. There are (7)_____ which can help managers to plan and implement (8)_____, and also to predict what kind of returns projects will generate. Another area which has been completely revolutionized by IT is communications. Now information can be sent all over the world at the touch of a button. Branches of a multinational company which might be located in different countries can now be connected to each other by means of a wide area (9)_____, creating an enormous virtual office which covers the globe.

Of course, this dependence on IT also has some disadvantages. Most business people do not have the very specialized skills to detect and solve the (10)_____ which a completely integrated IT system can pose. For this reason, IT departments often have to spend large portions of their budgets hiring specialists who can look for and put forward (11)_____ to these problems, and make (12)_____ to increase the security and stability of a company's computers, (13)_____ , and (14)_____ .

 有沒有覺得這篇文章似曾相識？！你可以再次閱讀 task 1 的文章來核對你的答案。

好了，本單元到此結束。希望你學會了如何談論、寫作關於資訊工程的用語。在繼續進行下一個單元之前，回到單元一開始的學習目標清單，檢視自己是否都已達成目標。

工具篇：本章重點語彙

1. function 的搭配詞組

與動詞搭配

have 有	**function** 功能
provide 提供	

與形容詞搭配

search 搜尋的	**function** 功能
extra 額外的	

2. system 的搭配詞組

與動詞搭配

create 創造	**system** 系統
enter sth. into 輸入……到	

與形容詞搭配

operating 操作的	**system** 系統
information 資訊的	
control 控制的	

複合名詞

system utility 系統效能

system function 系統功能

system change 系統改變

system integration 系統整合

3. program 的搭配詞組

與動詞搭配

write 寫	
design 設計	**program 程式**
test 測試	

與形容詞搭配

word processing 文字處理	
spreadsheet 試算表	
computer 電腦	
antivirus 防毒	**program 程式**
email 電子郵件	
shareware 分享軟體	

複合名詞

program designer 設式設計師

program documentation 程式說明文件

4. network 的搭配詞組

與動詞搭配

expand 擴張	**network 網路**
maintain 維護	

與形容詞搭配

peer-to-peer 對等型	
client-server 主從型	**network 網路**
local area 區域	
wireless local area 區域無線	

複合名詞

network protocol 網路協議

network topology 網路形態

5. data 的搭配詞組

與動詞搭配

look at 看	
record 記錄	**data 資料**
process 處理	
examine 檢視	

與形容詞搭配

supporting 輔助的	
additional 額外的	**data 資料**
raw 原始的	

複合名詞

data base 資料庫

data bank 資料庫

data entry 資料輸入

data field 資料欄位

data gathering 資料蒐集

data collection 資料蒐集

data processing 資料處理

data storage 資料儲存

data storage capacity 資料儲存空間

6. information 的搭配詞組

與動詞搭配

provide 提供	
divulge 揭發、洩漏	**information 資訊**
withhold 保留、扣住	
have 有	

	information 資訊
inside 內部的	
background 背景的	
personal 個人的	

複合名詞

information management 資訊管理

information processing 資訊處理

information service 資訊服務

information system 資訊系統

information technology 資訊科技

人力資源 HR

Hiring people is an art, not a science, and resumes can't tell you whether someone will fit into a company's culture.

Howard Schultz

assessment 評估	department 部門	development 發展
director 董事	employee 員工	experience 經驗
issue 議題	job 工作	level 程度
manager 經理	personnel 人事	salary 薪資
skill 技能	staff 職員	

這些是本單元我們要學的關鍵名詞。你將學習如何使用這些關鍵名詞來說、寫關於人力資源的議題。看完本單元，你將達到以下的學習目標：

☐ 瞭解與關鍵字彙一起使用的主要搭配詞
☐ 瞭解一些關鍵字彙組成的複合名詞
☐ 能夠運用同義字提升英文表達的豐富性
☐ 運用關鍵字彙與它們的搭配詞，做一些聽力與口說的練習
☐ 能夠有信心地使用關鍵名詞來談論與寫作人力資源的議題

上手篇

一開始我們先來練習閱讀文段中的關鍵字彙。

Task 1 請閱讀這篇關於人力資源管理重要議題的短文。找出當中的關鍵字彙，並注意這些字彙在文中如何被使用。

Human resources is a relatively new field in business. It refers to more than just hiring and firing. It is the active management of the company's main and most important resource: its people.

HR managers know that when key employees leave a company, they take with them valuable experience and advanced skills. This is a loss for the company in many ways. First, apart from the loss of experience and skills, which cannot really be measured in financial terms, there is a financial cost incurred in recruiting and training new personnel. Secondly, if the former employee takes a job with a new company, those same skills and that same experience may benefit a competitor. It is in the company's best interests, therefore, to try to reduce staff turnover and to retain their experienced staff. This is known as "staff retention," and it is one of the key issues in modern HR management.

HR people try to increase staff retention by a number of different methods. First, and most importantly, they try to offer good salaries, salaries which are commensurate with the industry standard, and also with the employee's age and skills. However, companies often find it difficult to meet these salary costs.

Secondly, they try to ensure good staff morale by promoting employee development through training, job swap schemes (where employees can move to another department for a while), social events and other benefits. However, there are also costs associated with this as well. Training an employee represents a financial investment in that employee, and if the employee leaves, the company looses its investment.

A third method of ensuring staff retention is promotion. Most modern companies now have very strict performance measurement procedures and standards. In these procedures, HR managers undertake comprehensive annual assessments of employees' performance. They work with department managers to determine the level of performance reached in key areas. Those employees who perform well, can often get promoted after a few years. These senior staff members tend to have much greater loyalty to the company and are usually less likely to leave.

中譯

人力資源是商務中相當新的一個領域。它代表的不只是雇用與解聘，而是積極主動管理公司主要且最重要的資源：人力。

人資經理認為當重要員工離開公司，他們隨之帶走的是寶貴的經驗與先進的技能。從許多方面看來，這是公司的一大損失。第一，除了無法以金錢衡量的經驗與技能上的損失，在招聘與訓練新人事上會產生財務成本。第二，如果前任員工在新公司找到工作，這些相同的技能與經驗可能嘉惠公司的競爭者。因此，為了公司的最大利益應該要試著降低職員的轉職率，留住經驗豐富的職員。這就是大家所知的「職員慰留」，而且這是現代人資管理的重要議題之一。

人資部門人員以許多不同的方法來提高職員的留任。首先，也是最重要的，他們試著提供高薪，薪資比照工業標準，且隨著職員年紀與技能調整。然而，公司通常都覺得這些薪資成本難以達成。

第二，他們試著以訓練、工作交換方案（即員工可以轉調至另一個部門一段時

日）、社交活動與其他福利來增進職員發展，確保員工有好的工作士氣。然而，這也會有相關的成本產生。訓練一名員工代表投資金錢在該名員工身上，因此如果員工離職，公司就失去它的投資。

第三個確保職員留任的辦法就是升遷。現在大部分現代化公司皆有很嚴格的績效衡量程序與標準。在這些程序中，人資經理對員工們的表現進行全面的年度評估。他們與部門經理合作，以決定在重要領域裡的績效達成度。表現優良的員工通常會在幾年後得到升遷。資深職員一般對於公司會有更大的忠誠度，而且通常比較不會離職。

➔ 配對練習

在這個部分我們要來學 9 個關鍵名詞。我們先把焦點放在與這些關鍵名詞搭配使用的動詞上。

Task 2 請將左欄動詞與最常搭配的名詞配對。請看範例。

have	
lay off	staff
manage	personnel
sack	employee
transfer	

請參看書末「解答」核對答案。「工具篇」附有中譯可供參考。

Task 3 請將左欄動詞與最常搭配的名詞配對。

broaden	
change	
develop	skills
do	job
exercise	experience
gain	

learn	•		
look for	•		
provide	•	•	**skills**
quit	•	•	**job**
require	•	•	**experience**
share	•		

 請參看書末「解答」核對答案。

Task 4 請將左欄動詞與最常搭配的名詞配對。

determine	•		
get	•		
maintain	•		
manage	•	•	**department**
move to	•	•	**level**
offer	•	•	**salary**
reach	•		
review	•		
work in	•		

 請核對答案。記住，搭配詞組並沒有一定的法則說明某些字可以搭配使用，某些字不行。重要的是，把那些搭配在一起的詞組學起來，當成固定用語來使用。把你在前面 task 裡配錯的組合記錄下來，然後加強研讀它們的正確型式。

有些字彙在前幾個單元裡你或許見過。在這裡提供更多與它們一起搭配使用的字彙，得以變化出不同的組合來應付商務活動中的不同任務。

下一個 task 要幫助你學會在文段中使用與這些關鍵名詞搭配的動詞。

Task 5 請以先前 task 當中的關鍵名詞完成這些句子。想想這些名詞應該使用單數還是複數。

- After one year, we will review your (1)_____ .
- As the personnel manager, your job is to manage (2)_____ .
- I gained useful (3)_____ by working on a multinational team.
- My (4)_____ now is much higher than it was at my previous job.
- I hope this job will allow me to broaden my (5)_____ .
- I manage the HR (6)_____ .
- I need a job which is going to allow me to exercise my English (7)_____ .
- I quit my (8)_____ last month.
- I recently moved to another (9)_____ , and changed my job.
- I was able to develop my communication (10)_____ in that job.
- I would like to change my (11)_____ . I am bored with this one.
- I would like to learn some new (12)_____ .
- I've been looking for a (13)_____ for 18 months now.
- If the recession continues, we will have to start laying off (14)_____ .
- Our job in this department is to support the sales (15)_____ so that they can do their job well.
- Please share your (16)_____ with us.
- We are planning to transfer some of our (17)_____ to China.
- We can provide you with the (18)_____ of working in an international company.
- We have a (19)_____ of 300 in the Taipei office alone.
- We need to try and maintain our current (20)_____ of output.
- We offer very good (21)_____ .
- We will sack any (22)_____ who steals company information.
- What (23)_____ do you work in?
- What kind of (24)_____ do you require for this job?
- You did an excellent (25)_____ on that report. Well done!
- You have reached a very high (26)_____ of expertise in this job.

- Your previous experience will determine the (27)_____ of salary you will get in this job.

請核對答案。你可以把句子裡的動詞畫底線，幫助自己記憶 verb-noun 搭配詞組的用法。

學完動詞，現在我們要把焦點轉到與關鍵字彙搭配使用的形容詞。

Task 6 請將左欄形容詞與最常搭配的名詞配對。請看範例。

company
general
line
managing
non-executive
project
senior

manager
director

請參看書末「解答」核對答案。「工具篇」附有中譯可供參考。

Task 7 請將左欄形容詞與最常搭配的名詞配對。

considerable
full-time
good
necessary
practical
relevant
a set of
temporary
valuable

skills
job
experience

請參看「解答」核對答案。

Task 8　請將左欄形容詞與最常搭配的名詞配對。

acceptable •
advertising •
annual •
average •
certain •
entry •
finance •
marketing •
starting •

• department
• level
• salary

 請核對答案。將前面 task 裡答錯的組合記錄下來，確實地改正並研讀正確詞組。你可以過幾天後重新複習「配對練習」單元，看看自己還記得多少。

Task 9　請以先前 task 當中的關鍵名詞完成這些句子。想想這些名詞應該使用單數還是複數。

- At the moment it's only part time, but I hope it will turn into a full time (1)＿＿＿＿＿ .
- Have we reached an acceptable (2)＿＿＿＿＿ of revenue yet?
- He doesn't have any decision making power. He's just a non-executive (3)＿＿＿＿＿ .
- He has considerable communication (4)＿＿＿＿＿ . He can persuade anybody to do anything.
- I am the project (5)＿＿＿＿＿ on this project.
- I can't apply for this job as I don't have any relevant (6)＿＿＿＿＿ .
- I gained valuable (7)＿＿＿＿＿ in that job.
- I love the advertising (8)＿＿＿＿＿ because the people there are so creative.
- I'm sorry, but I don't think you have the necessary (9)＿＿＿＿＿ for this job.

- If you have any problems, you should first talk to your line (10)_____.
- It's a really good (11)_____. I love working there.
- It's an entry-(12)_____ job, so the salary will not be that great.
- The accounting (13)_____ is short one staff member. Do you want to talk to them?
- The annual (14)_____ is pretty high.
- The average (15)_____ in this industry is high.
- The general (16)_____ is very ill.
- The managing (17)_____ is a woman.
- The marketing (18)_____ is in another building.
- This is a VIP club, for company (19)_____ only.
- We are having a meeting for senior (20)_____ to talk about strategy.
- We are looking for someone with a particular set of (21)_____.
- We need a certain (22)_____ of expertise in this position.
- You have a great academic resume, but do you have any practical (23)_____?
- You will get a starting (24)_____ of NT$1.5 million.

請核對答案。你可以把句子裡的動詞、形容詞畫底線，幫助自己記憶這些詞組的用法。

現在我們來學一些用在不同商業任務中的形容詞，它們可與 department、director 和 manager 搭配使用。

Task 10 請將表格中的形容詞與 department、director 和 manager 結合，並從下列句子挑選合適句意者做配對。請看範例。

accounts	finance	legal	R&D
advertising	HR	marketing	sales
	IT	personnel	service

例：This person is in charge of the finances, including taxes and billing.
   finance director/finance manager

1. This department deals with the customers and their orders. _____

2. This person manages a team which creates advertising posters and TV commercials. _____

3. This department is responsible for making sure there are enough people to do the work the company needs to do, and for keeping staff costs down. _____

4. This person is in charge of finding new employees, staff training, and staff development. _____

5. This person manages all the computers in the company, as well as all the systems and networks, and also the IT staff. _____

6. This department deals with all the company's contracts and other legal issues. _____

7. This department deals with creating demand for the company's products. It plans strategy and creates campaigns. _____

8. This person is in charge of a team of people that sells goods or services to customers. _____

9. This department creates new products for the company. _____

請核對答案。

Task 11 請將每個搭配詞組與最恰當的描述配對，有些詞組可以重複使用。請看範例。

administrative skills	management skills	presentation skills
communication skills	negotiating skills	technical skills
interpersonal skills	organizational skills	time-management skills
leadership skills	people skills	

1. You are an excellent organizer. *organizational skills*
2. You are never late and you are very good at planning ahead.
_____

3. You are really good at creating relationships. _____

4. You are really good at motivating people and helping them to work together. _____

5. You are very good at getting what you want. _____

6. You are very good at organizing processes and systems and keeping records. _____

7. You are very good at talking with other people and getting your message across. _____

8. You can work any kind of machine or equipment. _____

9. You deliver excellent presentations. _____

請參照「解答」。

學完與關鍵字彙搭配的動詞、形容詞，接下來我們要學習的是從關鍵字彙擴展出的複合名詞。熟悉這些複合名詞，活用關鍵字彙的能力也會倍增。

Task 12　請將左欄字彙與最常搭配的名詞配對。請看範例。右欄中有些名詞可以重複使用。

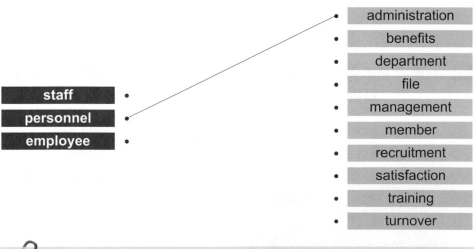

請核對答案。「工具篇」附有中譯供參考。

Task 13 請將左欄字彙與最常搭配的名詞配對。

- cut
- description
- head
- interview
- manager
- meeting
- opportunity
- prospects
- raise
- review
- satisfaction
- scale
- security
- vacancy

- salary •
- job •
- department •

 請參照「解答」核對答案。

Task 14 請研讀這兩個句子。然後使用先前 task 裡的複合名詞，按照相同方式重寫下列句子，使句意不變。請看範例。

例： We have 28 members of staff in this department.
　　→ We have 28 staff members in this department.

1. Administering personnel is interesting because you're always dealing with people.

　＿＿＿＿＿＿＿＿＿＿＿＿＿＿＿＿＿＿＿＿＿＿＿＿＿＿＿＿＿＿

2. Can I please see the file that the personnel department keeps on me?

　＿＿＿＿＿＿＿＿＿＿＿＿＿＿＿＿＿＿＿＿＿＿＿＿＿＿＿＿＿＿

3. Have you read the description of the job?

　＿＿＿＿＿＿＿＿＿＿＿＿＿＿＿＿＿＿＿＿＿＿＿＿＿＿＿＿＿＿

4. I don't think the satisfaction of the employees is very high here.

_____

5. I got a raise of my salary.

_____

6. I had an interview for a job today.

_____

7. I have a lot of satisfaction from my job.

_____

8. I have good security in my job. I don't think they will fire me.

_____

9. I studied the management of personnel in college.

_____

10. I was wondering if you had any opportunities for jobs here?

_____

11. Managing the staff is the job of the HR manager, not the finance director.

_____

12. One of the biggest areas of our budget is training for the staff.

_____

13. Recruiting staff is the hardest part of my job.

_____

14. The benefits of employees are quite good, including a car and a laptop!

_____

15. The management of employees is part of every department manager's job.

_____

16. There is a lot of turnover among the employees in this company.

_____

17. This is the department of personnel. It's quite new.

_____

18. We are doing a lot of training of employees this month.

_____

19. We are going to have a review of salaries. You may get a cut in your salary.

_____

20. We have a scale for salaries here. Your bonus will follow the guidelines on that.

_____

21. When I leave college I will have very good prospects for a job.

_____

 請參看「解答」核對答案。

➔ 語言的提升

在接下來的部分，我們要來做 personnel、staff 和 employee 這三個同義字彙的練習。雖然這些字的意思很相近，但用法有些不同。

Staff 與 personnel 是複數、不可數名詞。不能在它們後面加 s，而且必須使用複數動詞。它們通常代表群組，不能用來指稱個人。雖然不可數，但可以和數字合用。

Employee 則是一個可數名詞。複數型要在後面加 s。以下有一些範例：

Task 15 請研讀這些例句，辨認哪些句子是正確的，哪些不是。

1. Our personnel are the most important part of this company.
2. Personnel is important.

3. Personnels are important.

4. What's the name of that personnel?

5. Our staff are all experts at their jobs.

6. Our staffs are all experts at their jobs.

7. Our staff is all experts at their jobs.

8. He is a senior staff.

9. Two hundred personnel are not going to be enough.

10. Three staff are missing after the typhoon.

11. We have many employees.

12. He's an excellent employee.

 請參看「解答」核對答案。

我們更仔細地來看這些同義字彙，一開始先學與它們搭配的動詞，接著再學形容詞。

Task 16 請先研讀表格學會下列搭配用法，然後從右欄挑選適當的名詞完成下列句子。注意名詞的型式正確與否。

hire employ retain	**staff** **personnel**
retain motivate encourage	**staff** **employee**
recruit train have	**staff** **employee** **personnel**

• A good manager should know how to motivate his (1)_____.

• At the moment we are recruiting (2)_____.

- It's difficult to retain (3)＿＿＿＿＿＿ when our competitors are offering higher salaries.
- Most of our HR budget goes into training new (4)＿＿＿＿＿＿.
- We employ 300 (5)＿＿＿＿＿＿ in this office.
- We have some foreign (6)＿＿＿＿＿＿.
- We need to hire extra (7)＿＿＿＿＿＿ for the busy holiday period.
- We try to encourage our (8)＿＿＿＿＿＿ to have outside interests, hobbies, and so on.

請參看「解答」核對答案。

Task 17 請先研讀表格學會下列搭配用法，然後從右欄挑選適當的名詞完成下列句子。注意名詞的型式正確與否。

senior junior administrative clerical engineering technical executive legal sales	**staff** **personnel**
full-time part-time temporary	**staff** **employee**
existing key new	**employee** **personnel**

- Most of the junior (1)＿＿＿＿＿＿ come from the same college.
- Most senior (2)＿＿＿＿＿＿ in this company have been here more than ten years.

- Salaries for new (3)_____ will go up, but salaries for existing (4)_____ will stay the same.
- We have seven administrative and clerical (5)_____, five hundred technical and engineering (6)_____, three legal and executive (7)_____, twenty sales (8)_____. That makes a total staff of 530.
- We have too many full-time (9)_____, and not enough part-time (10)_____. We might need to change that ratio.
- We lost some of our key (11)_____ last year.
- We will need to hire some temporary (12)_____ to deal with the Christmas rush.

請參看「解答」核對答案。

接著我們來練習從文段中聽出關鍵字彙。能夠聽出使用中的關鍵字彙,熟悉它們的發音和語調,自然能更有信心地使用這些字彙。

🎧 23、24

Task 18 王茱莉是一家台灣財務公司的人力資源經理。她接受訪問談論她的工作。請聽這兩部分的訪談,並將你聽到在本單元學過的關鍵字彙打 ✓,然後回答下列問題:

▶ 茱莉在這個工作中的主要任務是什麼?

▶ 關於招聘程序她怎麼說?

▶ 關於解決紛爭她怎麼說?

▶ 關於職員留職停薪她怎麼說?

assessment	(	)	job	(	)
department	(	)	level	(	)
development	(	)	manager	(	)
director	(	)	personnel	(	)
employee	(	)	salary	(	)
experience	(	)	skill	(	)
issue	(	)	staff	(	)

建議你聽的時候先不要對照錄音稿喔。如果無法一次就聽懂，可以多聽幾次直到更能掌握訪談內容。在做接下來的 task 時你會覺得容易一些。

🎧 23

Task 19 請再聽一次第一部分的訪談，聽聽茉莉用了哪些與關鍵名詞搭配使用的動詞與形容詞，請把你聽到的填入下面表格。如範例。

recruiting		personnel
	-	staff
	new	employees
	set of	skills
		salary
		experience
		director

請參看「解答」，也可以閱讀對話的錄音稿。閱讀時，可將搭配詞組畫底線，幫助自己更注意它們的用法。

🎧 24

Task 20 請再聽一次第二部分的訪談，聽聽茉莉用了哪些與關鍵名詞搭配使用的動詞與形容詞，請把你聽到的填入下面表格。如範例。

tackling		issues
	line	manager
		department
		self-assessments
		job
		development
		level

請參看「解答」，也可以閱讀對話的錄音稿。閱讀時，可將搭配詞組畫底線，幫助自己更注意它們的用法。

⊙ 強化練習

Task 21 這裡有一些關於訪談的問題。想像你是王茱莉，利用 task 19 與 task 20 的搭配詞組來回答問題。記得替自己錄音。

Part 1

1. Can you tell us a bit about your job, Julie?
2. What part of your job do you like the best?
3. Can you tell us a bit about the recruitment process?
4. What do you offer employees?
5. What do you find challenging about recruiting for high-level positions?

Part 2

1. OK, so now tell us what you don't like about your job?
2. How do you solve disputes?
3. How do you measure performance?
4. How do you deal with staff retention?

 聽取你替自己錄音的內容。聽聽你是否把搭配詞組說對了。如果你覺得說得不夠正確，試著再練習一次。然後比較這兩次的錄音看看自己是否進步了。

Task 22 請用本單元學過的詞彙填入這篇文章裡的空格。有些字可以重複使用。

Human resources is a relatively new field in business. It refers to more than just hiring and firing. It is the active management of the company's main and most important resource: its people.

HR managers know that when key (1)＿＿＿＿＿ leave a company, they take with them valuable (2)＿＿＿＿＿ and advanced (3)＿＿＿＿＿. This is a loss for the company in many ways. First, apart from the loss of experience and skills, which cannot really be measured in financial terms, there is a financial cost incurred in recruiting and training new (4)_____. Secondly, if the former employee takes a (5)_____ with a new company, those same skills and that same experience may benefit a competitor. It is in the company's best interests, therefore, to try to reduce staff turnover and to retain their experienced (6)_____. This is known as "staff retention," and it is one of the key (7)_____ in modern HR management.

HR people try to increase staff retention by a number of different methods. First, and most importantly, they try to offer good (8)_____, salaries which are commensurate with the industry standard, and also with the employee's age and skills. However, companies often find it difficult to meet these salary costs.

Secondly, they try to ensure good staff morale by promoting employee (9)_____ through training, job swap schemes (where employees can move to another (10)_____ for a while), social events and other benefits. However, there are also costs associated with this as well. Training an employee represents a financial investment in that employee, and if the employee leaves, the company looses its investment.

A third method of ensuring staff retention is promotion. Most modern companies now have very strict performance measurement procedures and standards. In these procedures, HR managers undertake comprehensive annual (11)_____ of employees' performance. They work with department (12)_____ to determine the (13)_____ of performance reached in key areas. Those employees who perform well, can often get promoted after a few years. These senior staff members tend to have much greater loyalty to the company and are usually less likely to leave.

有沒有覺得這篇文章似曾相識？！你可以再次閱讀 task 1 的文章來核對你的答案。

好了，本單元到此結束。希望你已經學會如何談論、寫作人力資源議題的用語。請回到本單元一開始的學習目標清單，檢視自己是否都達成目標了。

工具篇：本章重點語彙

1. staff 的搭配詞組

與動詞搭配

have 有 hire 雇用 employ 雇用 retain 慰留 motivate 激勵 encourage 鼓勵 train 訓練	**staff** 員工（集合稱）

與形容詞搭配

senior 資深的 junior 初階的 administrative 管理的 clerical 文書的 engineering 工程的 technical 技術的 executive 管理的 legal 法律的 sales 業務的 full-time 全職的 part-time 兼職的 temporary 暫時的	**staff** 員工（集合稱）

複合名詞

staff member 員工

staff recruitment 員工招募

staff management 員工管理

staff training 員工訓練

2. personnel 的搭配詞組

與動詞搭配

	personnel
have 有	員工（集合稱）
manage 管理	
hire 雇用	
employ 雇用	
recruit 招募	
retain 慰留	
train 訓練	

與形容詞搭配

	personnel
senior 資深的	員工（集合稱）
junior 初階的	
administrative 管理的	
clerical 文書的	
engineering 工程的	
technical 技術的	
executive 管理的	
legal 法律的	
sales 業務的	
existing 現有的	
key 主要的	
new 新的	

複合名詞

personnel department 人事部門

personnel management 人事管理

personnel administration 人事管理

personnel file 人事檔案

3. employee 的搭配詞組

與動詞搭配

recruit 招募
sack 解雇
lay off 解聘
transfer 調職
retain 慰留
motivate 激勵
encourage 鼓勵
train 訓練

employee 員工

與形容詞搭配

full-time 全職的
part-time 兼職的
tcmporary 暫時的
existing 現有的
key 主要的
new 新的

employee 員工

複合名詞

employee turnover 員工轉職率

employee satisfaction 員工滿意度

employee training 員工訓練

employee benefits 員工福利

employee management 員工管理

4. skill 的搭配詞組

與動詞搭配

develop 發展
learn 學習
exercise 運用
require 需要

skills 技能

necessary 必要的	
considerable 大量的	**skills** 技能
a set of 一整套的	

5. job 的搭配詞組

與動詞搭配

do 做	
look for 找	
quit 辭	**job** 工作
change 換	

與形容詞搭配

good 好的	
full-time 全職的	**job** 工作
temporary 暫時的	

複合名詞

job description 工作描述

job interview 工作面試

job opportunity 工作機會

job prospects 工作遠景

job satisfaction 工作滿意度

job security 工作穩定性

job vacancy 職位空缺

6. experience 的搭配詞組

與動詞搭配

share 分享	
broaden 增廣	
provide 提供	**experience** 經驗
gain 獲得	

valuable 寶貴的	
relevant 相關的	experience 經驗
practical 實用的	

7. department 的搭配詞組

與動詞搭配

work in 在……工作	
manage 管理	department 部門
move to 轉調至	

與形容詞搭配

finance 財務	
advertising 廣告	department 部門
marketing 行銷	

複合名詞

department manager 部門經理

department head 部門主管

department meeting 部門會議

8. level 的搭配詞組

與動詞搭配

reach 達到	
maintain 維持	level 水平
determine 決定	

與形容詞搭配

acceptable 可接受的	
certain 特定的	level 水平
entry 入門的	

9. salary 的搭配詞組

get 得到	
offer 提供	**salary 薪資**
review 審視	

與形容詞搭配

annual 每年的	
average 平均的	**salary 薪資**
starting 開始的	

複合名詞

salary raise 加薪

salary scale 薪資等級

salary review 薪資審查

salary cut 減薪

10. manager 的搭配詞組

與形容詞搭配

project 專案	
line 產品線、直屬上級的	
senior 資深的	**manager 經理**
general 一般的	

11. director 的搭配詞組

與形容詞搭配

managing 管理的	
non-executive 非執行	**director 董事**
company 公司的	

錄音稿 Transcripts

Unit 1　工作程序 Job Procedures

🎧 **02**

OK, well I'm a sales person in a pharmaceutical company. In my job I have to read reports on new drugs, and then I have to give presentations on them to doctors. I have lots of appointments with customers, usually doctors in most cases. I also hold negotiations, again, sometimes with doctors, when they are interested in buying some of my products.

Actually, I don't go to meetings very often, as I'm usually on the road somewhere. I make lots of trips, all over Taiwan. If I can't go to a meeting, then I just read through the minutes and make sure I know what's going on. I report to my manager at the end of every week. As for proposals, I sometimes have to read proposals from the marketing department, but I usually ignore them. Ha ha! In my view, selling is about what happens between me and my customer, not some fancy proposal from marketing. The only procedure I carry out, I guess, is completing the weekly activity sheet. This is where I let my boss know what I've been doing during the week.

Uh, I never draw up agendas because I'm not involved in meetings, really, and I never implement systems. That's for the IT guys, right?

中譯

好，嗯我在藥品公司當銷售人員。在我的工作中，我必須讀取新藥品的報告，然後向醫生做藥品的簡報。我要訪問很多客戶，通常大部分是醫生。我也會進行談判，有時候是跟醫生，如果他們有興趣買我的產品的話。

事實上，我不太常開會，因為我經常都是外出到某個地方。我在全台灣大大小小的地方旅行過很多趟。如果我沒法開會，那我會讀讀會議記錄，確定自己知道發生什麼事就好了。每週結束前我要向我的經理報告。至於提案，有時候我得讀取來自行銷部的提案，但是我通常不加以理會。哈！在我看來，銷售純粹就是我和我客戶之間的事，而不是什麼行銷部精心設計的提案。我唯一執行的例行工作程序，我想，就是完成工作週報表。這是為了讓我的老闆知道這一週之內我都在做什麼。

呃，我從來不用擬議程因為我沒跟會議沒什麼關係，說真的，我也從來不用安裝什麼系統。那是資訊人員要做的，對不對？

🎧 03

Hi, I'm an office manager and assistant to a department manager in a trading company. OK, let's see, mmm. Yes, I often have to arrange meetings and confirm my boss's appointments. His schedule changes all the time so I have to confirm that his appointments are still going ahead. Oh, and of course I have to inform my boss about the changes to his schedule. I mean, it wouldn't be much use if I didn't tell him, right? Ha ha! Sometimes he might call me or leave a memo and ask me to put something on an agenda for a meeting. If the meeting is in the office, then I take the minutes and then write them up afterwards. Yes, I arrange his business trips, you know, book flights and hotels and all that. I receive reports when they arrive by courier, and I have to sign for them. Luckily I don't attend his presentations. They're really boring, I've heard, ha ha. I don't have to write proposals. And no, I don't conduct negotiations. He does, though. Follow procedures, well I guess I have my own procedures that I follow. And yes, I did establish a filing system for all the documents that come into our office.

中譯

嗨，我是一家貿易公司的辦公室經理兼部門經理的助理。好，咱們來看看，嗯，是的，我通常得安排會議並敲定我老闆的約會。他的時間表老是在變所以我必須確定接下來的預約是否依舊進行。喔，當然了，我必須通知我老闆他時間表上的變動，我是說，如果我沒告訴他，那就沒什麼用了，不是嗎？哈！有時候他可能會打電話給我，或是留下一張便條要我將某件事排入會議議程裡。如果會議在辦公室裡開，那我會做筆記，之後再寫成完整會議記錄。是的，我安排他出差的行程，你知道的，訂機票與飯店等等那些事。當快遞送報告來的時候我負責簽收。幸好，我不用參加他的簡報，我聽說，它們都很無趣，哈哈。我不用寫提案，我也不用處理談判的事情，但是他要。例行的程序，嗯我想我有我的工作程序要遵守。還有，對了，我將所有進入到我們辦公室的檔案都建立了歸檔系統。

04

Yes, I'm a department manager and I don't have a lot of time for this kind of thing. What do you want to know? Um? Oh, I see. Well, yes, yes yes yes no. Hm? Oh, I see. You want me to speak. OK.

I never miss appointments, it's very rude. I might have to change them, but I never miss them. Well, I'm the manager of this department, but when my boss is away I have to act as manager for three departments. As I said, I'm really very busy. About meetings, yes, I approve agendas which my staff give me, I chair the department meetings, and I sign the minutes of the previous meetings, if I think they're accurate.

Negotiations? Well, sometimes I open negations, but I usually let my staff conduct them. I see lots of presentations from my team, some of them are terrible. Oh yes, I have introduced lots of procedures into the department since I started working here, and developed quite a few systems. The department is really much more efficient now.

I submit a quarterly report to my manager, and I put together proposals all the time. There are so many improvements to be made around here. Cut short a trip? Yes, if there's an emergency at the office, then I will cut short a trip to come back to sort it out, yes. I mean, nobody else can do it!

中譯

對，我是部門經理，對這種事我沒有太多時間。你想知道什麼？呃？喔，我知道了。嗯，對、對、對，不。喔，我瞭解。你要我談談。好吧。

我從不會錯過預約的會面，那是很沒禮貌的。我可能得更改預約，但是我從不會錯過。嗯，我是該部門的經理，但是當我老闆不在時，我得擔任三個部門的經理。就像我所說的，我真的非常忙。關於會議，是的，我要批閱同意我部屬給我的議程，我要主持部門會議，我要簽核上一次會議的記錄，如果我認為它們是正確無誤的話。

談判？嗯有時候我會開啓談判，但是我通常讓我的部屬去進行。我看了很多我團隊做的簡報，有一些真是糟糕。喔，對了，自從我開始在這裡工作，我引進許多

工作程序到部門來，並且發展相當多的系統。部門現在真得有效率多了。

我要呈交季報告給我的經理，且我經常整合提案。這裡有許多要改善的地方。會不會縮短出差行程？會，如果辦公室有緊急事項，那我會縮短行程回來解決，沒錯，我的意思是，沒有其他人可以處理！

🎧 **05**

Well, I'm having a very busy day today. I'm currently making a trip to the South. I've had three appointments today already and I'm now conducting negotiations with one of the main hospitals in the south of Taiwan.

I've just finished giving my presentation to the medical team from the hospital, and they are talking about it now, so I'm having a break. I'm just taking some time out here in the waiting room. I'm reading this report on some medical trials on a new drug while I'm waiting. I'm also reading this proposal, but it's so boring, I can't finish it. I've just informed my manager by email that the negotiation is going well.

I've read through the minutes from the last department meeting, and I've put a couple of issues on the agenda for the next one. I'm arranging a meeting for tomorrow at 4:00, but I can't get a hold of one of the key participants. I'm waiting for her to return my call. I hope she calls back before the negotiations start up again. I really love my Blackberry! I can do all this even though I'm out of the office!

中譯

嗯，我今天非常地忙碌。目前我正前往南部。今天我已經有三個約會了，而我現在正與南台灣其中一家主要的醫院談判。

我剛完成向醫院醫療團隊做的簡報，他們現在正在討論，所以我在休息。我在等候室裡消磨一點時間。等的時候，我在讀一篇關於一項新藥品的試驗報告。我也在閱讀一篇提案，但是很無聊。我讀不下去。我剛剛用 email 通知我經理談判進行得很順利。

我讀了上一次部門會議的記錄，且我為下一個會議議程加入了一些議題。我正在

安排明天四點的一場會議，但是我無法聯絡上其中一名主要的參加者。我在等她回覆我的電話。我希望她能在談判再次開始之前打給我。我真是喜歡我的黑莓機！即使不在辦公室裡我照樣可以處理所有這些事！

🎧 06

Well, let's see, yesterday? Mmmm one day is pretty much like another around here. Let's see, oh yes, yesterday I drew up an agenda for the AGM. I also went to three meetings and took minutes for all of them. Too many meetings. Actually, I don't see why I have to go, but my boss says he likes me to be there, so I have to go …

OK, then what happened? Oh, I worked late, so I missed my hairdresser appointment at 5 o'clock. I didn't hold or open any negotiations, no, and I didn't attend any presentations. I probably received about four reports, which I passed to him. Oh, I also arranged a trip for him to Hong Kong. That's it. Exciting my life, isn't it! Ha ha!

中譯

嗯，我們來看看，昨天？嗯……在這裡一天跟其他天實在沒什麼兩樣。我們來看看，喔，對了，昨天我替 AGM 擬定議程。我還參加了三個會議，且全部做了記錄。太多會議了。事實上，我不懂為什麼我必須參加，但是我老闆說他喜歡我在哪裡，所以我得去……。

好，接著發生了什麼事呢？喔，我工作得太晚以致於錯過與我美髮師五點的預約。我沒有主持或開啟任何的談判，沒有，而且我沒有參加任何的簡報。我大概收到四份報告，我把它們轉給老闆看了。喔，我還幫他安排一趟到香港的出差。就這樣。真是精彩的生活，不是嗎！哈！

🎧 07

Well, looking at my day planner for tomorrow, as you can see it's rather full. This is because I'm a very important and busy woman. Now what do you want to know? My schedule for tomorrow. At 9:00 I'm chairing a meeting of the department heads. Heavens! That reminds me I still have to approve the agenda. Make a mental note of that. Um, then after that I'm going to prepare a presentation about the wonderful work we have done in this department. I've also got to submit my proposal to the president of the company by lunchtime tomorrow.

In the afternoon, I'm writing a report. So as you can see, terribly busy, and terribly terribly important!

中譯

嗯，看看我明天的日程安排，如你所見的，實在相當滿。這是因為我是一位非常重要且忙碌的女人。你想要知道什麼？我明天的時間表。九點的時候我要主持一場部門首長的會議。老天！這可提醒了我，我還得批准議程。要把這件事記在腦子裡。嗯，然後接下來，我要替我們部門所完成的傑出工作準備簡報。明天午餐前我還得呈交我的提案給公司總裁。

下ㄣ，我要寫一篇報告。所以，如你所見的，忙碌極ㄌ，且非常非常重要！

Unit 2　商務對談 Business Talk

 08

1. Can you please get to the point?
2. I have a number of concerns with this.
3. I have a number of key points here.
4. I have already expressed my main concern.
5. I would really like to emphasize this point.
6. I'd like to share my concerns with you.
7. My general point is …
8. Please stick to the main point.
9. The key point I want to make here is …
10. This is of serious concern to us.
11. We need to address the primary concern of …

12. You've raised a controversial point there.
13. You've raised a legitimate concern.

中譯

1. 可不可以請您講重點？
2. 關於這件事我有幾點顧慮。
3. 我這邊有幾個重點要說明。
4. 我已經表明了我主要的顧慮。
5. 我非常想強調這點。
6. 我想要跟你分享我的顧慮。
7. 我主要的論點是……。
8. 請回到主要論點。
9. 我在這邊要說明的主要重點是……。
10. 這是我們嚴重關切的事。
11. 我們必須聲明關於……的主要顧慮。
12. 你提出了一個頗具爭議的論點。
13. 你提出了一個合理的顧慮。

🎧 09

1. Can we please deal with the immediate question of …
2. Can you clarify your current position on this issue?
3. Here I would just like to outline our earlier position.
4. I apologize for putting you in an embarrassing position.
5. I don't know how to answer that tricky question.
6. I think I have already clearly stated my position on this.
7. I'd like to explain my position on this.
8. We need to consider two crucial questions now.
9. Well, I find myself in an awkward position.
10. You've asked a very good question.
11. You've raised a complex question there.

中譯

1. 請問我們可不可以處理當前……的問題

2. 您可不可以說明目前您在這項議題上的立場？

3. 在這裡我只是要略述我們早先的看法。

4. 我感到抱歉讓你陷入一個尷尬的立場。

5. 我不知道如何回答那個麻煩的提問。

6. 我想我已經清楚地說明了我對這件事的看法。

7. 我想解釋我對這件事的看法。

8. 我們現在必須考慮兩個重要的問題。

9. 嗯，我覺得自己身處窘境。

10. 你問了一個相當好的問題。

11. 你提出了一個複雜的問題。

🎧 10

1. Anyone have any ideas about how to solve this problem?

2. Does anyone have any suggestions for this?

3. During my presentation, I'll be presenting a range of issues.

4. I have a number of concerns.

5. I'd like to begin by briefing you on the current situation.

6. I'd like to make a couple of recommendations at this point.

7. I'd like to make a suggestion here, if I may.

8. I'd like to move on to the next point on the agenda now.

9. I'd like to offer a recommendation.

10. I'd like to open this meeting by …

11. I'd like to take this opportunity to welcome …

12. Let's just briefly review the present situation.

13. Let's look at the effect of this on our business.

14. There is no easy solution.

15. We are facing a number of difficult challenges.

16. We have a number of options at this point.

17. What are our options?

18. Please stick to the agenda.

19. The key issue is …

1. 有沒有任何人對於怎麼解決這個問題有任何看法的？
2. 有沒有人對於這個有任何意見？
3. 在我的簡報中我將報告一系列的議題。
4. 我有幾點關切的事項。
5. 我想一開始跟您簡單介紹一下目前的情況。
6. 現在我想提出一些建議。
7. 如果可以的話，我想在此提出建議。
8. 現在我要繼續議程裡的下一個項目。
9. 我要提供一點建議。
10. 我想以……來開始這場會議。
11. 我想利用這個機會來歡迎……
12. 我們簡要地來檢視一下目前的狀況。
13. 我們來看看這件事對我們生意的影響。
14. 沒有簡單的解決方案。
15. 我們面臨了幾個嚴峻的挑戰。
16. 我們現在有幾個選擇。
17. 我們有哪些選擇？
18. 請緊守討論議程。
19. 主要的議題是……

🎧 **11**

Sam: I'd like to open this meeting by making sure everyone has a copy of the agenda. Yes, OK let's get going. Oh, before we start, I'd like to take this opportunity to welcome Mike to the team. Welcome Mike.

Mike: Thanks. Hi everybody.

Sam: OK, the purpose of this meeting is to discuss the new product specs. We are facing a number of difficult challenges with the project. The client has changed the specs several times, and there are now several different versions floating around. The factory has one set, we have at least three sets, and the client will probably ask for more changes in the future.

Mary: Yes, you know I called my contact there and he said they're still not really sure what they want. They're going through structural changes and the boss is always away on vacation with his secretary and they can't even decide what kind of plants to have in their new staff canteen …

John : Mary, sorry to interrupt, but can you please get to the point? We all have a lot of stuff to do. Please stick to the agenda.

Sam: OK, well basically I've outlined the position. Anyone have any ideas about how to solve this problem?

John: Yes. I think we should just wait until they know what they want. Just put the project on hold.

Jane: I have a number of concerns with this. This is our biggest project at the moment. More than half our staff are working on it. If we put the project on hold, how will it affect our business?

Sam: I see your point. There's no easy solution. What are our options? Does anyone else have any suggestions for this?

Mike: I'd like to offer a recommendation.

Sam: Yes, Mike, please go ahead.

Mike: Why don't we just …

中譯

山姆：會議一開始我想確定是否每個人都有一份討論議程。是，好，我們繼續。喔，在我們開始之前，我想藉這個機會歡迎麥克來到我們團隊。歡迎麥克。

麥克：謝謝。嗨，大家好。

山姆：好，本會議的目的是討論新產品的設計規格。關於這個專案，我們面臨了幾個嚴峻的挑戰。客戶已經更改規格幾次了，而現在有許多不同的版本在流通。工廠有一組，我們至少有三組，而客戶將來可能還會要求更多的改變。

瑪麗：對啊，你知道我打給我的聯絡窗口，他說他們仍然不是非常確定他們想要的樣子。他們正進行結構性的重整，而老闆卻老是跟他的秘書去度假，他們甚至無法決定他們新的員工餐廳要放哪一種植物……

約翰：瑪麗，抱歉打岔妳的話，但可不可以請妳說重點？我們都有很多的事情要做。請緊守討論議程。

山姆：好，嗯，基本上，我已經略述了情況。有沒有任何人對於怎麼解決這個問題有任何看法的？

約翰：有，我認為我們應該等到他們搞清楚想要的是什麼再開始，就先擱置這個專案吧。

珍妮：關於這件事我有幾點顧慮。這是我們目前最大的專案，超過一半的員工都在執行這個案子。如果我們把這個案子擱置，對於我們的生意將會帶來什麼影響？

山姆：我瞭解妳的看法。這件事沒有簡單的解決方法。我們有哪些選擇？有沒有其他人對於這件事有任何意見？

麥克：我想提供一個建議。

山姆：是的，麥克，請說。

麥克：我們何不就……

🎧 **12**

Now, I'd like to brief you on the current situation in the Japanese market. There are a number of factors influencing this market. First, the market is flooded with cheaper goods from Korea. Our products are just too expensive. Look at this slide. These figures show that our prices are the highest in the market. Second, our brand presence is not strong enough to support such prices. Here you can see the results of some market research we carried out. The analysis reveals quite clearly that the consumer associates our products with low quality and low value. It seems the product recall we had last year really had a negative impact on our business. Now, as I see it, the key issue is what to do about this situation. Does anyone have any questions?

中譯

現在，我想跟您簡單介紹一下目前日本市場的情況。有幾個因素影響著這個市場。第一，市場上充斥著從韓國來的更便宜的商品。我們的產品就是太貴了。看看這張投影片。這些數據顯示我們的價格在市場上是最高的。第二，我們的品牌呈現不足以支撐這樣的價格。這裡您可以看到我們所做的一些市場研究結果。研究分析相當清楚地指出，消費者認為我們的產品品質低且價值低。看起來去年產

品因缺陷回收的動作對我們的生意的確造成負面影響。現在，依我看來，主要的
議題在於這個情況該如何解決。有沒有任何人有任何提問？

Unit 3　專案管理 Project Management

 13

Today we're going to take a look at how to manage a project. Project management consists of two phases, the planning stage, and the implementation stage. Let's begin with the planning stage.

In many ways, the success or failure of your project is determined by how well you plan the project. You need to begin by writing a proposal. In order for your proposal to be accepted, you need to make sure the proposal is written professionally and presented professionally. What do you need to include when writing a proposal for a new project?

You need to begin by describing the background situation. How does your proposed project fit into the overall strategic direction of the company? How will it benefit the company? You should do some detailed assessments of the current market situation to show that you're aware of market needs, and also assess the present financial situation of the company: How much will your project cost the company? How will the company benefit financially?

When you've described the background, then you need to present the proposal itself. Make clear recommendations here, and make sure that you put forward very practical suggestions: include information about who is going to do what by when.

If your proposal is aimed at solving a problem within the company, make sure you clearly identify the main problem that you want to tackle, and when putting forward your solutions, make sure they are realistic. Can they be achieved within the budget and the timeframe?

今天我們要來看如何管理一個專案。專案管理包含兩個階段：計畫階段與執行階段。我們先從計畫階段開始。

從許多方面來看，你的專案是成功還是失敗，取決於你的計畫有多周詳。你得從寫提案開始。為了讓你的提案能夠被接受，你必須確保將提案寫得很專業，並且很專業地呈現出來。所以，當你為一個新案子寫提案時需要包含什麼要件呢？

你得從描述背景環境開始。考慮你的提案計畫如何配合公司的整體策略方向。它將如何使公司受益？你應該針對目前的市場情形作一些詳細的評估，表示你注意到市場的需求，並且評估公司現今的財務狀況。你的案子會花公司多少錢？公司在財務上如何獲利？

當你描述完背景之後，接著你要替你的提案做簡報。這當中要使你的建言清楚易懂，確定你提出了非常實用的建議，包括關於誰要在什麼時間點做什麼事情的訊息。

如果你的提案是針對解決公司內部的問題，確定你清楚指出你想處理的問題，然後當你提出你的解決方案時，確定它們是實際可行的。它們是否能在預算之內，以及時間範圍內達成？

🎧 **14**

Make sure you also include some flexibility in your plan. Remember, the unexpected always happens, so you need to plan for this. Try to identify in advance what specific issues might arise during the project. For example, how are you going to avoid unnecessary delays? How do you intend to manage possible changes to the product or deal with sudden changes to the circumstances of the project? What other major challenges do you think you might meet? Highlight these issues and make sure you have strategies in place for dealing with them. Also, and most importantly, don't forget to estimate the costs of implementing the project. Set a tight budget and plan a timeline of key stages for the project.

Remember, the more carefully you plan the project, and the more detailed the proposal is, the easier it will be to implement, and the greater the chance of success.

Now let's move on to the second part of my talk today, which is about implementing a project.

During the implementation of the project, try hard to keep within budget by making sure costs don't go up. If you experience unexpected delays or encounter some event which you could not foresee — and there is always something that goes wrong — don't panic, but try to make up the time later in the process. If you need to make necessary changes, implement them as smoothly and as efficiently as possible.

Schedule regular team meetings to keep your team motivated and to keep the project moving forward. Make sure you have agendas for your meetings to keep the meetings efficient. Keep accurate minutes of all the meetings, as this will make it easier for you to write your reports, and to keep track of your team and the project status. Inform your line manager of the project status by writing frequent status or progress reports.

中譯

要注意在你的計畫中保留一些彈性。記得，意外總是突如其來，所以對此你需要備案。試著預先辯識出在計畫中有哪些特定的議題會出現。例如：你如何避免不必要的延遲？你打算要怎麼應付產品可能的改變或處理專案中環境突如其來的變動？你認為你可能還會遇到什麼其他重大的挑戰？強調這些議題並且確定你有應付的備用策略。還有，最重要的是，別忘了估算執行這個專案所需的成本。訂下嚴格的預算並為專案的重要階段定下時程。

記得，你計畫得越仔細，且提案越詳細，就越容易執行，成功的機率也越大。

現在，我們進入到我今天談話內容的第二部分，關於案子的執行。

專案執行的期間，要努力使成本控制在預算內不增高。如果你經歷到無預期的延遲或遇到一些你無法預見的事，不好的事總是會發生，這時候別驚慌，而是在過程中稍後彌補。如果你需要做必要的改變，盡量平穩且有效率地去執行。

安排定時的團隊會議，讓你的團隊保持動力且促進計畫繼續進行。確定你開會時準備了議程，好讓會議有效率地進行。將所有的會議做確實的會議記錄，如此能幫助你更容易寫報告、掌握你的團隊與專案近況。藉由經常地寫情況或進度報告來告知你的直屬經理專案的進度狀況。

Unit 4　策略管理 Strategic Management

 15

Thank you for coming everybody. I want to just briefly chat to you today about my development plan for the future. When I started the company ten years ago, business was easy as we were only one of the few players in the market. We have all been working hard over the last few years to develop the thriving business we have today. My sincere thanks to you all for your hard work over the years. However, hard times are ahead of us. It's getting more and more difficult to attract good business. The market is getting tougher and more competitive. This poses a considerable challenge, especially if we want to support sustainable development of the company, and of the market we operate in. There are two viable options we can consider. Firstly, I'm proposing a department merger of the sales and marketing departments. Secondly, I think we should seek a strategic alliance with one of the other players in the market.

Murmurs from audience.

What I want to do first is to clarify some of the more complicated issues. The proposed merger will bring about fundamental changes to our systems. In particular, it will improve the day-to-day management of the company by only having one department instead of two. Now, I am aware that this proposal may cause some concern, especially about staff redundancies, but I hope you guys as senior managers will be able to minimize the negative effect of staff cuts. Tracy has been promoted to assistant manager of the new department. I'm sure she will do a fantastic job.

Applause from audience.

OK, now let's talk about the alliance …

中譯

感謝大家光臨。今天我要與你們簡要地聊聊關於我對未來的發展計畫。十年前當我創辦公司的時候，由於我們只是市場中少數成員之一，做生意很容易。過去幾年來，大家一直都非常努力，才能發展到今日生意興隆的光景，向你們大家獻上我誠摯的感謝，感謝你們這些年來的努力。然而，我們目前面臨了艱難的時刻，要吸引到好生意是越來越困難了。市場變得越來越不好，競爭更為激烈。特別是如果我們想要持續支撐公司和我們操作的市場的發展，這些成為我們相當大的挑戰。我們有兩個可行的方案可考慮。第一，我提議將銷售與行銷部門合併。第二，我認為我們應該尋求與市場中其他成員的策略聯盟。

（聽眾一片喃喃聲。）

首先我要做的是釐清一些比較複雜的議題。這個合併的提案將會帶給我們系統重大的改變。特別是，以有一個部門，而非兩個部門來看，它將改善公司的日常管理。現在我注意到這個提案可能會引起一些關切，特別是員工過剩的問題，但是我希望你們身為高階經理能夠將裁員的負面影響減到最低。崔西升職為新部門的助理經理。我相信她會做得很好。

（聽眾一片掌聲。）

好，現在我們來談關於聯盟的事……

Unit 5　行銷 Marketing

 16

Interview with Ms. Zoe Chen, Part 1

Interviewer: So Zoe, you're responsible for the marketing of your company's products.

Zoe Chen: That's right.

Interviewer: Can you begin by telling us a little bit about your job. What does it involve for you?

Zoe Chen: Well, lots of things. I'm basically responsible for promoting two brands: one is an upmarket skincare product, and the other is a more popular mass-market brand in the Taiwan and greater China markets.

Interviewer: So how do you do that?

Zoe Chen: Well, I first get a research house to carry out some research. I need to be able to assess the market situation so that I can decide how to promote the brands. It takes me a long time to analyze the market data.

Interviewer: That part sounds kind of boring.

Zoe Chen: Ha ha. Well, it's not very exciting, but it's very important.

Interviewer: Uh-huh.

Zoe Chen: The market analysis provides a picture of the consumer, so that I can understand the needs of consumers a bit better. That's really important.

Interviewer: Why is that?

Zoe Chen: Well, you can't do good marketing unless you make a careful assessment of the market first. You have to understand the consumers, you know, what they want, what their desires and aspirations are, especially in this segment.

Interviewer: OK. Then what happens? Do you have to develop the marketing strategy yourself?

Zoe Chen: Actually no, not in this job. My marketing plan comes from the regional office. I have to match the plan to the local market, and then plan and organize a promotional campaign.

中譯

訪談陳柔依 Part 1

訪問員：柔依，妳負責的是你們公司產品的行銷。

陳柔依：是的。

訪問員：可不可以請妳跟我們說明一點妳的工作。妳需要做什麼事？

陳柔依：嗯，很多事。基本上我負責促銷兩個品牌：一個是頂端客戶的肌膚保養產品，另一個是在台灣與中國大陸比較大眾化市場的品牌。

訪問員：那麼妳怎麼進行？

陳柔依：嗯，首先我建立一個研究室來進行一些研究。我需要能夠評估市場情形，才能決定如何促銷這個品牌。分析市場資料花了我很長的時間。

訪問員：那個部分的工作聽起來有點無趣。

陳柔依：哈哈。是的，是不怎麼有趣，但是非常重要。

訪問員：嗯哼。

陳柔依：市場分析提供我對客戶的想像，如此我才能更加瞭解客戶的需要。那非常重要。

訪問員：為什麼？

陳柔依：嗯除非你先對市場做仔細評估，否則做不好行銷。你必須瞭解客戶，你知道的，他們想要的是什麼，他們的願望與他們所夢寐以求的是什麼，特別是在這一塊市場。

訪問員：好，接著是什麼？妳必須親自發展行銷策略嗎？

陳柔依：事實上不必，這份工作不需要。我的行銷計畫來自區域辦公室。我必須將計畫與當地的市場結合，然後計畫、組織一個促銷活動。

🎧 **17**

Interview with Ms. Zoe Chen, Part 2

Interviewer: Zoe, you just mentioned that as part of your job you have to plan and organize promotional campaigns. Can you tell us a little bit more about that? How does that work.

Zoe Chen: I use TV and media advertising, you know, print ads, such as magazine ads, and we usually also produce a couple of TV commercials per year for each brand.

Interviewer: Do you use international celebrities to endorse your products?

Zoe Chen: Well, it depends on the budget. Ha ha. My advertising budget is set by regional office, so if I have a big budget, then yes, but if I'm on a tight budget, then we just use local talent.

Interviewer: Do you get to meet the stars?

Zoe Chen: Sometimes, yes.

Interviewer: Wow, so cool. OK, tell us a little bit about the two markets you work in. Are they quite different or are they quite similar?

Zoe Chen: Well, the two economies are quite different aren't they. The Chinese economy is growing, while the Taiwanese economy is kind of sluggish at the moment, so that affects the markets.

Interviewer: Right.

Zoe Chen: A unique feature of the Taiwanese market, for instance, in my industry is the huge spending power of women. This is not the same in the Chinese market. We need to work harder there.

Interviewer: Really?

Zoe Chen: Yes, and the Chinese market is more price sensitive.

Interviewer: Price sensitive?

Zoe Chen: Yes, it means that we have to set the unit price of each product much lower and go for volume. The markets are quite different, and they are changing all the time, so I need to keep up with the changes. I'm basically always on the look out for great opportunities to promote the product.

Interviewer: Zoe, it's been great talking to you. By the way, do you use your company's products yourself?

Zoe Chen: Huh, yes I do actually. Why do you ask?

Interviewer: 'Cause you look fabulous.

Zoe Chen: Oh. Thanks.

中譯

訪談陳柔依 Part 2

訪問員：柔依，妳剛剛提到作為妳工作項目之一的是，妳必須計畫與組織促銷活動。關於這點妳能不能跟我們多說明一點？那是如何運作的。

陳柔依：我利用電視與媒體廣告，你知道的，平面廣告，例如雜誌廣告，我們通常每年還會為每個品牌拍攝幾則電視廣告。

訪問員：你們會不會聘請國際明星來代言你們的產品。

陳柔依：嗯，按預算而定。哈哈。我的廣告預算是由區域辦公室決定的，所以如果我有寬裕的預算，那我會，但如果預算很緊，那我們就使用當地的明星。

訪問員：妳有機會跟明星碰面嗎？

陳柔依：有時候會。

訪問員：哇，好酷。好，告訴我們一點關於妳工作的這兩個市場。它們是否非常不一樣或相當類似？

陳柔依：嗯，這兩個經濟體是相當不同的，不是嘛。中國的經濟正在成長，而台灣目前的經濟有點不振，所以影響到市場的表現。

訪問員：是的。

陳柔依：台灣市場有個獨特的特色，比如說依我們產業來看，女性擁有強大的消費力。這點跟中國市場不同。我們在那裡要加把勁。

訪問員：真的？

陳柔依：是，而且中國市場對價位更敏感。

訪問員：對價位敏感？

陳柔依：是的，這表示我們得將每項產品的單位價格調低，以追求數量。市場非常不同且經常在變，所以我必須跟上變動的腳步。基本上我總是在挖掘適當的機會來促銷產品。

訪問員：柔依，很高興跟妳說話。順便問一下，妳自己是否使用你們公司的產品呢？

陳柔依：哈，是的，我的確有用。你為什麼這樣問呢？

訪問員：因為妳看起來容光煥發。

陳柔依：喔，謝謝。

Unit 6 銷售業務 Sales

 18

George: Hi!

Mary: Hi!

George: Want a drink?

Mary: Sure. Thanks.

George: How was your day.

Mary: Terrible, terrible, and terrible.

George: Mine was great.

Mary:	I have this new customer, so I want to provide great after-sales service, you know, to really impress them, so I guaranteed next-day delivery.
George:	I made my first sale in my new job today. I went to visit a prospective client in his office. Really nice office, beautiful, 20th floor, great views, gorgeous secretary, you know.
Mary:	Uh-huh. The factory dispatched the order — a big bulk order — on time, but bad weather in the South China Sea caused a shipment delay.
George:	Really. So we were talking and I showed him all the features of the service we provide. I made him a great offer, and he accepted it almost immediately.
Mary:	Then when it finally made port, the whole consignment got delayed in customs because the sales invoice was not correctly completed.
George:	We completed the negotiation, and finalized the terms of the deal.
Mary:	Uh-huh. So I went over to the customs office to see if I could help them collect the consignment.
George:	I see. I got him to sign the contract immediately, and he even paid cash for it, 'cause I lied and told him we wouldn't be able to extend credit.
Mary:	Cool. I opened the container and found that the product was defective.
George:	Right! He agreed on the price and didn't even ask for a discount!
Mary:	Anyway, to cut a long story short, the customer said they are going to withhold payment until the problem is solved.
George:	So, I will be able to achieve my sales targets for this month! Whole thing only took thirty minutes! I used that new sales strategy I learned in training last week. It really works miracles!
Mary:	Terrible … terrible …
George:	It was so great!

喬治：嗨！

瑪麗：嗨！

喬治：要不要來一杯？

瑪麗：好啊。謝謝。

喬治：妳今天如何。

瑪麗：很糟、很糟、很糟。

喬治：我今天很好。

瑪麗：我有一個新客戶，所以我想提供絕佳的售後服務，你知道的，讓他們印象深刻，所以我保證貨品隔日送達。

喬治：我今天達成了我新工作的第一筆業績。我到一位可能成為買主的客戶的辦公室去拜訪。非常好的辦公室，你知道的，漂亮、高居第二十層樓、景觀佳、迷人的秘書小姐。

瑪麗：啊哼。工廠將訂單，一個量超大的訂單，準時發送了，但是糟糕的天氣在中國南海造成了船運延遲。

喬治：真的喔。於是我們談了一下，我將我們所提供的服務的所有特色秀給他看。我給他出一個好價錢，結果他幾乎立即接受了。

瑪麗：然後最後終於抵達港口，整批運送的貨品因為交易發貨單填的不正確，在過海關的時候延遲了。

喬治：我們完成了協商，談好了交易條件。

瑪麗：啊哼。所以我去海關辦事處看看我能否幫忙領取運送的貨品。

喬治：我瞭解。我讓他立即簽下合約，然後他甚至付了現金，因為我跟他撒謊說我們無法延長信貸。

瑪麗：真棒。我打開箱子發現產品有瑕疵。

喬治：對！他同意了價錢而且甚至沒有要求折扣！

瑪麗：反正，長話短說，客戶說他們要等問題解決了才肯付款。

喬治：所以，這個月我將能夠達到我的業績目標！整件事只花了三十分鐘！我用上禮拜在訓練中學到的新銷售策略。果真收到神效！

瑪麗：糟糕……糟糕……

喬治：真是太棒了！

Unit 7 生產 Production

🎧 19

Julie: OK, let's move on to the next point on the agenda now. I'd like to ask Mike from the production team to brief us on the situation at the factory now. Mike?

Mike: Thanks Julie. Well, as many of you may know, we have run into serious problems with the supplier recently. We have been using this local supplier for about ten years, and they are the leading manufacturer of the components we use in our products. However, recently they have hired a new manager who has implemented some changes which have affected us in the following ways. First, there have been a lot of long delays — they simply don't dispatch consignments on time. In the past, the supplier used to guarantee timely delivery, and they were pretty good about sticking to the schedule. But now they say they can no longer guarantee this. This means our production costs have risen. Second, we also noticed that we have shipped a greater number of defective products. Many of the basic functions simply don't work. We have tried to put in place stricter quality controls, but now we know for sure that the problem originates with their parts, not with our production process, which actually is pretty smooth.

Julie: So basically, Mike, what you're saying is that we have two problems with the supplier, delivery delays and the quality of the parts?

Mike: Yup.

Jeff: Have you tried reminding them of their obligation to honor the contract? Have you tried enforcing it?

Mike: Yes, we've tried that, but the terms of the contract don't cover delivery times. In the past we just used to rely on our relationship. But the new manager says there is no relationship.

Julie: Hmm. Can anyone else provide a solution to this?

Others: "No." "Not me." "Dunno." "Who knows?" "That's difficult."

茉莉： 好，我們現在繼續來看下一項議程。我想請來自生產團隊的麥克來為我們簡單說明一下目前工廠的情形。麥克？

麥克： 謝謝，茉莉。嗯，如同你們大家所知，最近我們和供應商有嚴重的問題。我們十年以來一直使用這個當地的供應商，他們也是我們產品使用的零件的主要製造商。然而，最近他們聘請了一名新經理實施一些改變，這對我們造成以下幾點影響。第一，長時間的延遲經常發生，他們根本就不準時發送貨品。在過去，供應商以往都保證及時送達，且他們非常能夠按照時間表運作。但是現在他們說他們不能保證這點了。這表示我們的生產成本增加了。第二，我也注意到我們的出貨有很大量的瑕疵品。許多基本功能根本就不能正常運作。我們試圖執行更嚴格的品質管控，但是現在我們確認問題出自於它們的零件，而不是我們的生產過程。實際上我們的生產過程相當順暢。

茉莉： 麥克，所以基本上，你所說的是我們和供應商有兩個問題，延遲送貨與零件品質？

麥克： 是的。

傑夫： 你有沒有試過提醒他們有義務要履行他們的合約？你有沒有試著去強制執行合約？

麥克： 有，我們試過，但是合約上的條件並不包含運送時間。以往我們習慣於信任我們彼此的關係。但是新經理說沒有這層關係存在。

茉莉： 嗯。有沒有任何人能夠對此提供解決辦法？

其他人：「沒有。」「我不行。」「不知道。」「誰知道啊？」「那太困難了。」

Unit 8 財務 Finance

🎧 20

Janice: Today I went to that private investment bank you told me about to see if I could raise some additional capital for our next big … development.

Paul: Oh. What did they say?

Janice: Well, we talked for three hours. I showed them our financial records for the last five years, told them that although we suffered a worse than expected loss in our first year, we generated good profits in the second year, that we earned better than expected profits for the last two years. I also showed them that our growth prospects for the next five years were looking good too.

Paul: And?

Janice: They wanted to know whether we will be able to achieve quick growth for the period of the loan.

Paul: And?

Janice: So I said that the figures speak for themselves. So we looked at the key figures some more.

Paul: And?

Janice: Well, they have to do all these checks, of course, because they want to minimize their potential risk. But at the same time, I know they want to get a maximum return on their investment. Then they asked what we needed the additional capital for.

Paul : So what did you tell them?

Janice: I told them that we wanted it to make some major investments in our factory, buy some equipment and so on.

Paul : Did they believe you?

Janice: Yes! (*laughter from both*) And they gave me the loan! (*more laughter*)

中譯

潔妮斯：今天我去你告訴我的那一家私人投資銀行，看看是否能籌措一些額外的資金給我們下一個大的……發展。

保羅：　喔，他們怎麼說？

潔妮斯：嗯，我們談了三個小時。我給他們看了我們過去五年來的財務記錄，告訴他們，雖然我們在第一年虧損得比預期的還嚴重，我們在第二年產出良好獲利，而在過去兩年裡，我們賺得比預期還要好的獲利。我還給他們看我們接下來五年的成長展望，看起來也非常好。

保羅：　然後呢？

潔妮斯：他們想知道我們是否能夠在借貸期間取得快速成長。

保羅：　然後呢？

潔妮斯：於是我說數字會說話。所以我們又多看了一些主要的數據。

保羅：　然後呢？

潔妮斯：嗯，他們必須做所有的檢驗，當然，因為他們想要盡可能減低潛在風險。但同時，我知道他們想要在投資上回收最大的獲利。於是他們問我們需要這筆額外的資金做什麼。

保羅：　所以妳怎麼跟他們說？

潔妮斯：我告訴他們我們想要在廠房上做重大的投資，買一些設備，等等。

保羅：　他們相信妳嗎？

潔妮斯：是啊！（兩人的笑聲）於是他們就給我貸款了！（更多的笑聲）

Unit 9　資訊工程 IT

🎧 21

Interviewer: So Jack, you work as the IT manager in an export company. Can you tell us a bit about your job?

Jack Lin: Sure. What do you want to know?

Interviewer: Well, why don't you tell us about the kinds of things you do everyday.

Jack Lin: OK. Well, let me see. I'm responsible for a number of things. I guess my main job is to manage the company's information system.

Interviewer: Errr … what's an information system?

Jack Lin: OK, well, we sell plastic and petrochemical products to the European market right? Every sale we make is recorded, you know, the number of units, the price, the buyer, the date, the delivery schedule, and so on. Traders input this detailed information into the system. My job is to maintain the system so that it runs smoothly all the time.

Interviewer: I see. So why is all this information necessary?

Jack Lin: Oh, well that's the cool part. The marketing department can analyze all this precise data to get relevant information about current market trends, you know, which countries in Europe prefer which products, what times of year certain products perform better than others. We can use this to control production in the factories.

Interviewer: Oh, yes, that is cool.

Jack Lin: Another thing is that the finance department can also analyze this data to predict price fluctuations in the market.

Interviewer: Wow! So how do you do all this stuff?

Jack Lin: Well, I wrote a software program.

Interviewer: You wrote a program?! All by yourself?

Jack Lin: Yes, I mean we developed the computer program together with the marketing, sales, production, and finance teams. They told me the program would have to perform certain functions, and then I wrote the program.

Interviewer: How long did it take?

Jack Lin: About three months, I guess. You know, there were lots of revisions and so on, and I had to keep providing extra functions as the other departments thought of more things.

中譯

訪問員：傑克，所以你在出口公司當資訊工程經理。你可不可以跟我們說一點關於你工作上的事？

林傑克：好的，你想知道什麼？

訪問員：嗯，你何不告訴我們你每天做的事。

林傑克：好，嗯，讓我想想。我負責很多事。我想我的主要工作是管理公司的資訊系統。

訪問員：哦……資訊系統是什麼呢？

林傑克：好，我們販售塑膠與石化產品到歐洲市場，對不對？我們的每一筆交易都會記錄下來，你知道的，像是單位數、價格、買方、日期、運送日程表，等等。交易員將這些資訊細節輸入系統。而我的工作就是維持系統讓它隨時運作順暢。

訪問員：我瞭解了。那麼為什麼所有這些資訊是必要的呢？

林傑克：喔，那可是有趣的部分。行銷部門可以藉由分析所有這些精確的數據而得到目前市場趨勢的相關資訊，你知道的，像是歐洲哪些國家偏好哪些產品，某一項產品在一年中哪些時間比其他產品賣得好。我們可利用這些來控制工廠的生產。

訪問員：喔，是啊，那太酷了。

林傑克：另一件事是財務部門也可以藉分析數據來預測市場的價格波動。

訪問員：哇！那麼你如何處理所有這些事呢？

林傑克：嗯，我寫了一套軟體程式。

訪問員：你寫了一套程式？！全都是由你一個人寫的？

林傑克：是的，我的意思是我們與行銷、銷售、生產與財務團隊一起發展這套電腦程式。他們告訴我程式要能執行哪些功能，然後我把程式寫出來。

訪問員：花了多少時間完成？

林傑克：我想，大約三個月。你知道的，總是有很多的修改等等，因為如果其他部門想到更多事情，我必須一直提供額外的功能。

🎧 **22**

Interviewer:	So what are you working on at the moment?
Jack Lin:	Well, I'm running a joint pilot project at the moment to make our information system global.
Interviewer:	What do you mean?
Jack Lin:	Well, we wanted to make it easier for our subsidiaries abroad to contact us and access our information. I hit upon an easy solution to this, which was to build a wide area network, which means that computers in all our global branches will be connected to each other.
Interviewer:	I see. And what's your role in this project?
Jack Lin:	Well, I'm coordinating this new project from this end, but we have several teams from other countries working on it together. We already have these kinds of networks in the different countries where we operate, but what we're trying to do is expand the networks and link them together. The team

has recently taken up one of my suggestions regarding security to make this easier.

Interviewer: I see. Anything else you have to do in your job?

Jack Lin: Yes, I also have to help the traders and sales staff to deal with unexpected IT problems. You know, when their computer breaks down, or they don't understand the system.

Interviewer: Does that happen often?

Jack Lin: Not really. Most of the people here are pretty computer literate. They can solve really common problems by themselves, but occasionally, they'll need me to work out an easy solution for them. I mean, sometimes they are too busy, so I have to step in and come up with more practical suggestions for issues they have.

Interviewer: Well, Jack, you sound like a really smart guy!

Jack Lin: Yes, my girlfriend thinks so too!

中譯

訪問員：那麼你目前在忙什麼？

林傑克：嗯，我目前正在執行一個聯合導航專案，讓我們的資訊系統全球化。

訪問員：你的意思是？

林傑克：嗯，我們想要幫助我們海外的分部更容易聯絡上我們與取得我們的資訊。對此，我想到一個簡單的解決方案，就是建立一個廣大區域的網絡，也就是說我們全球所有分部的電腦都將相互連結。

訪問員：原來如此。那你在這個專案中的角色是什麼？

林傑克：嗯，我在這端協調新專案的運作，但是我們有許多來自其他國家的團隊在共同進行。在我們營運的不同國家當中已經有這種網路的使用，但是我們嘗試要做的是擴大網路以及把它們連結在一起。團隊已經採用我的一個建議，使安全性更為簡易。

訪問員：瞭解。還有其他你工作中必須要做的事嗎？

林傑克：有的，我還得幫助交易員與銷售人員處理意外的資訊工程問題。你知道的，例如當他們的電腦當機，或是他們不瞭解系統的時候。

訪問員：這事經常發生嗎？

林傑克：並不會。這裡大部分人對電腦都有相當程度的使用認知。他們自己可以

解決相當常見的問題，但是偶爾他們需要我幫他們想出一個簡單的解決方式。我是說，有時候他們太忙了，所以我必須介入幫忙，想出更實用的點子來應付他們面對的問題。

訪問員：嗯，傑克，你聽起來是個十分聰明的傢伙！

林傑克：是阿，我的女朋友也這麼認為！

Unit 10　人力資源 HR

🎧 23

Interviewer: Can you tell us a bit about your job, Julie?

Julie Wang: Well, I'm the HR manager of a finance company. I'm responsible for recruiting new personnel at all levels of the company, and also for supporting the staff.

Interviewer: OK, so what part of your job do you like the best?

Julie Wang: Oh, I enjoy the recruitment process best.

Interviewer: Really, why?

Julie Wang: Well it's interesting to meet lots of new people, and to try to match the people you meet with the requirements of the company.

Interviewer: Can you tell us a bit more about that?

Julie Wang: OK, well, we recruit new employees from colleges around Taiwan. The recruitment process is quite intense for the candidates.

Interviewer: Why is that?

Julie Wang: Well, we require a particular set of skills, as you can imagine, and finding the right people can be quite difficult. We have to make sure we are getting the right people, you know, so that makes the interview process quite tough.

Interviewer: OK, so what do you offer your employees?

Julie Wang: Actually, compared to others in this industry, we offer a basic monthly salary that is lower compared to our competitors. But on the other hand we also provide our staff with valuable experience in working in finance.

Interviewer: And you recruit all levels of the company?

Julie Wang: Yes, for example last month we had to find and hire a new managing director. That was challenging.

Interviewer: Why?

Julie Wang: Well, most of the people I interviewed were older than me, and had more experience than me, so sometimes it felt like they were interviewing me, rather than me interviewing them.

Interviewer: Oh I see. That's tricky.

中譯

訪問員：茱莉，可否告訴我們一點關於妳的工作？

王茱莉：嗯，我是一家財務公司的人力資源經理。我負責替公司所有階層招募新員工，以及給職員支援。

訪問員：好，那麼妳最喜歡妳工作當中哪一部分？

王茱莉：喔，我最喜歡招募新人的過程。

訪問員：真的，為什麼？

王茱莉：嗯，能遇到很多新人，且試著將你遇到的人與公司的需要配對是很有趣的事。

訪問員：關於這點妳可不可以跟我們多說明一些？

王茱莉：好的，嗯，我們從台灣各地的大專院校招募新職員。招募過程對應徵者而言相當緊湊。

訪問員：那是為什麼呢？

王茱莉：嗯，我們要求一套特定的技能，所以你可以想像，找到適合的人就相當困難。我們得確定我們找到對的人，你知道的，所以讓面試過程變得更困難。

訪問員：好的，那妳提供什麼給妳的員工？

王茱莉：其實，比起業界其他公司，我們提供的基本月薪比我們的競爭者低。但另一方面，我們也提供我們的職員在財務方面寶貴的工作經驗。

訪問員：妳替公司各層級招募新人？

王茱莉：是的，比如說上個月我們得找尋與雇用一名新總經理。那非常具挑戰性。

訪問員：為什麼？

王茉莉：嗯，大部分我面試的人都比我年長，比我更有經驗，所以有時候像是他們在面試我，而不是我在面試他們。

訪問員：喔，原來是這樣。那真是不簡單。

🎧 **24**

Interviewer: OK, so now tell us what you don't like about your job.

Julie Wang: OK, well, I don't really like tackling complex issues involving disputes between managers and employees.

Interviewer: Does that happen often?

Julie Wang: No not really, but sometimes someone might have a problem with their work or their colleagues.

Interviewer: So how do you solve that?

Julie Wang: Well, I tell them first they have to inform their line manager of the problems. Then we try to solve them together. Sometimes we have to transfer people to another department.

Interviewer: I see, OK. I know that performance is a big issue in this company. Can you tell us a bit about that?

Julie Wang: Yes, well, this industry is very competitive, right, so we have to make sure that all our employees are working really hard. We ask our employees to carry out annual self-assessments, and then there is an assessment interview. In the interview we discuss the self-assessments to find out if the employee is happy. We also talk to the employee's manager to find out whether he or she is doing a good job.

Interviewer: How do you deal with staff retention?

Julie Wang: Well, it's a big issue. We try to support employee development, so we organize activities such as ping pong and hiking, you know. And we also do our best to provide a basic level of job satisfaction by involving people in multi-departmental projects and decision making.

Interviewer: I see, and are you satisfied with your job?

Julie Wang: Me? Oh well, ha ha. Sure!

訪問員：好，那麼現在告訴我們妳不喜歡妳工作的哪一部分。

王茱莉：好的，嗯，我不是很喜歡處理涉及經理與職員紛爭的複雜議題。

訪問員：那樣的事經常發生嗎？

王茱莉：不，並不會，但有時候有人可能會對他們的工作或他們的同事感到不滿。

訪問員：那麼妳如何解決？

王茱莉：嗯，我首先告訴他們得向他們的上級經理告知這個問題。然後我們試著一起解決。有時候我們必須將人員轉調至另一個部門。

訪問員：我瞭解了，好。我知道績效是公司高度重視的一件大事。關於這個，妳可不可以跟我們多說明一點？

王茱莉：好，嗯，這個產業非常競爭，是的，所以我們得確定我們所有員工都非常努力工作。我們要求員工執行年度自我評鑑，然後舉行評鑑的面試。在面試中我們討論自我評鑑的結果，看看員工是否快樂。我們也會和員工的經理談談，看看他或她的工作績效是否良好。

訪問員：妳如何處理留住職員的問題？

王茱莉：嗯，這是個大問題。我們試著支持職員的發展，所以我們組織了像是乒乓球與健行這些活動。還有，我們盡力藉著讓員工參與多部門專案與決策來提供基本的工作滿意度。

訪問員：我瞭解，那麼妳滿意妳的工作嗎？

王茱莉：我？喔，嗯，哈哈。當然！

解答 Answer Keys

Unit 1　工作程序 Job Procedures

Task 7

- draw up
- put something on
- approve

agenda

- go to
- arrange
- chair

meeting

- read through
- take
- sign

minutes

Task 8

- have
- confirm
- miss

appointment

- hold
- conduct
- open

negotiation

Task 9

- give
- attend
- see

presentation

- read
- receive
- submit

report

- read
- put together
- write

proposal

Task 10

• report to • act as • inform	**manager**

• go on • arrange • cut short	**trip**

Task 11

• implement • establish • develop	**system**

• carry out • follow • introduce	**procedure**

Task 15

completed results	uncompleted activities
I've had three appointments today already	I'm currently making a trip
I've just finished giving my presentation	I'm now conducting negotiations
I've just informed my manager	I'm reading this report
I've read through the minutes	I'm also reading this proposal
I've put a couple of issues on the agenda	I'm arranging a meeting

Task 28

1. negotiations
2. report
3. report
4. report
5. job
6. report
7. negotiations
8. negotiations
9. job
10. negotiations/job
11. job
12. negotiations
13. negotiations
14. negotiations
15. report
16. report
17. report
18. report
19. report

Task 29

- control
- billing
- delivery
- inventory

system

- complaints
- documentation
- emergency
- standard operating

procedure

- disastrous
- enjoyable
- weekend
- business

trip

Task 30

- ongoing
- lengthy
- intensive
- delicate

negotiation

- excellent
- effective
- short

presentation

Task 31

- departmental
- team
- board
- important
- urgent

meeting

- pressing
- important
- urgent

appointment

Task 32

1. meeting
2. appointment
3. meeting/appointment
4. trip
5. presentations
6. system
7. procedure
8. procedure
9. trip
10. system
11. procedure
12. procedure
13. trip
14. presentation
15. negotiations
16. system
17. negotiations
18. negotiations
19. negotiations
20. meeting
21. system
22. meeting
23. trip
24. presentation

Task 33

1. presentation package
2. presentation handout
3. presentation slides
4. presentation style
5. presentation skills

Task 34

1. I forgot the presentation handouts.
2. The presentation slides were very well designed.
3. The whole presentation package was very professional.
4. I like his presentation style. It's very clear and easy to follow.
5. You need to work on your presentations skills.

Task 35

Dear Johnny,

I hope you are well there and everything is still OK at home. I have been in the U.S. for three weeks now, working at my new job, and so far I am really enjoying it! The people here are very nice, and very helpful. Everyone has been so kind helping me to settle in to the company.

I want to tell you a little bit about my job, 'cause it's all so new and exciting to me! Mostly my duties are to assist the manager of the accounting department. It's a very junior job, but I think it will get better after a few months. At the moment I am learning how to **follow the procedures** and **implement the systems** they have here. There are so many of them, sometimes I get confused. Also, I have been learning how to **take minutes for meetings**, and how to draw up agendas for the meetings. I don't actually participate in the meetings, just listen and take notes, but it's good training for my English. My boss tells me I am **doing a great job**, so I must be doing something right!

I also have to **inform my manager** about changes to his schedule, and make and **confirm his appointments**. He's very busy, so I have to write a lot of emails for him, cancelling and changing his schedule. It's good that I studied email writing so hard at home! He has to **put together** quite a lot of **proposals**, **submit** tons of **reports**, and also **give presentations** so I have been helping him with that, you know, collecting data and running around for him.

Last week he had to **conduct important negotiations** with a client, and he took me along with him to watch and learn. It was so interesting to see how all these people do business together. So different from our country!

Next week, things will be a bit easier as he is **going on** a **business trip** for a week. I hope to have more time to write more to you then. Meanwhile, give lots of love to Mum and Dad and squeeze Baby Alice for me.

Lots of love.
Jade

Unit 2 商務對談 Business Talk

Task 1

- get to
- stick to
- have
- raise
- make
- emphasize

point

- have
- raise
- share
- address
- express
- be of

concern

Task 2

- general
- main
- key
- controversial

point

- main
- serious
- primary
- legitimate

concern

Task 5, 6

Verbs	Adjectives	
ask answer	good tricky	**question (inquiry)**
raise consider deal with	complex crucial immediate	**question (issue)**

Task 7, 8

Verbs	Adjectives	
explain outline state clarify	earlier current	**position (opinion)**
find oneself in put sb. in	awkward embarrassing	**position (situation)**

Task 11

factor	• be • influence n.p. • affect n.p. • contribute to n.p. • cause n.p. • lead to n.p. • explain n.p.
recommendation	• be • involve Ving • involve n.p. • include n.p. • include Ving

Task 12

figures	• represent n.p. • include n.p. • suggest n.p. • suggest that n. clause
analysis	• demonstrate n.p. • demonstrate that n. clause • provide n.p. • confirm n.p.

analysis	• confirm that n. clause
	• suggest n.p.
	• suggest that n. clause

Task 13

1. recommendations
2. recommendation
3. recommendation
4. analysis
5. analysis
6. analysis
7. analysis
8. recommendation
9. analysis
10. figures
11. recommendations/figures
12. factors
13. factors
14. factors
15. figures
16. factor
17. factor
18. factor
19. figures
20. factor
21. analysis

Task 15

1. The figures show	*a drop in sales.*
	the possibility of a recession.
	the market is shrinking.
	we need to increase our staff.
	a rise in prices.
	there are not enough sales staff.
2. The figures indicate	*a drop in sales.*
	the possibility of a recession.
	the market is shrinking.
	we need to increase our staff.
	a rise in prices.
	there are not enough sales staff.

3. The figures reveal	a drop in sales.
	the possibility of a recession.
	the market is shrinking.
	we need to increase our staff.
	a rise in prices.
	there are not enough sales staff.
4. The analysis shows that	the market is shrinking.
	we need to increase our staff.
	there are not enough sales staff.
5. The analysis indicates that	the market is shrinking.
	we need to increase our staff.
	there are not enough sales staff.
6. The analysis reveals that	the market is shrinking.
	we need to increase our staff.
	there are not enough sales staff.

Task 13

1. Anyone have any ideas about how to solve this problem?
2. Does anyone have any suggestions for this?
3. During my presentation I'll be presenting a range of issues.
4. I have a number of concerns.
5. I'd like to begin by briefing you on the current situation.
6. I'd like to make a couple of recommendations at this point.
7. I'd like to make a suggestion here, if I may.
8. I'd like to move on to the next point on the agenda now.
9. I'd like to offer a recommendation.
10. I'd like to open this meeting by …
11. I'd like to take this opportunity to welcome …
12. Let's just briefly review the present situation.
13. Let's look at the effect of this on our business.
14. There is no easy solution.
15. We are facing a number of difficult challenges.

16. We have a number of options at this point.
17. What are our options?
18. Please stick to the agenda.
19. The key issue is …

Unit 3 專案管理 Project Management

Task 2

- call
- chair
- call off

meeting

- go through
- stick to
- have

agenda

- read through
- accept
- sign

minutes

Task 3

- run
- coordinate
- implement

project

- review
- brief sb. on
- resolve

situation

- prepare
- read
- submit

report

Task 4

1. project	6. report	11. minutes	16. agenda
2. report	7. situation	12. meeting	17. situation
3. minutes	8. report	13. situation	18. project
4. project	9. agenda	14. minutes	
5. agenda	10. meeting	15. meeting	

Task 5

• new • major • joint	**project**
• present • difficult • particular	**situation**
• status • progress • full	**report**
• brief • team • departmental	**meeting**

Task 6

1. report	4. project	7. meeting	10. situation
2. meeting	5. situation	8. situation	11. project
3. report	6. meeting	9. report	12. project

Task 7

1. project status review
2. project team
3. project proposal
4. project coordinator
5. project leader, project manager
6. project status
7. project management

Task 8

1. <u>Project management</u> can be quite tricky sometimes.
2. The <u>project coordinator</u> needs to be able to communicate very well in English.
3. The <u>project team</u> has some excellent people.
4. I'd now like to tell you about the <u>project status</u>.
5. We are having a <u>project status review</u> next week.
6. The <u>project manager</u> does not know what she is doing.
7. This is my first time to be a <u>project leader</u>.
8. I outlined the problems in the <u>project proposal</u>.

Task 9, 10

• adopt • accept	**recommendation**
• put together • write	**proposal**
• act on • take up	**suggestion**
• put forward • make	**recommendation/proposal/ suggestion**

Task 11, 12

• firm • strong	**recommendation**
• draft • preliminary	**proposal**
• constructive • sensible	**suggestion**

Task 13

1. We have decided to accept your recommendation.
2. I'm writing a proposal at the moment.
3. We like your suggestion and we are going to take it up.
4. He made a strong recommendation for a bigger budget.
5. It's just a draft proposal. I'm still working on the details.
6. Does anyone have any constructive suggestions?

Task 16

1. new
2. background
3. detailed
4. current
5. present
6. clear
7. practical
8. main
9. realistic
10. specific
11. unnecessary
12. possible
13. sudden
14. major
15. tight
16. unexpected
17. necessary
18. regular
19. accurate

Unit 4 策略管理 Strategic Management

Task 2

- come into
- minimize
- produce
- take

effect

- choose
- consider
- explore
- limit

option

Task 3

- face
- meet
- pose
- resist

challenge

- address
- clarify
- decide
- raise

issue

Task 4

- bring about
- make
- manage
- resist

change

- await
- encourage
- stimulate
- support

development

Task 5

- act as
- appoint
- become
- be promoted to

manager

- provide
- improve
- oversee
- simplify

management

Task 6

- cancel
- complete
- propose

merger

- break off
- establish
- seek

alliance

Task 7

1. effect
2. manager
3. developments
4. options
5. development
6. management
7. manager
8. issue
9. alliance
10. merger
11. change
12. options
13. change
14. challenge
15. effect
16. alliance
17. management
18. challenge
19. issues
20. merger

Task 8

- direct
- negative
- positive
- significant

effect

- alternative
- best
- realistic
- viable

option

Task 9

- considerable
- exciting
- serious

challenge

- complicated
- controversial
- real

issue

Task 10

- fundamental
- major
- slow
- structural

change

- business
- product
- sustainable
- uneven

development

Task 11

- assistant
- line

manager

- day-to-day
- risk

management

Task 12

- company
- department

merger

- strategic
- strong

alliance

Task 13

1. merger
2. management
3. merger
4. manager

5. issue
6. challenge
7. development
8. management

9. challenge
10. development
11. option
12. option

13. effect	16. changes	19. change
14. effect	17. alliance	20. manager
15. issue	18. alliance	

Task 14

1. b	3. a	5. b
2. a	4. a	6. b

Task 15

- attract
- be bad for
- be good for
- conduct
- discuss
- do

business (process)

- build
- develop
- establish
- expand
- manage
- operate
- run
- start

business (thing)

Task 16

- good
- day-to-day

business (process)

- good
- thriving
- profitable
- lucrative

business (thing)

	business (thing)
• large • medium-sized • small	

Task 17

1. doing
2. good
3. develop/establish
4. are bad for
5. run/start
6. discussing
7. expand/build
8. do/attract
9. started/established
10. good/thriving/profitable/lucrative/large

Task 18

business (thing)	• community • enterprise • manager • plan • unit
business (process)	• administration • associate • confidence • cycle • strategy

Task 19

1. I am the business manager.
2. I have a good business plan.
3. I have a business strategy which will give us a lot of growth.

4. I studied business administration.
5. Business confidence was boosted after the election.
6. The business cycle follows the same pattern every year.
7. The foreign business community in Taiwan is quite small.

Task 20

development	• plan • program • project
company	• director • spokesperson • headquarters • car • policy • logo
management	• buy-out • team • strategy • consultancy • style • structure

Task 21

1. His management style is very different from mine.
2. I used to work for a management consultancy.
3. I lost my job in a management buy-out.
4. The company policy is to invest 35% of all profits back into the company.
5. The company spokesperson said they were not going to build here.
6. The management structure in this company is very complex. I want to simplify it.
7. This is part of a wider development project. We are working hard to improve the area.
8. You will be given a company car as part of your package.

Task 22, 23

• develop + expand	**business**
• form + found • start + establish • run + manage	**business/company**
• buy + acquire	**company**

Task 24, 25

• profitable + lucrative • good + thriving	**business**
• multinational + international • listed + public	**company**

Task 26

(suggested)

1. It's already a thriving business, but I'm trying to develop it so that it becomes really lucrative.
2. I established the business 20 years ago and managed it for 10 years.
3. We have just acquired a public company. It was very expensive, so I hope this will give us growth.
4. He is the CEO of a huge international company.

Task 29

started	the company
develop the thriving	business
attract good	business
poses a considerable	challenge
support sustainable	development
consider viable	options
propose a department	merger

seek a strategic	alliance
clarify some of the more complicated	issues
bring about fundamental	changes
improve the day-to-day	management
minimize the negative	effect
be promoted to assistant	manager

Unit 5　行銷 Marketing

Task 2

- create
- establish
- launch

brand

- cut
- raise
- set

price

- manufacture
- advertise
- distribute

product

Task 3

- begin
- launch

campaign

- allocate
- go over

budget

- develop
- implement

strategy

Task 4

- assess
- handle

situation

- come across
- grasp

opportunity

- include

feature

Task 5

- affect
- manage
- stimulate

economy

- enter
- establish
- flood

market

Task 6

- take out
- make
- run

ad

- develop
- dominate
- expand

market

- create
- get
- use

advertising

- improve
- do
- manage

marketing

Task 7

1. conducting
2. developing
3. establish
4. set

Task 8

- leading
- luxury
- mass-market

brand

- list
- retail
- wholesale

price

- branded
- defective
- natural

product

Task 9

- national
- public relations
- new

campaign

- annual
- training
- shoestring

budget

- business
- innovative
- long-term

strategy

Task 10

- complicated
- current

situation

- golden
- unexpected

opportunity

- distinguishing
- standard

feature

Task 11

| • developed
 • stable | **economy** |
| • overseas
 • small | **market** |

Task 12

| • misleading | **ad** | • competitive
 • large | **market** |
| • national
 • free | **advertising** | • aggressive
 • successful | **marketing** |

Task 13

1. local
2. innovative
3. unexpected
4. wholesale

Task 14

| **market** | • analysis
 • conditions
 • leader
 • research
 • share
 • segmentation |
| **marketing** | • activity
 • agency
 • campaign
 • department
 • plan
 • strategy
 • tool |

Task 15

1. We are using a range of marketing tools right now.
2. We are the market leader.
3. We are doing a lot of very interesting marketing activities right now.
4. The market share is too small.
5. Market segmentation is very important for helping us to reach the right consumers.
6. The market research shows we are still behind.
7. The marketing plan is ready. Want to take a look?
8. The marketing department is too small for this project.
9. The market conditions are hard.
10. I am doing some market analysis.
11. A good marketing strategy will help us to increase sales.

Task 16

1. research
2. analysis/assessment
3. analysis/assessment

Task 17

1. comprehensive
2. preliminary
3. rough
4. carry out, undertake
5. reveal, indicate, demonstrate

Task 18

(suggested)
1. We did comprehensive research into the situation and found no evidence of wrongdoing.
2. The analysis we undertook revealed that the product is overpriced.
3. This is only a general assessment.
4. The initial research indicates consumers like the product.
5. A detailed analysis demonstrated that the product needs more functionality

Task 21

marketing	company's products
promoting	two brands
popular mass-market	brand
carry out	research
assess	market situation
analyze	market data
market analysis	provides
do	good marketing
make	careful assessment
develop	marketing strategy
marketing	plan
local	market
plan and organize	promotional campaign

Task 23

plan and organize	promotional campaign
use	TV and media advertising
print	ads
magazine	ads
produce	TV commercials
set	advertising budget
have	big budget
be on	a tight budget
economy	is growing
sluggish	economy
unique	feature
price	sensitive
be on the look out for	great opportunities

Unit 6 銷售業務 Sales

Task 2

- develop
- prepare
- outline
- propose
- implement

strategy

- set
- meet
- reach
- exceed
- be above

target

Task 3

- accept
- arrange
- expect
- guarantee

delivery

- avoid
- be
- reduce
- experience

delay

Task 4

- accept
- consider

offer

- conclude
- secure

deal

- give
- offer

discount

Task 5

1. develops
2. implement
3. sets
4. meet
5. conclude
6. offer
7. consider
8. arrange
9. reduce

Task 6

- detailed
- innovative
- overall
- regional

strategy

- annual
- monthly
- quarterly
- revenue

target

Task 7

- prompt
- quick
- special

delivery

- long
- slight

delay

Task 8

- better
- conditional
- initial

offer

- the terms of the
- better

deal

- big
- substantial

discount

Task 9

1. overall
2. regional
3. revenue
4. better
5. substantial
6. The terms of the
7. prompt

Task 10

product		service	
	• category		• agreement
	• development		• center
	• information		• charge
	• line		• contract
	• range		• representative

Task 11

sales		delivery	
	• forecast		• address
	• pitch		• charge
	• promotion		• date
	• rep		• note
	• tax		• schedule
	• volume		

order	
	• book
	• form
	• number

Task 12

discount		price	
	• voucher		• hike
	• card		• freeze
	• price		• war
			• list

Task 13

cash	
	• card
	• cow
	• discount
	• dispenser
	• flow

cash	
	• inflow
	• injection
	• limit
	• outflow
	• reserve

credit	
	• agreement
	• card
	• crunch

credit	
	• limit
	• rating
	• risk

Task 14

1. Can you let me see the price list?
2. Do you have a discount card?
3. I have reached my credit limit.
4. Please check the delivery address.
5. The service charge is too high. Can you reduce it a bit?
6. The delivery date is wrong. It should have arrived yesterday.
7. The order number is NTV20056.
8. The cash outflow is greater than the cash inflow.
9. The sales volume is not high enough.
10. We are doing a sales promotion right now.
11. We are in the product development stage. It will be ready in a few months.
12. We have a brand new service center. You should pay us a visit soon.
13. We need a cash injection: revenue is down.

Task 15

1. customer
2. client
3. corporate
4. private
5. major
6. regular
7. potential/prospective

Task 16, 17

• collect + receive

• dispatch + send

consignment

- take + accept
- ensure + guarantee

delivery

- large + huge
- whole + entire

consignment

- quick + speedy
- prompt + timely

delivery

Task 20

1. Can you ensure speedy delivery?
2. Please be ready to accept prompt delivery.
3. Did you collect that huge consignment of goods I dispatched to you last week?
4. The entire consignment you sent last week was rotten.

Task 21

(suggested)

1. We offer a great service.
2. We need to work harder if we are going to achieve our targets this quarter.
3. I am finalizing the deal with them at the moment.
4. I received a substantial discount on this purchase.
5. Let's go for a drink to celebrate when we complete the deal.
6. My sales results have exceeded the monthly target!
7. I have no choice but to reject this offer.
8. I'll strike a deal with you, OK?

Task 22

1. approach a prospective customer
2. introduce the product
3. show the product features
4. quote a price
5. conduct a negotiation
6. agree on a price
7. close the sale
8. draw up and sign the contract
9. dispatch the order
10. track the consignment
11. accept payment
12. issue a sales invoice
13. provide after-sales service

Task 24

George	Mary
make my first sale	have a new customer
visit a prospective client	provide great after-sales service
show all the features	guarantee next-day delivery
provide service	dispatch a big bulk order
make a great offer	complete the sales invoice correctly
complete the negotiation	collect the consignment
finalize the terms of the deal	be a defective product
sign the contract	withhold payment
pay cash	
extend credit	
agree on the price	
ask for a discount	
achieve my sales targets	
use a new sales strategy	

Unit 7 ｜ 生產 Production

Task 2

- advertise
- create demand for
- develop   **product**
- distribute
- manufacture

- begin
- boost
- cease   **production**
- increase
- outsource

Task 3

- arrange
- expect
- guarantee   **delivery**
- make
- take

- accompany
- collect
- deliver   **consignment**
- dispatch
- receive

Task 4

- exercise
- have
- implement
- maintain
- put in place

control

- exercise
- fulfill
- have
- perform
- provide

function

Task 5

1. outsourcing
2. manufacture

3. put in place
4. ensure

5. shipping
6. provide

Task 6

- branded
- defective
- finished
- innovative

product

- full
- smooth

production

Task 7

- early
- fast
- recorded
- special

delivery

- large
- particular
- single
- whole

consignment

Task 8

- cost
- effective
- strict
- tight

control

- administrative
- basic
- main
- useful

function

Task 9

1. strict
2. defective
3. smooth
4. Large
5. valuable
6. speedy
7. primary

Task 10

product	• category
	• development
	• information
	• line
	• range
production	• capability
	• capacity
	• cost
	• line
	• manager
	• process
	• schedule
	• team
	• unit

Task 11

1. The production cost is too high. We need to try to reduce it.
2. This product line includes shampoo, conditioner, hairspray, and gel.
3. The production process was developed in our German factory.
4. The production schedule is already delayed.
5. The production team consists of three people.
6. We produce a full product range for the company.

Task 12

1. line
2. range
3. category
4. line
5. capability
6. capacity

encounter + come up against
solve + sort out **problem**
pose + cause

hit upon + find **solution**
reject + rule out

unexpected + unforeseen
basic + main **problem**
tricky + serious

clever + neat **solution**
feasible + viable

Task 17

1. We need to sort out the basic problem before we proceed.
2. We have come up against an unforeseen problem.
3. The production team have hit upon a clever solution.
4. We ruled out this solution last time. It's just not viable.

Task 18

1. The contract specifies the terms of our agreement.
2. I think we should switch suppliers. We need a more reliable one.
3. You will have extra costs if you want special delivery of the raw material.
4. We found a way to reduce production costs, and now they are falling.
5. There might be long delays if you choose this shipping method.
6. Unexpected production delays have arisen, for which we apologize.
7. We are the largest manufacturer of this type of product.
8. Manufacturers produced too much of this product. Now there is a surplus and the price has dropped.

run into serious	problems	-
have been using local	supplier	-
leading	manufacturer	-
have been long	delays	-
dispatch	consignments	-
guarantee timely	delivery	-
production	costs	have risen
defective	products	-
put in place stricter quality	controls	-
-	production process	is pretty smooth
honor/enforce	contract	-
terms of the	contract	don't cover
provide	solution	-

Unit 8　財務 Finance

Task 2

- estimate
- have
- meet
- reduce

cost

- borrow sth. from
- go to
- instruct
- negotiate with

bank

Task 3

- issue
- get
- process
- submit

invoice

- suspend
- remit
- withhold
- spread

payment

Task 4

- avoid
- involve
- minimize
- take

risk

- earn
- get
- maximize
- yield

return

Task 5

- examine
- look at
- process
- store

data

- adjust
- arrive at
- compare
- see

figures

Task 6

- assess
- damage
- enhance
- improve

prospects

- achieve
- experience
- see
- stimulate

growth

Task 7

- arrange
- obtain
- provide

financing

- borrow
- invest
- raise
- repay

capital

- increase
- protect
- recoup

investment

Task 8

1. reducing
2. invest
3. minimize
4. maximize
5. examine
6. assess
7. borrowing

Task 9

- administrative
- heavy
- production
- running

cost

- commercial
- international
- investment
- overseas

bank

- original
- sales
- tax
- VAT

invoice

- interest
- late
- monthly
- overtime

payment

- calculated
- minimal
- serious

risk

- annual
- guaranteed
- maximum

return

- comprehensive
- detailed
- financial
- raw

data

- key
- official
- sales
- trading

figures

Task 13

- economic
- exciting
- gloomy
- growth

prospects

- continued
- quick
- steady
- sustainable

growth

Task 14

- corporate
- personal

finance

- share
- venture
- working

capital

- foreign
- initial
- sound

investment

Task 15

1. running
2. calculated
3. guaranteed
4. financial
5. growth
6. investment

Task 16

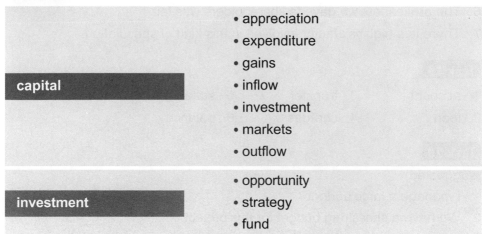

capital

- appreciation
- expenditure
- gains
- inflow
- investment
- markets
- outflow

investment

- opportunity
- strategy
- fund

growth	• rate
	• forecast
	• target

Task 17

profit	• margin
	• forecast
	• growth
	• share

risk	• factor
	• rating
	• assessment
	• management

Task 18

1. It's an investment fund. I have invested quite a lot in it already.
2. Our capital inflow has been good this year.
3. We tried to raise some money in the capital markets, but our stock price didn't reach the target price.
4. We had a high capital expenditure because we built a new factory.
5. The growth forecast for the economy was too optimistic.
6. The profit share we gave to shareholders was fair.
7. There is a high risk factor involved in this kind of speculation.

Task 19

| 1. account | 3. transfer | 5. statement | 7. card |
| 2. loan | 4. charges | 6. balance | |

Task 20

(suggested)

1. I manage a large budget.
2. We have a shoestring budget for this project.
3. I have strict instructions not to allow anyone to exceed their budget.

4. This investment should achieve a higher return.
5. I want to earn a better return on investment this time.
6. We need to attract some more investment to the company.
7. This new project will need a substantial investment.
8. Last year the company experienced a sustained growth of 3%.
9. We need to promote quick growth in this market if we can.

Task 21, 22

• suffer + incur • make up + cover	**loss**
• announce + report • make (U.K.)*	**profit/loss**
• earn + generate • increase + maximize • make (U.S.)	**profit**

* "make a loss" 爲英式用法。

Task 23, 24

• heavy + worse than expected	**loss**
• net + pre-tax	**profit/loss**
• great + good	**profit**

Task 25

1. We need to maximize profits.
2. The whole group incurred worse than expected losses.
3. The fund reported half-yearly pre-tax profits of NT$30 million.
4. I hope we can cover the loss next year.
5. We invest the profits we generate in overseas funds.

private investment	bank	
raise some additional	capital	
suffered a worse than expected	loss	
generated good	profits	
earned better than expected	profits	
growth	prospects	were looking good
achieve quick	growth	
looked at the key	figures	
minimize their potential	risk	
get a maximum	return	
needed the additional	capital	
make major	investments	

Unit 9 資訊工程 IT

Task 2

• have • provide	**function**	• write • design • test	**program**
• create • enter sth. into	**system**	• expand • maintain	**network**

Task 3

• look at • record • process • examine	**data**	• provide • divulge • withhold • have	**information**

Task 4

1. system
2. program
3. data
4. program
5. information
6. programs
7. data
8. information
9. data
10. information
11. network
12. data
13. functions
14. system
15. functions
16. information
17. network

Task 5

• search • extra	**function**
• operating • information • control	**system**
• word processing • spreadsheet • computer • antivirus • email • shareware	**program**
• peer-to-peer • client-server • local area • wireless local area	**network**

Task 6

• supporting • additional • raw	**data**	• inside • background • personal	**information**

Task 4

1. data
2. system
3. network
4. information
5. system
6. programs
7. data
8. information

9. systems
10. program
11. network
12. functions

13. function
14. data
15. network

16. program
17. program
18. network

19. program
20. program
21. information

Task 8

network	• protocol • topology
program	• designer • documentation
system	• utility • function • change • integration

Task 9

information	• management • processing • service • system • technology
data	• base • bank • collection • entry • field • gathering • processing • storage • storage capacity

Task 10

1. network protocol
2. program documentation
3. program designer
4. information service
5. system utility
6. data storage capacity
7. system integration
8. data entry
9. network topology
10. data field
11. information system

Task 11

1. Data entry is probably the most boring job in IT.
2. You must make sure you enter the data into the correct data field.
3. Our data storage capacity is too low.
4. We offer an information service for new users.
5. The information system here is very complex.
6. The network protocol we use in this company is Ethernet.
7. The network topology cannot really deal with the number of computers we have. We probably need to change it.
8. Let's ask the program designer. Maybe he can help us.
9. If we had the program documentation, we would be able to understand how it works.
10. The system integration is almost complete.

Task 12

1. build - develop
2. manage - maintain

Task 13

1. provide - offer
2. run - work
3. allow - enable

Task 14

1. How long will it take to improve the network?
2. It's a difficult system to maintain.
3. My job is to manage the network. It's a big network, so it takes up all my time.
4. Over the years we have built an excellent system for the company.
5. The program allows you to save your work in different formats.
6. The program runs really well now.

7. The system enables anyone to access it from anywhere in the building.
8. The system is not running very smoothly.
9. The system offers a platform for further growth.
10. We need to spend some money on upgrading the system.
11. What other functions does the program provide?

Task 16

manage	company's information	system
input	detailed	information
maintain	-	system
analyze	precise	data
get	relevant	information
wrote	software	program
developed	computer	program
perform	certain	functions
providing	extra	functions

Task 17

running a	joint pilot	project
hit upon an	easy	solution
build	wide area	network
coordinating	new	project
expand	-	networks
taken up	-	suggestions
deal with	unexpected IT	problems
solve	common	problems
work out	easy	solution
come up with	practical	suggestions

Unit 10　人力資源 HR

Task 2

• have	**staff**
• sack • transfer • lay off	**employee**

• manage	**personnel**

Task 3

• develop • learn • exercise • require	**skills**
• do • look for • quit • change	**job**
• share • broaden • provide • gain	**experience**

Task 4

• work in • manage • move to	**department**
• reach • maintain • determine	**level**
• get • offer • review	**salary**

1. salary	8. job	15. staff	22. employee
2. personnel	9. department	16. experience	23. department
3. experience	10. skills	17. employees	24. skills
4. salary	11. job	18. experience	25. job
5. experience	12. skills	19. staff	26. level
6. department	13. job	20. level	27. level
7. skills	14. employees	21. salaries	

Task 6

project
line
senior
general   **manager**

managing
non-executive
company   **director**

Task 7

necessary
considerable
a set of   **skills**

good
full-time
temporary   **job**

valuable
relevant
practical   **experience**

Task 8

finance advertising marketing	**department**
acceptable certain entry	**level**
annual average starting	**salary**

Task 9

1. job	7. experience	13. department	19. directors
2. level	8. department	14. salary	20. managers
3. director	9. skills	15. salary	21. skills
4. skills	10. manager	16. manager	22. level
5. manager	11. job	17. director	23. experience
6. experience	12. level	18. department	24. salary

Task 10

1. service department
2. advertising director/advertising manager
3. HR department
4. personnel manager/personnel director
5. IT director/IT manager
6. legal department
7. marketing department
8. sales director/sales manager
9. R&D department

Task 11

2. time-management skills
3. interpersonal skills/people skills

4. leadership skills/management skills
5. negotiating skills
6. administrative skills/organizational skills/management skills
7. communication skills
8. technical skills
9. presentation skills

Task 12

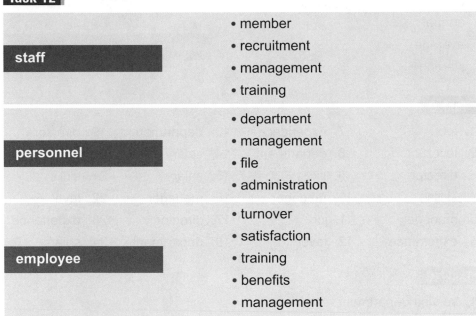

staff
- member
- recruitment
- management
- training

personnel
- department
- management
- file
- administration

employee
- turnover
- satisfaction
- training
- benefits
- management

Task 13

salary
- raise
- scale
- review
- cut

job
- description
- interview
- opportunity
- prospects

job
- satisfaction
- security
- vacancy

department
- manager
- head
- meeting

Task 14

1. Personnel administration is interesting because you're always dealing with people.
2. Can I please see my personnel file?
3. Have you read the job description?
4. I don't think employee satisfaction is very high here.
5. I got a salary raise.
6. I had a job interview today.
7. I have a lot of job satisfaction.
8. I have good job security. I don't think they will fire me.
9. I studied personnel management in college.
10. I was wondering if you had any job opportunities here?
11. Staff management is the job of the HR manager, not the finance director.
12. One of the biggest areas of our budget is staff training.
13. Staff recruitment is the hardest part of my job.
14. The employee benefits are quite good, including a car and a laptop!
15. Employee management is part of every department manager's job.
16. There is a lot of employee turnover in this company.
17. This is the personnel department. It's quite new.
18. We are doing a lot of employee training this month.
19. We are going to have a salary review. You may get a salary cut.
20. We have a salary scale here. Your bonus will follow the guidelines on that.
21. When I leave college I will have very good job prospects.

Task 15

1. correct
2. not correct
3. not correct
4. not correct
5. correct
6. not correct
7. not correct
8. not correct
9. correct
10. correct
11. correct
12. correct

Task 16

1. staff/employees
2. employees/staff/personnel
3. staff/employees
4. employees/staff/personnel
5. staff/personnel
6. employees/staff/personnel
7. staff/personnel
8. staff/employees

Task 17

1. staff/personnel
2. staff/personnel
3. employees/personnel
4. employees/personnel
5. staff/personnel
6. staff/personnel
7. staff/personnel
8. staff/personnel
9. employees/staff
10. employees/staff
11. employees/personnel
12. staff/employees

Task 19

recruiting	new	personnel
supporting	-	staff
recruit	new	employees
require	set of	skills
offer	basic monthly	salary
provide	valuable	experience
hire	new managing	director

Task 20

tackling	complex	issues
inform	line	manager
transfer people to	another	department
carry out	annual	self-assessments
doing a	good	job
support	employee	development
provide a	basic	level

Notes

Notes

國家圖書館出版品預行編目資料

商英教父的單字勝經 / Quentin Brand 作；杜文田譯.
—— 初版. —— 臺北市：貝塔, 2008.09
面； 公分
ISBN 978-957-729-706-8（平裝附光碟片）

1. 商業英文　2. 詞彙

805.12 97014406

商英教父的單字勝經

作　　者 / Quentin Brand
譯　　者 / 杜文田
執行編輯 / 陳家仁

出　　版 / 貝塔出版有限公司
地　　址 / 台北市 100 館前路 12 號 11 樓
電　　話 / (02) 2314-2525
傳　　真 / (02) 2312-3535
客服專線 / (02) 2314-3535
客服信箱 / btservice@betamedia.com.tw
郵撥帳號 / 19493777
帳戶名稱 / 貝塔出版有限公司

總 經 銷 / 時報文化出版企業股份有限公司
地　　址 / 桃園縣龜山鄉萬壽路二段 351 號
電　　話 / (02) 2306-6842

出版日期 / 2008 年 9 月初版一刷
定　　價 / 420 元
ISBN：978-957-729-706-8

商英教父的單字勝經
Copyright 2008 by Quentin Brand
Published by Beta Multimedia Publishing

貝塔網址：www.betamedia.com.tw

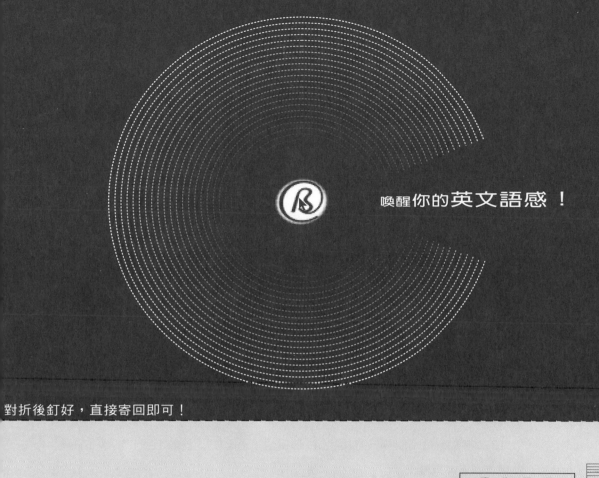

喚醒你的英文語感！

對折後釘好，直接寄回即可！

100 台北市中正區館前路12號11樓

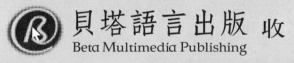

貝塔語言出版 收
Beta Multimedia Publishing

寄件者住址 □□□

貝塔語言出版
Beta Multimedia Publishing

讀者服務專線（02）2314-3535　　讀者服務傳真（02）2312-3535
客戶服務信箱　btservice@betamedia.com.tw
www.betamedia.com.tw

謝謝您購買本書！！

貝塔語言擁有最優良之英文學習書籍，為提供您最佳的英語學習資訊，您可填妥此表後寄回（免貼郵票）將可不定期收到本公司最新發行書訊及活動訊息！

姓名：_____　性別：□男 □女　生日：_____年_____月_____日

電話：(公)_____(宅)_____(手機)_____

電子信箱：_____

學歷：□高中職含以下　□專科　□大學　□研究所含以上

職業：□金融　□服務　□傳播　□製造　□資訊　□軍公教　□出版

　　　□自由　□教育　□學生　□其他

職級：□企業負責人　□高階主管　□中階主管　□職員　□專業人士

1. 您購買的書籍是？_____

2. 您從何處得知本產品？(可複選)

　　　□書店 □網路 □書展 □校園活動 □廣告信函 □他人推薦 □新聞報導 □其他

3. 您覺得本產品價格：

　　　□偏高 □合理 □偏低

4. 請問目前您每週花了多少時間學英語？

　　　□ 不到十分鐘 □ 十分鐘以上，但不到半小時 □ 半小時以上，但不到一小時

　　　□ 一小時以上，但不到兩小時 □ 兩個小時以上 □ 不一定

5. 通常在選擇語言學習書時，哪些因素是您會考慮的？

　　　□ 封面 □ 內容、實用性 □ 品牌 □ 媒體、朋友推薦 □ 價格□ 其他_____

6. 市面上您最需要的語言書種類為？

　　　□ 聽力 □ 閱讀 □ 文法 □ 口說 □ 寫作 □ 其他_____

7. 通常您會透過何種方式選購語言學習書籍？

　　　□ 書店門市 □ 網路書店 □ 郵購 □ 直接找出版社 □ 學校或公司團購

　　　□ 其他_____

8. 給我們的建議：_____

_____

喚醒你的英文語感 ！

Get a Feel for English !

喚醒你的英文語感！

Get a Feel for English !